INCOGNITO

KHALED TALIB

This is a work of fiction. Names, characters, places, and incidents are products of the author's imagination or are used fictitiously and are not to be construed as real. Any resemblance to actual events, locations, organizations, or persons, living or dead, is entirely coincidental.

World Castle Publishing, LLC
Pensacola, Florida
Copyright © Khaled Talib 2017
Hardback ISBN: 9781629896946
Paperback ISBN: 9781629896953
eBook ISBN: 9781629896960
First Edition World Castle Publishing, LLC, May 15, 2017
http://www.worldcastlepublishing.com
Licensing Notes
All rights reserved. No part of this book may be used or reproduced in any manner whatsoever without written permission, except in the case of brief quotations embodied in articles and reviews.
Cover: Karen Fuller
Editor: Erik Johnston

DEDICATION

For Imran Talib and Tetsu Liew

ACKNOWLEDGEMENTS

It is true. You should never say never. But that is what I did after my debut novel, *Smokescreen*, was published. I did not want to write another novel. The tediousness of writing made me want to throw in the towel and call it quits. Yet, somehow, I found a new level of enthusiasm to want to write another story... and *Incognito* came to be.

Writing the first novel was not an easy affair, but little did I realize that I had picked up some valuable lessons along the way that improved my skills. For that, I am indebted to many people. A giant thanks to August Tarrier in Philadelphia, who taught me how to take the first step; Diane O' Connell and her husband, Larry, in New York, who gave me confidence in writing my action scenes and explaining a variety of techniques like exposition and character building. A special thanks to my copy-editor, Elizabeth A. White in Savannah, Georgia, for making my words jump. I tip my hat to New York Times bestselling author Ruth Harris, who suggested the novel's title after I sought her advice from a list of possible ones. My gratitude to Eric Johnston, author and in-house editor at World Castle Publishing, for his patience. A salute to Karen Fuller, publisher of World Castle Publishing, for making this novel a reality.

I am also blessed to be part of a world community of writers, and I am appreciative of their indispensable support and friendship, which includes the International Thriller Writers and the Crime Writers Association.

This novel is a work of fiction, but the passages contain lessons to be learned in these interesting times. In the age of fake news, it is always advisable to question what has been deemed as the truth. Having been in the field of journalism and public relations, I am aware how perceptions can be built. Powerful technologies allow information to spread like wildfire these days, so it is always advisable not to make permanent decisions based on temporary emotion. It will help us avoid undesirable consequences, which can prevent regret.

Prologue

The cockroach peered into Pope Gregoire's nostrils, its feelers twitching wildly. His nose flared in reaction, sending the creature scurrying frantically into a corner. The old man opened his left eye wider, then his right. If this was purgatory, he'd expected to see the wings of an angel, at least—not that of a filthy insect.

He felt his own heartbeat in the throb of his palm. Clearly, the Angel of Death had not visited him yet. So where was he?

Confusion swirled about his head as he tracked the smell of earth amidst concrete. He couldn't tell whether it was day or night. The two fluorescent tubes on the ceiling manipulated the hour. There were no windows, and scarcely any air was admitted except through the slit under the metal door. He could hear nothing but his own breathing. He looked around in a daze, then dragged himself up slowly against the wall.

He saw into his blurry memory. Two black vans pulled up on a quiet street under the dark fabric of the sky. More than a dozen armed masked men in black jumped out. Bodies of his escorts, including several cardinals, members of the Swiss Guards and secret service men, began hitting the ground as muffled thumps sounded repeatedly around him. Screams and moans of pain accompanied columns of dark red blood thrown into the air.

His anxiety surged when a gunman aimed his weapon at him. First thought: Why would anyone want to harm a leader of peace, a man whose sole mission on earth was to distribute goodness and alleviate the sorrow and pain of others? Second thought: Fear. In the dark clouds of doubt, he questioned his own faith; what if he died and did not meet God? What if he had spent his entire life serving the wrong religion? Third thought: Fight back. If there was ever a time to retaliate, even if it meant killing someone, this would be the appropriate moment. Pope or no pope, he was a human being whose life was being threatened.

He saw into the gunman's cold eyes. His prayer for strength was interrupted by a sharp, stinging pain on his left cheek. A dart. As he pulled it out, two masked men rushed forward and grabbed his arms. He felt his mind tumbling, burrowing deeper and deeper into the chasm of despair. That's all he remembered.

As his senses grew more alert, he realized that he was in a cell. He looked down at his attire. He was still wearing the black cassock from the previous night. His body ached with fatigue, and he didn't feel clean. The world must not see him this way. He held the Pectoral Cross around his neck tightly. Who dared kidnap the Servant of the Servants of God? Whoever was holding him against his will wanted him alive for some reason—at least for now. God knows best.

Heavy footsteps sounded outside, and he glanced up as the metal door flung open. A man in a black mask and desert camouflage appeard and stood at the door.

"Your Holiness," said an Eastern European voice behind the mask.

"Your words don't match your hospitality," the old man said, feeling his throat dry. "Who're you? Why am I here?"

The masked man slipped both hands into his pants pockets and took several steps forward. "I just wanted to check on you. Do you require anything?"

"I need water," the old man said. "I also want to clean myself."

The masked man nodded. "I'm sorry for the discomfort.

It was the best we could do given the circumstances. Are you hungry?"

"No, I'm not. The least you could've done is to prepare a bed for an old man. I'll be very sick in a few days if I continue to sleep on this miserable floor. How long do you plan to keep me here?"

The cockroach ran past the mysterious host.

"It depends on whether the Vatican accepts our ultimatum or not," the masked man said, crushing the insect under his boot.

"What is it that you want?" the old man asked.

"Something bigger than the Vatican," the masked man replied. "You're like the cheese on the mouse trap."

"I don't understand."

"We're doing the thinking for you, so there's nothing for you to understand. But we expect the Vatican to comply."

"Expect? And if we don't?"

"Let's not think that far. Besides, a man of God shouldn't be afraid of anything."

"I can control my fear. It's time that defeats me. I have responsibilities. There are things I must do." The old man placed a hand on his left cheek and felt some swelling.

"It's the effect from the tranquilizer gun," the masked man said, removing his pale hands from his pockets. "The swelling will disappear in a few days."

"How did you know where I would be that night?" The old man removed the Pectoral Cross from around his neck and held it with both hands.

The masked man grunted. "Do you honestly think your disguise could fool me? Surely you're not naïve enoughto believe the Vatican is devoid of traitors." He pointed to the Pectoral Cross. "We'll need that cross as proof we have you."

"What happened to my escorts?" the old man asked.

"Most are dead. Maybe in the future, a modern-day Homer will write a story about it."

"May God forgive you," the old man said, staring at the frigid eyes peering out though the holes in the mask.

"Thanks for putting in a good word for me."

There was stillness between them.

"You have an Eastern European accent, but I can't detect your origin," the old man said.

The masked man turned and stepped out the door. Without looking back, he said, "If I wanted you to know who I am, why wear a mask? Get some rest; my men will attend to your needs. By the way, the media has gone crazy. They're all asking the same question: where in the world is the pope?"

"So am I."

PART ONE

CHAPTER ONE

The Pope is Missing

The emblazoned headline ran across the front page of the *Times*. Ayden Tanner read the corresponding article on his iPad as he sat in the departure lounge overlooking the tarmac at Heathrow Airport. The pope's mysterious disappearance had thrown the world into shock and confusion ever since news broke a day ago. He was last seen at his window waving to the crowd in Saint Peter's Square. A state of emergency had been declared in Italy. World leaders had offered "any necessary support" to find him.

On the row of seats in front of Ayden, several passengers watched segments of the Vatican press conference on a wall mounted flat-screen TV. A BBC female anchor was speaking to a male reporter standing outside the gates of Saint Peter's Square. Behind him, paramedics were carrying people out on stretchers as police acted to maintain calm. The reporter responded to the anchor's questions, while also offering his own assessment of the situation. He analyzed phrases and words used by Vatican officials during the press conference earlier.

The news ticker at the bottom of the screen streamed the latest developments: street protests; marches taking place around the world; soldiers deployed across Europe to cordon off kilometers of area; special dog units, helicopters and drones being used for search and rescue operations; candlelight vigils in various cities and towns from Latin America to the Philippines.

The foreign press, hungry for more information, swarmed the pope's birthplace, Annecy, France, in search of diverse angles and perspectives to boost their ratings. Interviews extended to the pope's siblings, relatives, and old friends.

Already ranked among the top global newsmakers, the news coverage of Pope Gregoire's disappearance had tripled his popularity. The pope had stolen the show. Like everyone else, Ayden had some questions on his mind. Did terrorists kidnap him? Had demands been made? Was it murder driven by internal Vatican politics? How could a world-famous man with a tight security detail simply vanish? Was it a gimmick to restore faith in the Church?

God help us all.

But Ayden Tanner… he didn't believe in God.

***

Ayden didn't expect to find a gun stashed in the aircraft lavatory compartment as he stood outside waiting for his turn. He didn't need it until later, so he expected his assignment partner, usually someone familiar with the ins and outs of the destination, to supply him with the necessary equipment upon landing. Unless hijacking the plane was in order. In those rare circumstances, a gun and other accessories would be made available on board. Such assignments could happen. But he wasn't a terrorist. He was just different — he didn't exist.

Finding the pope would be Ayden's seventh mission since joining the League of Invisible Knights. The secret organization functioned under the auspices of Anonymous, the international network of activists and hacktivists. Anonymous had set up this covert unit to bring about the triumph of good over evil. Despite its roguish reputation, Anonymous had gained popularity around the world as the power-giving voice to the silenced. It offered a new form of protest, preventing governments from absolute control.

Gossip and casual small talk filled his ears, rising even above the pilot's announcement that the plane would land shortly. All flights would be grounded until further notice due to the current weather conditions in Geneva. Inside the tight lavatory cubicle, Ayden ruminated about the pope. Unlike everyone else, he kept his theories to himself, eschewing the cheap talk from the facts. No good came from blurring truth and fiction.

The mirror reflected a thirty-five-year-old, reserved Englishman with jet-black hair. Once upon a time he was a blond. He would be again in a couple of weeks if he didn't re-dye his hair. He studied the stubble across the taut jawline of his pale, angular face. He was lucky to be breathing after his last assignment, five days ago. The mission in Myanmar was successful—the terrorist Buddhist monk was now dead—but Ayden came that close to death.

Dark circles had formed around his watery eyes. He felt his nose starting to get stuffy. A common cold on its way; nothing an aspirin couldn't cure.

The captain's voice came though the intercom again. Passengers and the cabin crew were advised to return to their seats and belt up.

Ayden walked across the aisle back to his seat. He hated taking off and landing moments. In fact, he hated the whole experience of flying, period. The increase in airport security amid fears of a terrorist attack made the experience of flying worse. Fear of the plane blowing up was the least of his worries. You die, you die. It was the hassle of screening that irked him most. But it made him a savvier traveler. He had learned to wear zipper boots to expedite through security. He never kept coins in his pockets. Who enjoyed walking back and forth through the screening machine? Travel light, travel smart. That was the new motto.

The plane landed smoothly. The immigration control office didn't give him a second look. Ayden's fake passport was top of the line.

Ayden passed through the barrier and walked out into the reception hall. Outside, his eyes searched for a limo driver holding a fictitious Greek name on a signboard: Demetrious Mallas.

Second row...a lean, pepper-haired man somewhere in his forties in an old, faded leather jacket and jeans. Ayden approached him.

"That's me." Ayden pointed to the signboard above the man's head.

"Welcome to Geneva," the limo driver said, pushing his way to the front. "Which hotel are you staying at?"

"*Les Hauts de Rive.*" Ayden gave the name of the small establishment.

"I know it." The limo driver stared at Ayden's carry-on bag. "No other luggage?"

"I travel light." *As if it was against the law.*

"Please wait near the taxi stand and I'll bring the car around," the limo driver said as he led Ayden toward the exit.

Outside, a cold draft of air blew across Ayden's face. His winter jacket offered mild protection against the bone-chilling winds. He put on his watch cap and gloves. He felt a bit of comfort wearing them despite his nasal congestion. Above him, the semi-dark skies swirled. Darker than England? No way.

Two middle-aged men who stood nearby were discussing the pope in French. It was a hot topic in Europe whether one was Catholic or not. The pope had gone into self-imposed exile, fed up with the Vatican's chicanery, one man said. He was murdered, the other said. It went on and on.

A woman standing outside one of the exit doors stared at Ayden. She reminded him of Mrs. Baylock, Damien Thorn's evil governess in the old movie *The Omen. Satan's Nanny.*

Satan's Nanny wore a starched and pallid face, with straight black hair sticking out from under her hat. Her eyes were hollow and black, including the white parts. He was imagining things.

Heavyset, she stood about five feet eight inches tall and wore a felt hat and a herringbone coat over a sweater with a scarf. Her tweed skirt fell below her knees.

Satan's Nanny cast a passing glance as she walked past him, then disappeared through one of the terminal's entrances. *Weird bitch.*

The taxi pulled up to the curb. Ayden opened the back passenger door and climbed in, placing his bag on the floor. The limo driver shifted gears as he pulled out and drove at a cautious speed, keeping the vehicle steady on the slippery road. Halfway out of the airport, he turned on the radio. Static interrupted the French-language news broadcast: the road would be snow-packed and icy, making everywhere impassable. Airborne debris would accompany high winds. A hailstorm could cause structural damage. Ayden understood French, just one of the many languages he spoke.

"You understand French?" The limo driver looked at Ayden through the rear mirror.

"No," Ayden lied.

"The weather is going to be very bad for a few days," the limo driver translated the radio broadcast. "Not a good time for a holiday. No skiing or other winter sports allowed."

Was the Swiss driver fishing for information? Every foreigner should know it was not a good time to visit Geneva. So why did Ayden come?

Ayden certainly wasn't about to volunteer that he'd come to meet a Vatican proxy, who was expected to brief him further about what happened to the pope. The proxy was sent on behalf of a cardinal whose identity should be protected, and thus could not be named.

A song played after the news.

"Mind turning off the radio, mate?" Ayden asked, unable to tolerate the static crackling sound.

The limo driver reached out to switch it off.

Ayden picked up the black duffel bag, unzipped it, and pulled out his iPad. He removed his gloves and began scrolling on the tablet, relying on his personal and untraceable Wi-Fi device. He read the latest news updates on the pope on several news sites. Pictures showed a medium-size old man with cotton thin hair with a wrinkled and puffy face. The dark patches around the cheeks were overshadowed by his button nose, which gave him a cheerful disposition even though the man was reputed to be tough.

Pope Gregoire was born to a French cheese-making family. As a young man, he had rescued a couple in a burning car. He graduated from Sorbonne University, Paris, with a Master's degree in art and museum studies. He commenced clergy training at the Seminary of Saint Marie Majeure in Strasbourg. Later, ordained a priest, he served in South America and the Philippines. In later years he was made bishop and then the archbishop of Paris, where he subsequently vied for the papacy. The pope had a penchant for chocolate and enjoyed landscape painting. He had been trained to decipher Morse code as a boy after joining the French resistance against the Nazis. He spoke English, Italian, German, and Latin.

The limousine traveled along *Cours de Rive.* The shops were closed, the place deserted. According to the GPS on Ayden's tactical watch, the car appeared to be taking a longer route than necessary.

"Why are we taking a longer route to the hotel?" Ayden asked, pretending to be familiar with the direction. He looked into the rear mirror. Their eyes met in reflection.

"Sorry, I forgot to tell you—there is a road accident along the usual way and traffic is bad down there." The driver pointed to the message board on the dashboard. He wasn't lying.

"Okay, no worries," Ayden said, putting the iPad away.

Snow crunched under the tires as the vehicle moved along the deserted street. Ayden became conscious of a faint sound of bells. Was it the public clock or a tram's bell? He ruled out the latter. The city was in a lockdown. No tram service today. It must've been the clock. Plenty of clocks and watches in this city.

The view looked the same everywhere: frost and snow covered the backdrop, even coating the spidery overhead tram wires. The groaning wind continuously brushed snow against the sidewalk. Rime clung on a bicycle chained to a street barrier outside a shop.

The sky grew darker and the driver turned on the headlights. He switched on the radio again, and they heard. Andrea Bocelli's "Con Te Partiro." The static crackling had gone away.

The vehicle stopped at a traffic light.

No other cars on the road, why even bother?

The limo driver began to cough wildly, then leaned forward and rested his head against the steering wheel, his arms flopping to the seat. He became lifeless.

"Hey, what's wrong?" Ayden leaned forward and nudged the man. No response.

Ayden climbed over into the front passenger seat. He pulled the limo driver back. "Hey mister—"

The limo driver opened his eyes wide and turned to look at Ayden. Eyes gleaming with malice, he jabbed a syringe into Ayden's neck.

Ayden's shock turned to anger. He put his hand on the driver's face and shoved hard against the door. The assailant's head hit the window, but the impact didn't subdue him. As they struggled, Ayden felt his eyelids grow heavy, his limbs weaker.

He slumped back against the passenger door, staring at the driver. The sound of Bocelli's song seemed to echo in his head as the world went dark.

CHAPTER TWO

Isabelle Gaugler entered her room, closed the door, and snapped on the light. Her booking at *Les Hauts de Rive* had also been arranged by the mysterious Mr. Somebody. She had read about the hotel on the net. Located along *Boulevard des Tranchees*, it was once a family lodge. With about twenty rooms, the hotel featured a light brown exterior with green shutters closed over its arch windows. The split foyer entryway led to a curvy staircase beside an ancient traction elevator with frames, trims, and controls. From the entrance, the left side of the foyer led to a corridor with more guestrooms. The right side corridor led to the reception parlor, the kitchen, and a small washroom. The owner's office was located opposite the reception parlor. The dining room, along the same side as the owner's office, occupied most of the space.

Isabelle tossed her bags on the bed, unzipped her leather jacket, and hung it on the back of a chair. A single strum of the harp signaled a text message on her cell phone. She took it out from her jeans' pocket and saw a video message. She sat on the edge of the bed and opened the file. A figure appeared wearing a Guy Fawkes mask with a hood over his head. Isabelle recognized Mr. Somebody's voice as the message started to play.

Greetings Isabelle. You have been assigned to find the pope.

The Vatican has arranged for someone to meet Ayden Tanner, your assignment partner, in Geneva. You will also be assisted by Guy Cisse. They should have checked into your hotel by now. Please liaise with them. As usual, please delete this message even though your phone is hack-proof.

She deleted the video, then sent a message to Ayden and Guy Cisse announcing her arrival and room number. Guy replied. No response from Ayden. Isabelle and Guy agreed to wait for Ayden before deciding the next step to take.

Isabelle put her cell phone on the bedside table and removed her boots before pulling the bed covers back and climbing in. Resting against the headboard, she reflected on the message from Mr. Somebody. She had a personal interest in this assignment. Born a Catholic, her faith had been shaky at times. People needed hope or they'd die. She was not ready to perish. More importantly, she needed a strong blessing. She felt dirty on the inside, and ashamed of her past. By rescuing the pope, perhaps God would forgive her.

She slid down, pulling a pillow over her head to allow blackness to overcome her.

Isabelle startled awake. The harsh, piercing light from the ceiling lamp stung her eyes. She glanced at her watch: 11 p.m. She couldn't believe how long she'd slept. Her eyes roved around the room. It took her a while to adjust to the interior. The old decor bothered her. So did the smell of wood accentuated by the heater. Save for the plasma TV on the wall, the interior was reminiscent of a classic vampire movie of the 1950s. A dull landscape painting hung behind the bed. The desk faced the wall beside the window. If only the hotel had a bar to chase away the boredom and miserable weather sabotaging her mood.

With heavy eyes she stood, stretched, and moved to the window. She drew the curtain aside and looked down. A woman in black stood on the pavement under the shadow of lights. Isabelle's wristwatch measured an outside temperature at 35.6 degrees Fahrenheit. Unless the woman had congenital insensitivity to pain, how could anyone withstand such intense cold?

A streetlamp flickered beside the bus stop abutting the hotel. Isabelle levered the window hinge off and pushed the panel open, rousing a squeak. She pulled the hinge back instinctively when the phone on the bedside table rang. She grabbed the receiver on the second ring.

"*Allo, Mademoiselle* Duchamp. This is the receptionist, Jonas Abegg," a young Swiss-French voice greeted her.

"*Allo*, Jonas. What is it?"

Isabelle had checked into the hotel as Camille Duchamp, a Belgian florist on a business trip.

"You left your powder case on the reception counter," Jonas said. "Shall I bring it up?"

"I'll come down," Isabelle said, looking for any excuse to leave the room.

She put on her boots and picked up her phone. As she headed toward the door, she slipped into the bathroom beside the short hallway.

Clad in a black thermal pullover above the jeans, Isabelle raked her long brown hair as she faced the mirror. At 5 feet 7 inches tall, the young Frenchwoman had high cheekbones, a well-bridged nose, and a small mouth. Her straight, nonchalant eyebrows rested above a pair of piercing green eyes, their seriousness lessened by the dimples on her cheeks.

Like Ayden, Isabelle's first meeting with Mr. Somebody was not coincidental. While feeding pigeons at Trafalgar Square one day, the mysterious individual had approached her. Everything else, as they say, was history.

Isabelle unlocked the door and stepped out into the hotel's

dim corridor. The wooden floor creaked under her as she headed toward the stairs. It was faster for her to take the stairs than the elevator, as her room was just one floor up from the foyer. Echoes of her steps bounced as she descended the concrete stairs.

Isabelle grew suspicious when she reached the bottom of the steps. A pair of stark eyes stared at her across the foyer. They belonged to the same woman in black who'd been standing outside the hotel earlier.

"Everything okay?" Isabelle asked.

No answer.

Isabelle noticed the glint of a knife in the woman's hand. The woman raised the weapon and hurled it straight at her.

Isabelle ducked sideways as the knife flew past over her shoulder, missing her by an inch. She bolted to the left and rushed through the door, which she slammed behind her hard and pressed her weight against the thick wood.

"What's going on?" Jonas poked out of the parlor door along the hallway. The young man, with brown hair and a boyish face, wore a pink sweater and a pair of jeans.

"Lock the door!" Isabelle blasted in French.

The receptionist looked ashen. "*Pardon*?"

"Trouble! Just lock it," Isabelle said.

"Please, come inside the parlor. I made coffee… relax," Jonas said calmly.

Isabelle's throat felt dry. "Listen to me. There's a woman outside with a knife. She tried to kill me."

Jonas stepped forward. "What kind of a joke is this? Look at the weather — who wants to hang outside right now?"

"Not a joke," Isabelle replied.

Jonas tilted his head. "Mademoiselle, please."

Isabelle pushed Jonas back with a flat palm. "Are you deaf?"

"Mademoiselle, rest assured, no harm will come to you," the receptionist said. "If there's a problem, I'll call the police. Are you on medication?"

"Don't be rude! I'm not crazy," Isabelle snapped. "She may not be alone."

Jonas sighed. "Is the person a hotel guest?"

"I don't know, and I don't care. Just don't open the door."

"Step aside, please. Let me check," Jonas said.

"No," Isabelle said stiffly. "If you open the door, trouble begins."

"We've never had trouble here except from unsatisfied customers."

The door thudded violently.

Isabelle grabbed Jonas by the shoulders. "Believe me now?"

Jonas's shoulders tightened. "I don't know what to believe, but I don't like the sound I just heard." He fumbled in his pocket for the keys. He removed a keychain, selected a long, thin piece, and inserted it into the keyhole. He turned the key twice and pulled it out.

Isabelle exhaled and stepped away from the door. "Thank you."

"I must call the police," Jonas said.

"They won't arrive in time," Isabelle said.

"I must notify them, it's procedure," Jonas said, harried.

"How many rooms are occupied right now?" Isabelle asked.

"Everybody checked out this morning except you and one other person, Monsieur Ferde Borsok."

Isabelle recognized the name—Guy's fake name. "What about the night staff? Who else is here with you?"

"I'm alone today. I don't think they'll all come. A few of them called me and said they won't come until the weather is fine. Anyway, I'm not expecting new guests. We are officially closed until further notice," Jonas said.

"Where's the hotel owner?"

"Monsieur Bertrand is in Zurich for a few days," Jonas

explained.

"We can't stay here tonight, it's not safe. Where can we go? Where do you live?"

Jonas's eyes widened. "I live here. Monsieur Bertrand gave me a room to offset some of my salary."

"We must leave," Isabelle said.

Jonas pursed his lips. "Let me try to call the police."

"*Merde*," Isabelle cursed in French. She scrambled her fingers inside her pants for her phone. Folding it around her fingers, she tapped the call screen once, then raised it up to her ear. "Trouble," she said, then listened for a while.

"Who did you call?" Jonas asked after Isabelle hung up.

"Monsieur Borsok."

Jonas raised a single arched brow. "You know him? How —?"

"Stop asking questions."

"I'm calling the police," Jonas said, darting into the receptionist room.

"The police, the police, the police — good luck," Isabelle muttered as she trailed him.

The small reception room contained an L-shaped counter with an antiquated switchboard flush against the wall behind it. Isabelle found her gold-plated powder case resting on the countertop beside a coffee flask and two cups. A key box hung on the wall behind Jonas's swivel chair. Behind it, postcards and Post-it notes plastered a corkboard. A satchel lay on the floor. A low table rested against the wall opposite the counter, flanked by two wooden chairs. Above it hung an old poster of a skier jumping off a slope. In the corner next to the window, a wooden hanger stood covered with jackets, mufflers, an umbrella, and several winter caps.

Jonas sat on the swivel chair and operated the switchboard. After putting on the headset, he plugged a cord into a socket. But his sense of hope was replaced by a long exasperating sigh. "The switchboard is dead," Jonas said.

"They must've cut the wires," Isabelle replied. "I expect a blackout soon too."

"You seem to know a lot about what's going on." Jonas stared at his phone on the desk. "I'll try calling them on my cellphone."

"How long before you get through?"

"What?"

"Weather like this, the police lines must be busy—it'll take hours to get through," Isabelle indicated.

"I must try." Jonas picked up the phone, pressed the emergency number, and set it on speaker mode, only to get a busy signal. He shut his eyes tightly, but his chest heaved rapidly as he endured the painful suspense.

"Don't panic," Isabelle said.

"Okay, don't panic. What shall I do?"

Isabelle didn't reply. She moved to the window and opened the latch. Blurred pinpricks of light illuminated the buildings beyond the courtyard. A recognizable face appeared in front of her. She stepped aside to let him in.

A beefy, light-skinned man with a shaved head climbed through the window Isabelle had opened. Standing six-feet tall, Guy Cisse had a chiseled face with a narrow nose, thin lips, and oblique eyes. He wore a brown leather jacket over a black thermal pullover, blue jeans, and mountain shoes. With an MPA57 submachine gun slung over his shoulder, he carried a haversack in one hand while the other held two large duffel bags. He rested the load on the floor.

"My God!" Jonas fixed his eyes on the computer's monitor. "Is this the woman you're talking about?"

Isabelle walked back and stood behind Jonas. The CCTV screen showed the woman in black and seven masked figures standing at the foyer. They were armed.

"*Oui*," Isabelle acknowledged, putting her hand on Jonas's

shoulder. "She brought friends, as I suspected."

"This makes me nervous," Jonas said. "I'll try to call the police again." Again, he got a busy signal.

The monitor showed the assailants axing one of the window shutters outside the hotel.

"What are they doing?" Isabelle asked.

"Trying to break one of the dining room windows," Jonas said, then turned to look at Guy by the window. "Why do you have a weapon?"

Guy ignored Jonas and turned to Isabelle. "Did Demetrious contact you?" He knelt, unzipped one of the bags, took out a chrome-plated Desert Eagle, several clips, and cartridges, and handed them to Isabelle.

"He didn't check in," Isabelle said, checking the gun.

"This ain't cool. He should've been here hours ago." Guy stepped behind the counter and stared at the screen.

"Mr. Somebody can locate him by GPS," Isabelle said. "Right now we have bigger problems."

"Someone forgot to lock the gates of hell," Guy said, looking at the monitor screen.

Isabelle tapped Jonas. "How did she get the password for the hotel entrance?"

"*Je ne sais pas.*" Jonas indicated he didn't know. "Maybe she spied on the other guests. Everyone's got the same password."

A howling wind whistled through the window gap. Isabelle strode to the window and closed it tight.

"Dude, we gotta bail," Guy said.

Jonas shook his head in confusion. "Bail?"

"I mean get the hell out of here—*jet,* now," Guy said. "Is there another way out of this place?"

Jonas pointed to the window. "Beyond the courtyard is a street. Climbing down the wall is going to be a problem."

"We make a rope," Isabelle said. "We take some bed sheets

and tie them together."

"It's a long way down. My room is a few doors away from Monsieur Borsok's. We can get two more sheets from there," Jonas said.

"*Allez!* We do it now," Isabelle said, rushing them. "After that, I'm going upstairs—my things are in my room." She swiped her powder case from the countertop.

"We don't have time," Guy said.

"We make the time—everything is in my bag," Isabelle insisted. "Besides, I'm not comfortable walking around with a leaking vagina. I need my tampons."

Glass shattered, jolting everyone.

"They've broken in." Jonas stared at the screen.

The screen showed a piece of the broken shutter on the pavement. The masked individuals were climbing into the dining room one at a time.

The sound of an axe splitting the dining room's door down the hallway increased their sense of insecurity. Guy rushed to the parlor door and peered out the hallway. "Lock this door."

Jonas darted to the door and shut it. He shoved a slim shaft into the keyhole and gave it two turns. He then removed the key and slipped it into his jeans pocket.

Ice pellets began to fall. All eyes turned to the window.

Guy looked at the hanger in the corner. "Those hailstones are nasty. Take those jackets, the ones with the hoods, and cover yourselves."

Isabelle and Jonas put on a jacket each and pulled the hoods over their heads.

Heavy footsteps clumped down the corridor. Then, splinters flew inside the door as a thumping sound shook the wood. The tip of the axe blade eventually bit through the door.

The lights went out. The noise outside disoriented everyone. The pounding was relentless.

Guy turned on his phone light and handed it to Isabelle. "Hold this," he said, then aimed the submachine gun at the door.

Jonas could be heard rummaging through the desk drawer. A strong light beamed from a large flashlight as he pointed it at the window. He picked up the satchel on the floor and then opened the window wide, popping his head outside. After looking left and right, he lifted one leg over the sill and then the other as ice pellets assailed him. Isabelle and Guy followed.

Outside, Isabelle returned Guy's phone to him and scuttled across the courtyard, with Jonas shining the flashlight in front of them as he led the way. Isabelle heaved herself up through the window into Guy's room as Jonas flashed the light into the room. She helped Jonas pull himself up, then tiptoed to the first bed.

Isabelle removed the heavy blankets from the twin beds and then stripped the sheets. They then crept out of the room and proceeded to Jonas's room to get the extras.

"Take the flashlight," Jonas said, handing it to her after they stepped out into the hallway again.

"What about you?" she asked.

"I'm familiar with this place, I can manage."

With the gun in the other hand, Isabelle grabbed the flashlight and walked to the end of the corridor. She turned and flashed the light across the hallway. Jonas was gone.

The sound of axe thudding grew louder as she neared the end of the hallway. She switched off the light and opened the door slowly, peeking out. Weapons gleaming, flashlights bobbing in their hands, the woman in black and accomplices stood outside the reception parlor's door as one of the accomplices swung an axe repeatedly on it.

The illumination gave Isabelle some visibility as she quietly stepped into the foyer. She turned on the flashlight as she treaded up the stairs to her room. She shut the door behind her, then crossed to the chair and grabbed her bag and jacket on it. She tossed the bag on the bed, unzipped it, and stuffed the jacket inside. Carrying the bag in one hand, she crossed the room to the door.

A ricochet of bullets tumbled through the air as Isabelle rushed down the stairs. She switched off the flashlight near the bottom, then veered to the right and darted into the other hallway.

The hailstorm continued to pound as Isabelle hurried across the courtyard toward the wall. Jonas was already there. As she passed the parlor's window, she ducked and crawled to avoid stray bullets. Guy, pressed against the wall beside the window, fired intermittently into the room.

"I'll catch up with you, don't wait for me," Guy said as she passed him.

Isabelle reached the wall, took the sheets from Jonas, and began braiding them one after the other, knotting the ends as tightly as possible. She tied one end of the rope to a railing and threw the other end over the wall. The rope hung slightly off the ground.

They tossed their bags over the wall, and they landed on the snow-foamy sidewalk without a sound.

Isabelle looked at Jonas. "After you."

"I don't know how to climb down."

"I don't have time to teach you," Isabelle said. "You live or die. Place hand-over-hand on the way down as you slide your feet. C'mon, let's go."

Isabelle turned to Guy and called out to him. Her voice dissipated amidst the hailstorm clatter and exchange of fire.

"I can't do it," Jonas cried. "It's too difficult."

"Please, you must try," Isabelle urged.

Flashlight beams bobbed through the parlor's windows. A masked face appeared with a gun in his hand. He aimed at Isabelle and fired. She ducked, but the bullet hit Jonas in the chest, knocking him over the edge. Isabelle reached for her gun and fired back. The bullet hissed through the air and hit the assailant's head.

Guy spun and fired repeatedly through the window.

Isabelle stuck her gun back into her waistband and quickly hoisted herself down. She landed on her feet, skidding slightly before maintaining balance. She removed her gun and looked at Jonas sprawled on the ground. His eyes were wide open, legs twisted under him. She should feel something. She tried... nothing. She knelt down and shut his eyes. She felt a thump beside her and swung her gun around. It was Guy.

The rope jerked. They looked up to see two masked figures looming over the wall. Isabelle and Guy pointed their guns upward and pulled their triggers simultaneously. The assailants jolted backward at the impact of the headshots.

They ran along the wall lined with frosted trees. Up ahead, a red Mini Cooper was pulling out of its spot between cars. The duo stepped off the sidewalk and stood in the center of the small road to block the vehicle. They raised their weapons at the driver to force him to stop. The car halted abruptly.

Guy opened the front passenger door and pushed the car seat down to let Isabelle slide into the back seat.

"What are you doing? Get out! I don't want trouble," the young male driver stammered as Guy shut the door after getting into the seat beside him. The tanned individual wore a black leather jacket, was no more than twenty-five, and had short dreadlocks.

"Drive." Guy pointed the submachine gun at the young man's face.

As the car moved, the incessant wiper blades chattered and jerked in motion to clear the layer of snow across the windshield. Suddenly, the driver jammed on the brakes. The headlights shone on a masked figure with a shotgun standing in front of the beams.

Guy leaned toward the driver and pressed his foot down on

the accelerator, forcing him to floor it. The engine screamed. Tires spun in the snow. The car lurched forward at the masked man with the shotgun, running him over as he fired at the windshield.

They ducked as the car crashed into the back of a parked vehicle.

Guy slid slowly back up his seat. He looked at the driver. "You okay, dawg?"

Stark fear kept the driver's eyes wide open, as if held by a speculum. "Am I okay? Are you crazy? You called me a dog?"

"I think you're disoriented." Guy turned to Isabelle. "You okay?"

"I'm fine," she said, pressing both sides of her temples, eyes half closed.

"Get out of my car," the driver pleaded.

Guy patted him. "You're in shock, dawg—take it easy. We won't harm you. We just need your help, that's all."

The driver slammed his fist on the dashboard. "I'm not in shock and I cannot help you. My name is Abebe, not dog. I came from Ethiopia. Life is good here, no trouble here. You understand? So leave me alone, please." He kept mulling over why they had dragged him into this mess.

"Sorry, dawg—situation." Guy took out his phone and keyed in a message to Mr. Somebody.

Isabelle leaned forward and peered over Guy's shoulder. A spidery map interface appeared with a red blinking cursor against a green screen. They watched the cursor move. And then, it stopped blinking.

"Where's Cemetery the Plain Palace?" Guy asked, staring intently at the map.

Isabelle leaned forward. "It's pronounced *Cimetiere de Plainpalais*," she said. "It's a cemetery."

Guy looked at Abebe. "Dawg, do you know how to get there?"

Abebe cringed. "Leave me alone. Why you call me a dog?"

"It's just slang for a friend with the same face," Guy said.

"I dunno what you talkin' about," Abebe said.

Isabelle leaned forward and pressed her gun's muzzle behind Abebe's ear. "Maybe this will help you focus."

"It's less than ten minutes from here," Abebe said apprehensively.

"Take us there now," Guy said.

"You bring trouble now for me." Abebe sat up straight, slid into reverse, and spun the car backward. "Oh my God, this is a crazy night, crazy people. I don't know who you people are—I don't want to know. Just don't kill me."

Guy brought his face up close to the driver. "Drive."

CHAPTER THREE

Ayden blinked languidly in the pitch blackness. His breathing began to feel tight. The feeling of compression slowly paralyzed his entire system. The inside of his mind felt dark and utterly soundless. He could hear his own heartbeat. He tried to sit up, and hit his head, slowly realizing he was in a coffin. Soil slipped through the slits, assailing his eyes, nose, mouth, and body. He snorted, blowing out the dirt from his nose, and blinked repetitively to shake off the remainder. He felt his duffel bag between his legs. Air was precious right now. He could only hope help would arrive in time.

Like every other member of the League of Invisible Knights, Ayden had been trained to withstand all kinds of torture. The founders had scouted him through the files of military, police, and intelligence organizations. Potential candidates were selected based on certain criteria. Above all, they must have heart. Anyone who failed the training program would have to repeat it. Traitors were dealt with severely.

Ayden agreed to participate in the league's program because he felt betrayed by the country he loved. His resume impressed the secret echelons of Anonymous. The former Special Air Services (SAS) commando had single-handedly rescued a group of Pashtun women and children in southern Afghanistan from a human trafficking gang. The display of chivalry didn't impress his superiors, especially since the culprits included Afghan officers. Lieutenant Ayden Tanner should have accepted the "culture" of the environment. Being a member of the league had some perks: a rent-free, three-bedroom apartment in Hampstead Village. Except for junk mail, his letterbox was always empty. The neighborhood stores and cafes knew him as John the Artist, since he was always seen at the art shop buying supplies. He hung his artworks all over his apartment walls. But no one had ever seen it. He never brought guests home. He was also John the Reader at a nearby bookstore. He read fast, all kinds of genres, fiction and nonfiction.

He couldn't recall how he ended up on the secret island. All he could remember was being kicked out of a bar one night in London after starting a drunken brawl. He found himself the next morning having coffee in the kitchen of a small cottage on the outskirts, with a man who simply introduced himself as Mr. Somebody. He spent the next few days in the cottage. Then one day he woke up on a beach with a man in a Guy Fawkes mask staring down at him. No doubt, Mr. Somebody had drugged him. He learned the reason later. The island's location must remain a secret. From the landscape, vegetation, and animals on it, he gathered he was still somewhere in the UK.

He spent the first three months in a wooden shack, isolated, disconnected from human contact. Rabbits, unusual looking butterflies, and foxes kept him company. He was given basic amenities and supplies to survive alone. He soon discovered the value of isolation. It helped cleanse his thoughts and removed impurities inside his soul.

At the end of the isolation period, Ayden was taken to meet other candidates and the training began. Under the tutelage of no-nonsense instructors he learned martial arts, espionage strategies, holistic security strategy, language proficiency and shibboleth, espionage parlance, and the art of disguise. Those were morning lessons. Afternoon lessons were more intensive. Lights out by ten.

Upon graduation, Ayden was given a special honor...death. An obituary in the newspaper reported his demise...a car accident during a road trip to Devon, it seemed. His body was buried in an Anglican cemetery. Even though he grew up to become a non-believer, the charade was necessary. It was easily fabricated since both his parents were dead. Having no siblings or other relatives made it easier. The only son of an Anglican pastor and a housewife mother, their memory continued to linger in his mind. He credited them for teaching him values even though he didn't agree with his father's beliefs.

***

Guy had instructed Abebe to park the Mini Cooper nose in at a roadside parking lot opposite the cemetery. The abundance of trees inside the cemetery diluted the lights from the streets and surrounding buildings. The hailstorm had temporarily stopped, but the wind remained relentless, whirling up particles and litter on the empty street.

They climbed over the short gate into the cemetery grounds. Walking along a winding stone path, Isabelle and Abebe relied on their phone lights for some form of visibility. The cursor on Guy's led them between tombstones, statues, and manicured lawns with benches.

They made a sharp turn and paused at a tombstone.

"This ain't cool," Guy said.

Isabelle shone the light on the headstone. "It's the wrong place to have a picnic."

Guy stepped forward and rested his hand on the headstone. It fell backward.

"The soil is soft. Some shit happened here. Help me dig, both of you," Guy ordered.

"You know what you're doing?" Abebe looked at Guy.

"This is an important grave. Geneva's Who's Who is buried here. They'll send us to jail—"

"Dig!" Guy shouted.

They pulled out grass patches and heaved chunks of soil with their bare hands. The task seemed to take forever. Around them, nothing stirred except the wind blowing through trees, causing boughs to bend. They finally reached the top of a wooden box lying four feet underground. Guy and Isabelle brushed the dirt from the top while Abebe removed the soil from around the sides. The coffin cover had been nailed shut.

"Yo, man, can you hear me? You okay in there?" Guy banged the lid with his fist a couple of times.

"I'm still alive, but my breathing is getting a bit tight," Ayden replied in a faint voice.

Guy felt along the sides of the cover. He retrieved a Swiss Army knife from his pocket and flicked one of the blades. Slipping the knife between the slits, he pried the lid up and stuck two fingers inside the gap, holding it open. "Can you try pushing the lid from inside?"

"I can't even move," Ayden said.

Guy looked at Abebe. "Come over here and help me."

Abebe knelt beside Guy and slipped his fingers under the lid. They began to apply force to open it.

The cover popped open. Ayden took a deep breath and then sat up slowly. He tossed his bag out and started to climb out.

"How long were you in there?" Guy asked, pulling Ayden up.

"About six hours," Ayden said, clearing his throat. "I was rationing my consumption of air. The limo driver from the airport drugged me. That's all I remember."

"We had our fair share of adventure at the hotel too," Guy said.

Ayden looked at the Ethiopian. "Who's he?"

"My name is Abebe," Dreadlocks said.

Guy looked at Abebe. "You live alone?"

"I have a roommate, but he's gone back to his country for the holidays," Abebe said, then slapped his face. "I talk too much. You want to stay with me, isn't it? Let's part ways right now. You *goodbye* this way, *I goodbye* that way. I've helped you save your friend. My job is done."

"Abebe, what do you do in Geneva?" Ayden asked.

"Assistant watchmaker."

"Fascinating," Ayden said. "Working for a famous watch company?"

"Ya."

"They pay you well?"

Abebe nodded. "It's okay."

"So why do you have a roommate?"

Silence.

"I'm just an apprentice," Abebe admitted. "The apartment is rented."

"An apprentice with a nice car," Isabelle said.

"It's not my car," Abebe said. "I'm taking care of it for my roommate."

"Tell you what, Abebe—a thousand euros if you let us stay for a few nights," Ayden said. "What say you?"

"Make it two thousand. I need to fix the broken windshield," Abebe said.

"Very well," Ayden said.

The trees began to sway wildly in the strong wind.

Ayden looked at Isabelle and Guy, then at the hole. "This is what happens when you don't book a five-star hotel. I'm feeling like a brass monkey. Let's get the hell out of here."

***

Voices in the kitchen woke Ayden up. He didn't mind, as he felt rested despite yesterday's ordeal. Unfortunately, sleeping on the carpeted floor had exacerbated his runny nose. Isabelle had taken the single bed.

Ayden looked at the Ziploc bag on the chair above a pile of clothes. Guy had given it to him last night. He picked up the bag then sat on the empty bed, pouring out the items: two wireless earpiece walkie-talkie sets, stacks of euros, a medical kit, passports of various European countries, an FNP-45 tactical pistol with a suppressor, and extra ammunition.

It suddenly occurred to him to check his phone. He grabbed the duffel bag on the floor and removed a shaving can. He twisted it open and retrieved the Android phone inside it. Thank goodness they had failed to find it there. It was on silent. A text message popped up from Rafael Rabolini, the Vatican press secretary. The message read:

Meet at Saint Moritz instead. Hans Hauser Café. Today at 3 p.m.

Ayden looked at his watch. It was 6:35 a.m. He replied *OK*, wondering if there was ample time since he was unfamiliar with the train schedules.

He entered the kitchen and found Isabelle eating a bowl of cornflakes at the round table. Without a drop of makeup, her face looked pale and dry, but she still looked radiant, somehow. Maybe it was the overall package. As team leader, he was privy to the individual agents' files in order to understand their psychology better. Twenty-nine years old, Isabelle had grown up in an orphanage in France. A former lieutenant in the French army, her Algerian posting was not rewarding. One evening during a routine patrol out in Sahel in the north east of Niger, she was gang raped and badly beaten by six of her fellow soldiers. She spent months in a military hospital. The scars were permanent, physically and mentally.

After she was discharged from the hospital, she wrote a fake suicide letter and sent it to her superior. She explained her reason for taking her own life—the army had betrayed her. The soldiers who raped her continued to walk free. She knew the reason—they were men with family connections. They could do no wrong. Isabelle's body was never found in the Seine, according to news reports.

She became a stowaway on several ships and eventually found her way to Thailand. She spent the next three years in Phuket. There, she underwent plastic surgery to reconstruct her face. She then enrolled in one of the martial arts camps. Her training included knife fighting and mixed blade throwing. Isabelle had a reason for the intense training—she had future plans.

She returned to France after hooking up with an Algerian she met in Bangkok, who arranged a safe passage back. It didn't take her long to find the six soldiers who'd defiled her. News reports on the deaths were always the same: hands and feet tied to the bed, penis sliced off and stuffed in their mouth. Payback.

Guy had a pastrami sandwich. Abebe, looking half asleep, sipped coffee intermittently while having an egg sandwich.

The round white clock on the wall ran five minutes behind his watch. The window shade above the sink was partially up. The storm had dissipated, but their minds remained unsettled.

Ayden sat down and raked his fingers through his black hair, then poured a cup of coffee. "Change of plans—we leave after breakfast." He didn't elaborate due to Abebe's presence. The less the Ethiopian knew about him and their mission, the safer for everybody.

"Don't forget my money," Abebe said.

"Did my personal physician tell you I have dementia or what?" Ayden replied cuttingly.

Abebe withdrew. "Sorry, I'm a little bit—"

"Obsessive-compulsive?"

"Why the change of plans?" Guy asked.

"Maybe he got stuck in the storm," Ayden replied without going into details.

"Who got stuck in the storm?" Abebe asked.

"Abebe, give it a rest," Ayden said.

"You people are secret agents?" Abebe scanned everyone. "Detective? Spies? Military? Must be some kind of international spy network, ah? One man with a Greek name, another sounding Austrian, and the French lady. Well, it's not my business. Since you didn't kill me, I assume you're on the side of good."

"We're nobody," Guy said.

Like the rest, Guy's file history had attracted the league to recruit him to become one of their anonymous specialists. Guy had been living in Geneva for a year as Ferde Borsok, supposedly an Austrian. The former US marine had escaped a maximum-security prison in Florence, Colorado, after being falsely convicted of a crime he didn't commit. One night, walking home from the gym in a Detroit suburb, he decided to stop at a 7-Eleven store. While he was there, three men entered the store to rob it. An off-duty cop who was present at the time was killed in the shootout, along with the cashier and two other customers. The store's cameras showed Guy entering only seconds before the armed robbers. Before the cop was shot, he managed to kill one of the robbers. The robber's gun fell and slid toward Guy, who was hiding behind a shelf. In his testimony, Guy said he grabbed the gun, the same one that killed the officer, for protection. Though the cameras covered the activity of people entering and exiting, and the register, there was no coverage to back up Guy's word that he was hiding and not responsible for the cop being shot. With four dead bodies and their families and the community screaming for blood, the jury was itching to convict someone. Since he entered the store at the same time and was found in possession of the weapon that killed the officer, he was their sacrificial lamb. He received life.

After escaping, Guy crossed the Canadian border and then found his way to Europe. He stayed in Norway for a couple of months working as a lumberjack. One morning during a weekend fishing trip, a mysterious individual approached him. He introduced himself as Mr. Somebody. From that day, Guy's life changed. He also underwent plastic surgery to reconstruct his features.

"Abebe, can you take us to the train station?" Ayden asked.

"You didn't notice the car's windshield?" Abebe said. "Take a taxi."

"I don't enjoy Swiss taxis," Ayden said. "Just turn on the car heater. Nobody's going to notice the car. They know how crappy the weather has been like."

"What kind of espionage organization do you work for that they don't even supply a fancy car?" Abebe asked.

Ayden raised an eyebrow in irritation. "You want your money or not?"

***

Underneath a wool hat, Chief Inspector Henri Guillaume adjusted his square spectacles on his bulbous nose as he knelt down and examined one of the bodies in the courtyard. The dead, half immersed in snow, had been unmasked. Shocked eyes stared at him. The detective was accompanied by several plainclothes officers and a team of forensic specialists. The purity of the snow didn't conceal the morbid atmosphere. His mind scoured for an explanation of what happened at *Les Hauts de Rive* last night. The station had received a call that the sound of gunfire had been heard. A patrol car arrived to find a body lying on the public sidewalk, and another in the middle of the street. The scene of investigation led to the hotel.

Detective Eglin Kugler stood beside him. He wore a beanie hat and a leather jacket, a white muffler swaddled around his neck. "They used bed sheets to go over the wall," said the thirty-something partner, pointing to the ledge across the courtyard. "The body on the sidewalk has been identified as Jonas Abegg, hotel's employee."

Eglin Kugler had trained as a schoolteacher, but later in life decided to switch careers. Born in Basel, his family had moved to Geneva after his father got a job as a senior watchmaker. He spent some years with the Swiss police and then got seconded to Interpol before switching back to the Geneva police, where he was promoted to detective.

"Who else worked here that night?" Guillaume groped his gloved hands.

"None of the staff showed up because of the storm."

"I noticed a few cameras around the hotel. Get the recorded security footage," Guillaume said.

Kugler nodded. "Working on it." He removed a small notebook from inside his jacket and ran through his notes. "We didn't find any identification on them." He pointed to the forensic team studying the other cadavers. "We found a shotgun near the body on the street. A car ran him over. No witnesses. By the way, did you hear what happened at *Cimetiere de Plainpalais?* Someone desecrated one of the graves."

"So? Lots of sick people out there," Guillaume said, lifting one of the dead man's icy, cold hands. He turned the palm upward. The fingertip on the right thumb had a tattoo: A dagger with wings.

"Looks familiar, doesn't it?" Guillaume said. "Thought you said no identification was found."

Kugler sighed and knelt down. "Yes, it does. How could I have missed that?"

"Wonder what brought *Sword* to a small hotel?" Guillaume reflected.

***

Back at the police headquarters in Boulevard Carl-Vogt, the

chief inspector had just hung up the phone when there was a knock on his door. He bid the person enter.

Kugler came in and sat opposite him. Legs crossed, he whipped out his trusted notebook. "Two hotel guests didn't check out that night—Ferde Borsok, an Austrian, and Camille Duchamp, a Belgian. The other guests left before the storm. One guest was a no-show, a Greek named Demetrious Mallas. However, airport immigration said he entered the country."

"Maybe he checked in elsewhere at the last minute?" Guillaume said.

"We're trying to track him down. If the other two didn't get killed, where did they go?"

"Maybe Sword took them."

"Want me to inform the Italians?" Kugler asked.

Guillaume nodded. "We should. Why do I get a feeling this case has something to do with the pope's disappearance?"

***

Kugler stepped out of Guillaume's office and stood behind the door thinking. The chief inspector's last statement made sense. The case appeared to be related to the pope's disappearance. He knew Guillaume was right, especially after seeing those tiny tattoos on the dead men's right thumbs. How could he have missed that? It was embarrassing. He hated the fact Guillaume was the one who spotted it when he had earlier examined the bodies. He was younger, stronger, and sharper. Yet the chief inspector had managed to outdo him today. He didn't resent Guillaume, although he found his methods slow. Understandably, the chief inspector was overly cautious about everything and relied too much on protocol. Then again, Kugler knew the partnership was necessary. He needed someone to take the reins or he would just continue with his loose cannon ways. In reality, his problem was not Guillaume, but his lack of patience. He wished, though, the man would do something about the odor of smoke from his body.

Chapter Four

At Gare Cornavin Station, the specialists were greeted by hurried faces as trains whistled and the intercom intermittently spat out announcements. They expected to reach Saint Moritz in the evening.

Ayden and Guy wore black and white suits underneath winter coats. The rabbi disguises came complete with sidelocks, moustaches, and beards. Keeping with the Jewish concept of tzniut—modesty in dress and behavior—Isabelle wore a white headscarf and a long cream gown underneath her black winter jacket.

Ayden led everyone toward the platform gate. Several police personnel in dark tactical attire had positioned themselves in front of it, studying every passing face. As they approached, two officers with sidearms blocked their path.

"Your tickets, please." One of the officers hooked his thumb in his waistband as he looked at Ayden.

Ayden handed over the tickets.

"Where are you going?" the other officer asked.

"Saint Moritz, for a religious convention," Ayden replied, faking a guttural voice.

The officer raised his brows. "Where are you staying?"

"*The Kulm*," Ayden said, referring to the famous hotel.

"Where are you from?"

"Israel." Ayden couldn't help feel he was being interrogated.

The officer tilted his head and whispered to his partner holding the tickets, who responded with a nod. "Who is this woman?" He pointed at Isabelle.

"My wife," Ayden said. "She's also my personal assistant."

"And that one?" The officer pointed to Guy.

Ayden looked at Guy, and then back at the officer. "Rabbi Shlomo is originally from Ethiopia. He's now an Israeli citizen."

The officer stared at Ayden. He then stepped aside and gestured for them to pass. The officer holding the tickets raised a hand. "One moment please."

"Is there a problem?" Ayden asked.

The officer stretched out his hand, palm upward. "May I see your passport?"

Ayden handed over the fake Israeli passport.

"Which airline did you fly in on?" the officer with the tickets asked.

Ayden stomped his foot on the ground. "Ya, I see what's going on here. You've got a problem with my face. It's always different when it comes to us," he barked. "For centuries we suffered in Europe. *Ya Ha' Shem! Ya Ha' Shem!* When will this racism end?"

The commotion started to attract a crowd around the gate.

"Go, go." The officer returned the tickets and stepped aside.

They didn't look back as they passed the gate and walked across the platform. The soothing sound of the compressor's hum replaced the din of shrieks by the time they reached the center of the carriage. They tossed their bags on the overhead rack and settled down. Ayden sat by the window with Isabelle beside him. Guy sat opposite them. Not a word was spoken among them until the train moved. Then, they each broke into a smile.

The wheels rattled and jerked as the carriage surrendered to the pull of the engines. The momentum picked up gradually, rolling out of the station, transitioning from cityscape to a vast swath of countryside with rugged cliffs, lakes, villages, and some farms clinging to steep edges.

Ayden stood and removed the iPad from his bag, then settled again and began to read the news. He turned the screen and showed a news link to Isabelle and Guy. An article in the *Tribune de Geneva* reported the incident at *Les Hauts de Rive.*

Isabelle took the device from Ayden and thumbed the screen. "The police are not saying much," she whispered.

"Probably holding back information." Guy slouched with an elbow on the armrest. "Or they've got no clue what went down."

"*Unidentified bodies with gunshot wounds found in hotel...*" Isabelle read the article under her breath. "They're searching for two hotel guests who didn't check out: an Austrian male and a Belgian female. That's us."

"Good luck to them," Ayden said.

Guy looked at Ayden. "Did the Vatican guy tell you anything else about the pope when he messaged you?"

"No, he didn't," Ayden said, shaking his head.

"An inside job, that's what I think," Guy said. "No secret the pope was unpopular with his inner circle. He was a tough guy who wanted to clean up the administration."

"Maybe the Mafia wasn't happy with him, so one family decided to do something," Isabelle added. "He did ostracize them, you know."

"Don't talk tosh. I don't want to speculate," Ayden said. "The Vatican's list of scandals is longer than the Mahabharata. I'm looking at various scenarios. Keeping an open mind."

"Considering the pope's tight security detail, don't you find it strange that the inner circle doesn't know anything?" Isabelle said, returning the iPad to Ayden. "Maybe they hid his body inside the Vatican after murdering him," Isabelle suggested. "I read one of the popes created a secret passage inside the Vatican centuries ago."

"I don't know, but I don't think they can move a body without being detected," Ayden responded. "There are surveillance cameras everywhere. In any case, let's stick to the facts. Once I meet that Vatican bloke I'll know more. Rafael Rabolini, that's his name...the Vatican press secretary."

"Or maybe he went into monastic silence because of some big scandal and nobody wants to talk about it," Isabelle continued stubbornly.

Ayden sighed. "Bloody mommy. You don't know when to stop, do you?"

Isabelle raised her hand in apology.

"We also have to find a way to talk to the Swiss Guards," Ayden said. "Find out as much as we can."

"Not going to happen through the front door," Guy said. "There's also the danger that if we speak to one, the rest will find out. Are we prepared for how that's going to turn out?"

Ayden nodded. "We'll learn more when I meet this Rabolini chap."

The ride eventually rocked everyone to sleep except Ayden. His mind raced, thinking about the assignment. A few questions popped into his head. Who buried him? Who sent those assassins to the hotel? Since Mr. Somebody had arranged the limo pickup from the airport, how could it have gone wrong? Was there an infiltrator in the league? What about Rabolini? Could he be trusted?

Thoughts of Maria crept in. Her death had affected him badly. They had met during a safari trip in Dubai. One thing led to another, as the story goes. It was a short story. She was gone. Dead. Somehow, Maria's memory had a way of breaking through. The emotional scar churned an intractable conflict inside him. He tried to convey strength and confidence outside, but he could feel the ruse fading in spite of his efforts. The endorphins

he experienced during workout sessions were temporary relief —
he could never truly push away that feeling of regret. For a
period of time, he had prescribedhimself an over-the-counter
antidepressant, *Paxil*. But he stopped when he realized it was
making him an addict.

Ayden tilted his head against the window and stared out into
the open space. The locomotive crossed a viaduct and thundered
into a tunnel. It emerged along a silvery sheen between mountains.
As his mind drifted, a large bird soared over an alpine rim in
the distance. An eagle? He couldn't be sure. Swooping down the
mountains, the bird was followed by another. They coordinated
and flew side by side. Making a precipitous descent, they headed
toward the train as snow sputtered below, forming parallel lines.
No bird could do that. Only a jet could. But they were not jets.
They were men in jetpack wingsuits.

The two wingsuit pilots climbed again and flew over the
train, then veered over the pine trees and swerved to the other
side. Passengers stood and piled over to the other side of the
carriage to get a better view of the exhibition. All phone cameras
and conventional ones were out.

As the fliers drew closer, the machine gun turrets mounted
under their fiberglass wingsuits became visible.

Ayden nudged Isabelle and Guy awake. "Get up. Trouble!"

The marauders began strafing the train carriage. Windows
shattered as bullets crashed all around, showering pointed shards
of glass inside. Cries, moans, and screams filled the enclosure.

Guy pulled Isabelle to the floorboard as Ayden jumped over
the seats in the next row. Crouched in the leg space, his heart rate
began to rev as the assault continued.

The train slammed on its brakes and halted with a screech,
sending bags, cutlery, and cups across tables onto the floor.

"Why did the train stop?" Guy asked loudly.

"There could be an obstacle ahead," Ayden replied.

The carriage doors hissed open and a young train conductor rushed in. He removed his hat and dropped it at the sight of the massacre. Inching forward, trance-like, he began to hyperventilate as he spoke. "A tree fell across the tracks ahead, and —"

Guy grabbed the train conductor's ankle and pulled him to the floor as the snarling screams from the jetpack engines drew closer again.

Feeling the veins in his neck throbbing, Ayden crawled toward Guy and Isabelle.

"That tree didn't fall by itself. We better move." Ayden pointed to the exit.

After taking their belongings, they scuttled toward a large rock in front of the pine forest about fifty meters ahead. Guy held the train conductor's arm as their legs sunk into the crunchy snow. Some passengers had taken cover under the train, while others had rushed into the forest.

"They're not going to stop until they get us," Ayden said.

"How'd they find us?" Guy asked.

"I don't care to find out right now. I just want those wingsuit pilots gone," Ayden said.

"How? All we have are guns," Isabelle said, tightening her scarf.

"If I could climb one of those trees, I could reach them," Ayden said, pointing behind her.

The raiders dived toward the train again, strafing a massive amount of holes in the carriage walls before flying past.

"They're going to turn around again," Ayden said. "Let's move to the other side of the rock."

They shifted to the other side, their backs now toward the train.

Ayden looked at Isabelle and Guy. "Now's my chance to —"

Guy didn't wait for Ayden to finish his sentence. After dashing into the woods, the tall, matted pine needles made him invisible.

The silence was overbearing as they waited for a signal from Guy.

The raiders reappeared, circling over an opening in the forest. As they began to nose down, the sound of Guy's submachine gun echoed throughout the forest. One of the jetpack wingsuits swiveled before hitting the ground, sending shards of fire and fragments bouncing. The second raider left an echo trail tearing the sky as he retreated. And then...silence.

Ayden looked at the forest canopy. Cupping his hands around his mouth, he shouted at Guy. "Hey!"

"*Yeah?*" Guy's reply sounded distant.

"He knows you're up there!"

"*I know!*"

Isabelle pointed to the right. "Three o'clock."

Ayden stood and rushed toward the forest. Stepping on broken branches, pinecones and needles, he scurried past several dozen passengers behind dead trees and fallen fronds. He began climbing a tree a few feet away from Guy. As the second raider hovered above, Ayden aimed his *FNP-45* and emptied the magazine.

Fire engulfed the wingsuit, discharging a thick black smoke. It wobbled and vanished behind a line of trees. A ball of blue and orange fire came immediately after a rumbling explosion. Below, a chorus of cheers and applause erupted.

As Ayden and Guy approached, the train conductor stood from behind the rock, looking stunned. "Excuse me, who are you people?" he asked.

"Nobody," Ayden replied.

The train conductor's eyebrows furrowed in confusion. "Nobody? I've never seen rabbis in action before."

Ayden smiled. "Neither have I."

***

They discarded their disguises and hitched a ride to Saint Moritz after reaching a nearby village. The train conductor and engineers had insisted everyone wait for the police and emergency services to arrive. That was not going to happen in their case.

The ride dropped them at Saint Moritz train station late that evening. A bus at the depot beside the station then took them to *Hotel Stille*, a ski dorm. Ayden had booked the hotel through the Internet using another fictitious name.

The ski dorm was located along Via Surpunt, a quiet street near the edge of the woods. The path to it was covered in knee-deep snow. Inside, a chirpy male receptionist named Knipp greeted them through a cutout window in the wall.

Their third floor walk-up room opened to a small tiled foyer connecting to the kitchenette. A short corridor with a bathroom on the side led to a bedroom with two beds in-between bedside tables. The view overlooked the dark mountain peaks and a parking lot below. Later, an extra bed was sent up.

Hours after checking in, Ayden made his way by bus downtown to *Hans Hauser* in Dorf, the up-market center. The restaurant's patio, encased by boutiques along the winding cobblestone paths, was filled with customers in colorful winter clothes. Slow sips of coffee and wine and small bites of cakes and sandwiches entwined with casual conversations. Halfway through his hot drink, a male waiter approached and gave Ayden the bill folder.

"I didn't ask for the bill." Ayden stared at the waiter.

The waiter narrowed his eyes and glanced sideways. "Take the folder," he said subtly.

Ayden opened it and read the message scribbled inside on a piece of paper.

Go behind the building.

Get in the taxi.

A taxi waited for him at the side of a small road. Inside, a middle-aged driver sat wearing a feathered hat. Ayden sat in the back seat. This time around, however, he was prepared for any surprises.

The Leaning Tower of Saint Moritz dates back to the 12th century. It was part of an old church named after Saint Maurice that was destroyed in the 1800s. Perched on a green lawn, it stands more than thirty meters high and is covered by a landslide protection wall to prevent further listing.

A man wearing a brown Alpine hat and a black overcoat sat quietly on a bench near the tower as a soft breeze whispered through the trees. Two birds on a short branch chirped at one another.

"Switzerland also has a leaning tower, did you know that? This tower is older than the Tower of Pisa, yet one is more famous than the other," the man said.

Dried leaves fell from surrounding trees, skittering across the snow-covered garden as a cold draft stirred the air.

Ayden ignored the history lesson. "Are you Rabolini?"

"Pleased to meet you, Demetrious." Rabolini tapped on the bench to gesture for Ayden to sit beside him. "I heard about the train incident. It's all over the news. I knew you would be on that train. For your safety, I decided to meet here instead, in case they followed you."

Rabolini was somewhere in his thirties, six feet tall, with strong Italian features — round face, black hair, brown-eyes, with an Armenoid nose.

Ayden looked around. "What happened to the pope?"

"He was kidnapped. The kidnappers have given us demands," Rabolini said, his tone low and careful.

"What kind of demands?"

"For you to understand the situation, I must start from the

beginning."

"If you must, though I hate long stories," Ayden said.

"Have you heard of Vatican II?"

"I'm not a member of your church — explain it," Ayden said.

"Vatican II, opened on 11 October 1962 and signed on 8 December 1965, was an assembly of Roman Catholic leaders who came together to reform doctrinal issues. They also discussed Islam. The Church chose to acknowledge it as a member of the brotherhood, because Muslims believe in the same God of Abraham. *Nostra Aetate* is the declaration on the Church's relation with non-Christian religions."

"Sounds peaceful so far. What's the problem?"

"The kidnappers want the Vatican to denounce Islam. They want us to downgrade the status of Islam. If we don't, they'll execute the pope publicly. Then the Muslim world will be blamed for it."

"Over the years, the politicians and the media have tried to desensitize people about Muslims. You blame them for this and that, and foreign armies continue to make incursions here and there. Don't get a shock if you wake up one day to find a new Saladin...and then it'll be too late. So who's orchestrating this shenanigan?" Ayden rested his elbow on the chair's rail.

"There are many anti-Islam organizations. One that stands out is Sword, the most powerful terrorist organization in Europe. Their actions will no doubt resonate with many Europeans who dislike having Muslims as neighbors. Fascists have attacked mosques, shops, businesses, and people."

"Tell me, who heads this organization, Sword?" Ayden inquired.

"We don't know. Someone contacted us and arranged a meeting one night at Borghese Park in Rome."

"Who attended?" Ayden asked without expecting an answer.

"Masked men — no faces. On my side, I'm not at liberty to say.

All I know is that I was told to meet you because an arrangement was made. The person does not wish for anyone to know your services have been engaged. I can tell you he's a cardinal."

"I know that part," Ayden said, sensing something out of order, but unable to place it. Rabolini made no secret he was withholding information, yet Ayden couldn't shake the feeling he was hiding something more. Perhaps he was reading too much into the man's response.

"Eyes are watching, questions are being asked. Rumors will fly, stories will change. That's why it was arranged for us to meet far away," Rabolini said.

"It's amazing they pulled it off considering the pope's security," Ayden said. "Our organization tried to track him down. We hacked every intelligence agency around the world, including their satellite systems." He shook his head. "Nothing. We even used key loggers to track input of keywords and phrases associated with the situation. Whoever kidnapped the pope took every precaution to make sure he could not be found."

"It puzzles us too," Rabolini said.

"I heard there are secret tunnels running under the Vatican. Maybe that's how they got the pope? In other words, the kidnappers had inside help."

"I can't discount the possibility. But those tunnels were sealed a long time ago. We've got round-the-clock guards stationed everywhere. Our surveillance cameras missed nothing," Rabolini said.

"Did the kidnappers give any proof they have the pope?"

"Yes, they showed the Pectoral Cross, which—"

"Just a moment." Ayden felt his cell phone buzz inside his jacket. He reached into a pocket and took it out. It wasn't a call, it was a warning signal. The screen blinked blood red.

Rabolini moved his head closer to look at the screen. "What's happening to your phone?"

Ayden glared at Rabolini. "What's in your jacket?"

Rabolini showed his puzzlement. "I have my phone, my wallet, and the keys to my flat. Why?"

"Take them out, show them to me."

As Rabolini emptied his pockets, Ayden's phone began to beep.

"That's how they tracked us," Ayden said, holding up Rabolini's phone.

"What is it?" Rabolini raised his eyebrows.

Ayden dismantled the phone, placed the SIM card on the ground, and crushed it under his boot. "They intercepted your phone. They were tracking your movements and reading your text messages. That's how they knew I was coming to Geneva."

Rabolini's eyes widened. He stood and looked around suspiciously. "That means they know we're here right now. What about yours?"

"Mine is a special phone," Ayden said, also standing. "We better leave." He gave Rabolini a plain white business card. "In case you didn't memorize my phone number."

Rabolini looked at the card. "It's blank."

"Just heat it and the text will appear," Ayden said. "Get a new phone, but don't leave gossip on it. Let's arrange to meet again."

"The taxi driver can take you back to your hotel," Rabolini said, taking the card.

"Not a wise idea for me to return with him. Got to find another way back," Ayden said. "What about you?"

"I'm familiar with this place. I know how to disappear."

"Stay alive. Trust no one."

INCOGNITO

CHAPTER FIVE

Back at the ski dorm, the sunset spread colored rays over the mountaintop before darkness descended over Saint Moritz. Lights went on in several apartment buildings across the inconspicuous, quiet street of Via Surpunt.

"So that's how they tracked us, Rabolini's phone," Ayden explained to Guy and Isabelle as they sat on the bed opposite him. They were both in casual attire with their backs against the wall, legs up. "From what I understood from Rabolini, this is an international plot being organized by a European terrorist organization. So scratch the mafia out of the list. Even so, I don't think everyone in the Vatican is completely innocent."

"That means some of the closest people to the pope," Guy said.

"We'll start with the Swiss Guard commander. I wish Mr. Somebody would let me know the name of the cardinal he spoke with."

"Colonel Bastien Frei—that's the name of the Swiss Guard commander," Guy said. "I read about him on the net today."

"Proud of your research, are you?" Ayden gave a sardonic smile.

"Apart from dodging bullets," Guy replied. "Just because you've got a James Bond accent doesn't mean you're more intelligent than me."

"Pack your bags, we're going to Vatican City tomorrow," Ayden said.

"Can we detour to Milan first? I hear the stores are having a nice sale." Isabelle fluttered her eyelashes.

Ayden squinted at her. "I wish we could, I would love a manicure."

"You guys go ahead. I'll stay here and check out the nightlife," Guy said, shaking his head and snapping his fingers. "You know, I mean really check it out."

"This is not R and R time."

"Man, seriously? We're in Saint Moritz, where the rich and George Clooney hang out. Just for five minutes," Guy said.

"Don't think your girlfriend is going to like that," Ayden said.

"Hey, do you see me wearing a ring?" Guy smiled devilishly as he showed the ring finger of his left hand.

Isabelle's eyes flashed irately at Guy. "You're disgusting—pig."

Guy's prurient innuendo angered Isabelle. Something about the way men talked about women always stirred her up. Subconsciously, it may have had to do with her brutal rape. Since that time, she had looked at men differently. She tried convincing herself not all men were alike, but she also knew that few cared for a woman's mind. Though she still found men attractive, she had resisted getting to know anyone since the attack. For now, every male on the planet was the enemy until proven innocent, the two in front of her included.

"Whoa, what's up with that?" Guy looked at her.

Lines appeared on Isabelle's forehead as she glared at him. "Women are not goods. They have feelings, you know. They also have a mind."

"Just chill, I was just talkin'," Guy said.

Isabelle slipped off the bed and marched to the kitchenette.

Ayden followed her and watched her prepare coffee. "Need help?"

"I'm fine," Isabelle said. "Men—vicious animals in disguise, yet created in the likeness of God."

"I didn't write the Bible, but I see your point," Ayden quipped. "What happened back there?"

"It's nothing," Isabelle said, slamming a palm on the counter.

"That was nothing too?" Ayden said sarcastically. "I don't know what Guy said to rile you up, but I don't think he meant to hurt you." Ayden could sense her body tense with suppressed anger.

She stared at him intensely. "He has a girlfriend, no?"

"Yes."

"So why does he talk about getting lucky with other women?"

"It's just Guy being Guy. That's how he talks. You should know him by now. He says things he doesn't mean and forgets it in five minutes."

She pointed a finger at him. "I hate it when a man insults a woman's dignity. If you want to eat a hamburger, you go to a fast food place. If you want to have a woman, you must appreciate her character. You understand?"

Ayden nodded. "Yes, I do. But what's really bothering you?"

"Let's forget about it," Isabelle said.

"This is about your past? I read your file," Ayden said.

"So you know my pain. My luck meeting the monsters," Isabelle said.

"I know what you've been through, but don't get overly sensitive. It's just talk," Ayden said. "C'mon, you're one of the guys—maybe prettier than us—but one of the guys."

Isabelle smiled, embarrassed.

"Yeah, we're crew right? We're a team. No dis intended."

"Okay."

"We all have our stories," Ayden said. "I knew someone. My

bee's knees. She was embedded with the Iraqi army when their convoy was obliterated by a Sukhoi fighter jet along the Iraqi-Syrian border. The one regret I had was not revealing to her my real name."

"I'm sorry to hear that, but what does bee's knees mean?"

Ayden smiled. "It's an expression to mean someone who is everything to you."

"I like this expression."

"We can't jeopardize the mission. Everybody needs to focus," Ayden reminded her. "All of us have stories, some tagged with pain. Don't let it eat at you. Keep moving forward."

"Don't worry. I'm French — it's my nature to lose my temper," Isabelle said. "We don't keep it inside us like you people across the channel."

Ayden rested his head on the refrigerator. "I'm going to ignore that last statement." He took a step forward. Just as he was about to put his arms around her, she raised her palm to stop him. "Your words are nice. But I don't need your sympathy. I got my revenge already."

"Fine."

"I hope God forgives me for what I did," Isabelle said.

"If he exists, I'm sure he will. You're too good looking to be in hell."

"Tell me, how do you live daily?" Isabelle asked. "I have my faith. It gives me hope."

Ayden smiled. "My hobbies, food, movies, travel, and regular exercise."

"It's enough for you?"

"Yes, it is."

They stepped out of the kitchen.

"Jesus Christ. French people are a bunch of tight-asses," Guy said.

The room went silent. Isabelle sat at the edge of the bed across from Guy and locked eyes with him as she sipped her coffee. Ayden stood in-between them, facing Guy as he handed the extra mug to him. With a finger to his lips, he signaled to be silent. He then stepped aside.

Guy looked at Isabelle. "Sorry."

Her eyes softened. "No problem."

"You know, at the end of the day, all we have is each other. We're uncertain about our past, but we have a new future. Personally, I'm not comfortable with my present state, having to use fake names all the time. Man — wish I was back in the States. No matter how bad or good it's been to me, it's still home. This is the price I pay every single day, even though I am somewhat free here. If I go back, they'll take my body, but I've been here so long they've already locked up my soul. So I might say shit and stuff, but that don't mean I think less of any of you."

"Forget about it," Isabelle said.

Ayden took a sip of the coffee. "Bloody mommy. Too much sugar in the coffee."

***

The F-16 swooped down on the convoy, frantically firing at the welded-steel body of the armored personnel carrier driving with a convoy though the desert terrain. The pounding left Maria, the other journalists, and the infantrymen frightened and confused. The fighter jet could be heard tearing through the sky. In that instant, a giant fireball erupted from inside the carrier, turning the air to liquid fire, burning Maria's face —

Ayden shuddered as he sat straight up on the extra bed. Sweat ran down his face and body. It was a recurring dream. He took a moment to compose himself, then looked at his watch — 6 a.m. He rose. Wearing a white T-shirt and flannel sleep pants, he crept into the bathroom, did his thing, and then headed to the kitchenette.

Ayden put the kettle in the sink and turned on the faucet. He picked up a mug and a coffee packet from the plastic tray. His fingers searched for sugar. None left. The idea of having coffee without sugar was blasphemous. If the room had a phone he could get housekeeping to send some up. It didn't.

He dragged himself back into the bedroom, put on his pullover, slipped into his jeans and boots, and headed out.

He walked across the hall to the stairs and went down to the empty dining room as breakfast was being prepared. In front of the cutout kitchen window, a long table displayed bread, two flasks of coffee and tea, pitchers of milk and juices, and baskets filled with packets of butter, jam, and apricot.

A side door squeaked opened. Two males in kitchen uniforms appeared carrying chafing dishes. They ignored Ayden while arranging the utensils on the table. They stepped back inside, then returned once more with additional utensils and disappeared again.

Ayden picked up a few packets of sugar stacked in a caddy on one of the dining tables. As he turned to walk out, a sudden rush of boots jolted him. A dozen armed men in winterized jumpsuit and balaclavas ran up the flight of stairs. He faded into the background, then crept under a round table covered with a cloth.

Peeping through the cover's vertical slit, he saw the kitchen's side door open. The two kitchen staff members reappeared.

Two masked men entered. They spoke to the employees in Swiss-German. A man in a gray mask inquired if the rooms on each floor were connected to a stairwell. One of the kitchen staff explained the only way down was through the stairs in the middle.

Ayden heard loud voices in the foyer. Knipp, the receptionist, appeared, demanding an explanation for the men's behavior.

Big mistake, Ayden thought.

Gray Mask turned and fired three rounds into Knipp. Blood

splattered on the carpeted floor as his body hit the ground.

The two kitchen workers bolted toward the side door. Gray Mask's submachine gun cut them down before they reached it. Their bodies jerked spastically after falling forward, and then went limp. The other man, in a black mask, opened the side door and marched through. Gray Mask proceeded toward the foyer.

Ayden rolled out from under the table and lunged behind Gray Mask. He grabbed the killer's right arm and twisted it behind him, forcing him to drop the submachine gun. Ayden coiled his other arm around Gray Mask's neck, applying pressure on his windpipe. He then lifted Gray Mask slightly upward, immobilizing him with shortness of breath, and pulled him back between the tables.

Black Mask reappeared and aimed his weapon at Ayden. More masked men gathered inside, weapons at the ready. They stood side by side in a semicircle.

"Drop your weapons," Ayden said.

"You better let him go. You don't stand a chance," Black Mask said.

Gray Mask's breathing grew more ragged as Ayden lifted him farther off the ground.

"If you choose to test me—"

"Stop," Black Mask said. He put his weapon on the ground, then turned to his accomplices and ordered them to disarm.

"Don't forget your sidearms," Ayden said, noticing their thigh holsters. "Two of you collect the weapons and put them on the table here." He moved his head to indicate the table nearest to him on the right.

Two men stepped forward and collected the weapons, then placed the pile on the table.

Ayden instructed them to remove the magazines and scatter them all over the room.

Ayden stared at Black Mask. "Where are my mates?"

"Outside," Black Mask said.

"Bring them here, and get a car ready for us," Ayden said.

Semi-clothed, Guy and Isabelle rushed in with their belongings and approached Ayden, flanking him. Guy removed Gray Mask's handgun from his leg strap and pressed its tip against his rib cage as Ayden continued to hold the hostage in a chokehold.

"We're leaving now with your friend. I need not explain to you the rules, but I might as well say it since the culture here might be different — don't follow us or your friend gets it," Ayden said. "Where's the car?"

One of the masked men stepped forward and handed a key to Isabelle. "White Renault."

With the temperature tightening their skin, Ayden marched the hostage toward the car. Their bodies ran haywire with the morning bitterness, coffee deprivation, and other disruptions. They first trudged toward the back of the white Renault and dumped their bags in the boot. Guy then took hold of Gray Mask's arm and dragged him into the backseat of the car as Isabelle got in from the other side.

Driving past mounds of snow on both sides of the pavement, Ayden kept an eye on the rearview. As the car lurched onto the highway, two cars followed.

"Son of a bitch. I told them not to follow us," Ayden said.

Through the rearview mirror, he looked at Gray Mask. "What do you want from us?"

No answer.

Isabelle slapped the back of the hostage's head. "Answer him."

Guy removed the mask, revealing a brawny-faced man with black hair and a slight scar across his forehead.

"Are you a member of Sword?" Ayden asked.

The man remained silent.

Guy elbowed the man's ribs.

The man moaned. "Yes," he finally said with a thick German accent.

"Who sent you? Why? How'd you find us?" Ayden asked.

"We hacked Rabolini's phone. We followed you back to the dorm after your meeting with him."

"How'd you know we were on the train?"

"We knew what time you were meeting Rabolini based on the text messages. We expected you to be on that train," the man simpered.

Isabelle tapped him in the head. "Names. We want names."

The captive's eyebrows contorted. "You better kill me — don't expect me to reveal anything more."

"We won't kill you," Ayden said. "But we'll make sure you never walk again."

"I can't tell you."

"Trust me, the pain we're going to inflict on you is not worth protecting the sender's identity," Ayden said, looking into the rearview again. The two cars continued to trail them.

"Nothing can be more painful than betrayal," the man said.

Guy elbowed him across the cheek. Stretching his jaws wide, the man looked angrily at Guy. "Beat me if you like, I won't tell you anything."

"Your friends tried to kill us back on the train," Ayden said. "Why do you want to detain us now?" Ayden's blue eyes focused on the German's livid face.

"I have nothing more to say to—"

The rear window shattered as a bullet zinged through the car, hitting the back of the German's head. He slumped down and hung between the front seats. Blood spattered on the transmission area, dashboard, and on everyone. A second bullet hit the passenger's side mirror, shattering it.

"Get down!" Ayden felt his breathing deepen. The rearview

mirror showed a masked man with an Uzi leaning out of a pursuing car's passenger window.

Guy and Isabelle slithered down low in the backseat. Ayden tightened his grip on the steering wheel as metal ripped from bullets tearing through it. Reading a left exit sign up ahead, he stepped harder on the accelerator.

The car screeched as Ayden made a sharp turn into an uneven road. He drove between snow-covered fields with bare trees toward an intersection, then swerved to the right to connect to another quiet road.

"Everyone okay?" Ayden asked without looking back.

"You know, dawg, no matter how much trouble I get into, I never feel immune to bullets," Guy replied.

"You're not supposed to," Ayden said.

A second round of bullets hit, obliterating the rear window. Guy and Isabelle covered their faces and heads from the raining pieces of glass.

"Use his body to cover the rear," Isabelle said, looking at the dead man.

"Do it," Ayden responded, realizing it would also hinder his visibility.

As a hail of bullets continued to pound the car, Isabelle and Guy lifted the dead man's body and shoved it in the space between the back seat and the rear window. Blood continued to drip from the body, dripping down the seat and soaking the carpeted space as bullets thumped into the cadaver's flesh.

"Think one of you can get that bastard?" Ayden asked.

Isabelle leaned over the backseat. In a quick motion she lifted herself and perched her weapon on the dead man's waist. She fired two shots. Ayden watched in the driver's side mirror as the Uzi bounced on the road and the gunman slumped, his torso hanging out the window of the pursuing vehicle.

Isabelle crouched back and looked at Guy's matted, damp

hair and clothes. "You've got blood in your hair."

Guy wiped his hair and looked at his fingers. He looked at the blood covering Isabelle's cheeks. "You've got some on your cheeks too."

Isabelle picked up the gray balaclava on the floorboard and began wiping her face. When she was done, she leaned forward and spoke to Ayden. "Where're we going now?" Isabelle asked.

"As far as the gas in this car can take us," Ayden said.

The second chase car was stepping up. Another shooter appeared from the passenger's open window.

A shadow fell across the road in front of them as a black helicopter passed over the top of the pursuing vehicle and hovered in front of it.

"There's a helicopter behind us," Ayden said.

"Shit," Guy said.

"It seems to be trying to slow down the car," Ayden said.

"Police?" Isabelle asked.

"I can't tell," Ayden said.

The sound of helicopter blades beating the air suddenly intermingled with machine gun fire. The second pursuit car began to swerve, then slid off the left side of the road and struck a tree.

"This is unexpected," Ayden said. "It fired on the car!" Ayden pressed the accelerator further and watched the speedometer climb to one-thirty.

The helicopter rose above his view and hovered in front of them. Then, it rose up higher into the air, turned to the right, and was gone.

Seeing a cable car sign up ahead, Ayden made a sharp turn to the left and pulled into a parking lot.

Ayden opened the car boot from the inside and then rushed with the others to the back of the car. They put on their jackets, pulling up the hoods to cover the bloodstains, took their belongings, and sprinted for the building's glass door.

The sign on the building read: *Muottas Muragl* (Mount Muragl), a funicular station carrying passengers along a cliff railway to the mountaintop and back. The old ticket master seemed to take forever to process their tickets. When he finally handed them the tickets, they dashed through the turnstile and ascended to the platform, which was filled with people waiting for an oncoming cable car descending soundlessly on the sloped track.

The cable car's multiple doors rasped open on the far side to let returning passengers out. A moment later, the other doors swung open to let passengers in. A uniformed attendant waved the passengers forward. They strode in calmly through several doors, perching themselves on the rows of benches.

Ayden's eyes caught sight of the arrival of several men wearing caps and sunglasses on the platform. Their presence made him feel uncomfortable. It didn't take long to confirm his suspicions when the men reached inside their jackets and pulled out guns.

"Gun!" Ayden yelled.

They lunged into the cable car. People ran for cover in every direction. Shrieks commingled with the sound of the human stampede. The screams grew so loud Ayden could feel his eardrums tremble.

The clumping of boots on top of the cable car's roof alerted them. Suddenly, two of the assailants peered over the carriage's edge, weapons pointing inside. The trio fired by reflex, sending both assailants slumping to the ground.

The car's doors slid closed and it lurched into motion.

"They could still reach us — this is too slow," Guy complained, staring through the rear window as the carriage moved on the steel lines through the Samedan forest.

The remaining assailants jumped on the cantilevered stairway and ran after the carriage.

"The carriage will not protect us," Isabelle said, staring at their trackers. "Let's not forget all these other passengers."

"As long as we have the high ground, there's hope," Ayden said.

Sunrays trickled through the cabin windows now and then before slinking behind a cluster of frosted pines. Everyone felt warm in their attire, but just as Guy was about to unzip his jacket, Ayden discouraged him, fearing the sight of blood might scare the passengers.

A bullet drilled through the glass window, spraying shattered glass inward. It bounced off a metal pole and embedded in a wall. The passengers crouched lower and covered their heads, their voices wailing in fear.

"Too close, that one," Ayden said.

"Why don't we shoot back?" Guy said.

Looking at the passengers, Ayden's first thought was their safety. A retaliatory measure could have an adverse effect. "Let's wait till they get closer," he finally said.

A building loomed at the top of the slope, featuring a long glass terrace amidst a sprawling vanilla backdrop.

"What's that?" Isabelle pointed to the building.

"Looks like a hotel," Ayden said.

"*Hotel Romantik,* a ski resort," said a teenage skier wearing an orange visor. "Who're you people? What's going on?"

"Take it easy and stay down," Ayden ordered. He removed his Android phone and clicked on the map app. "We can trek the Engadin Mountains to Tirano, the nearest border town in Italy."

"With no snow boots we won't last long out there," Isabelle said.

"We'll have to make do."

The carriage halted, but the doors did not open. The cabin filled with indignation when the intercom crackled an announcement. "We are sorry for the inconvenience. This is due to some mechanical issue with the lines. Our engineers are trying their best to fix the problem," the voice said in Swiss-German. The message was repeated in Swiss-French.

"What kind of BS is that?" Guy asked, annoyed.

"Probably an auto response," Ayden said.

A loud whine of helicopter blades hovered above them.

Ayden popped his head out the shattered window and looked up. "It's the same helicopter."

The helicopter hovered in the air. Then it began to move sideways, raining instant death on the trackers in a hail of high-powered caliber rounds. In less than a minute, bodies lay dead across the mountain slope. The helicopter turned a full circle, then pushed forward toward the funicular.

A crewman in a black jumpsuit and helmet peered out of the craft and threw out a rope ladder, signaling for Ayden to climb up as the helicopter remained stationary above them.

"Shall we or shall we not?" Ayden mumbled, staring at the man. "He didn't kill us, so why not?" He knocked the remaining shards out of the window with his gun's butt, then reached out and grabbed the rope ladder. He turned to Guy. "You go first."

Guy climbed quickly, followed by Isabelle. When Isabelle was midway up, Ayden grabbed the bottom rung and pulled himself up. He turned to the young skier and gave him a salute. The teenager reciprocated with a V sign.

Once they were all on the helicopter, the crewman raised the ladder up and slid the door closed as the helicopter ascended higher.

"*Ciao.*"

A well-built man wearing a pair of blue sunglasses greeted them as the crewman returned to the cockpit. Sitting near the door with a seat belt strapped on, their rescuer wore a black turtleneck above brown leather pants and black boots. A gun in

INCOGNITO

a shoulder holster was strapped around his torso. Hair combed back with sideburns shaved high, his most distinctive feature was his thin and long nose, which protruded from a tight face, giving him a snobbish look. His squinty, fiery green eyes were set deep, hinting at a conniving attitude. The man turned to the pilot and made a swirling motion with his index finger. The pilot tilted to the left and increased forward speed. Destination: unknown.

The man looked at Isabelle and Guy as they removed their hoods. "You've got blood on your face."

"It's a long story. I'll tell you about it over coffee later," Guy said.

The man looked down his nose at Ayden. "My name is Mauro Cavallo. I'm the chief of *Servizio Informazioni del Vaticano,* the Vatican intelligence service."

"You guys are as mythical as the Loch Ness Monster. Yes, I've heard of The Entity, once upon a time also known as The Holy Alliance," Ayden said. "Founded by Pope Pius the Fifth in the 16th century, if I'm not wrong."

"You know a lot about us, I see," Cavallo said.

"I read a lot. Bad habit of mine," Ayden replied. "Some say you're as ruthless as any other spy agency—assassinations, kidnapping, poisoning, arms sales, money laundering. True or not, who knows?"

"I know, and that's all that matters," Cavallo said in a self-assured manner.

Ayden pulled down his hood and unzipped his jacket. "It's clear you've no plans to hurt us. So why did you save us?"

"We'll talk more soon," Cavallo replied.

Ayden knew what Cavallo meant. Talk more meant trading information, playing mind games, trying to size each other up. Ayden was in no mood to entertain him. All he wanted right now was a hot shower and a cup of coffee.

CHAPTER SIX

The mild sun lit Senator Willem Van Der Haas's gold-flecked blue eyes as he bounded across the cobblestone courtyard toward the exit. He had just attended a parliamentary session at The Hague's Binnenhof building. The Dutch immigration and integration policies continued to be a hot topic, with the Netherlands divided in its response to the growing number of African and Arab refugees in the country. On any other day he would've stopped to chat with the press, invite them for coffee at a nearby café, or scheduled a Q&A in his office. Not today. He was not in the mood for them. During the parliamentary session earlier he'd received distressing news about what happened in Saint Moritz. Sword lost men. He didn't utter a single word as he headed toward the waiting Lexus.

The man stood five feet nine inches tall, had slicked back golden hair, and his eyes were closer to his wide, furrowed forehead than his snub nose. Originally from the town of Zaanse Schans, the Dutch senator was the second son of a couple who owned a tourist pub. With a degree in law and political and international relations, he rose to the rank of senator after beginning his career in foreign affairs. Van Der Haas was well liked and respected by the general population, as he had championed their rights, including issues on housing, gender equality, and same-sex marriage. The forty-six-year-old had a penchant for ganja and cigars.

Van Der Haas slammed the car door shut. The reporters knocked on the tinted glass window as the vehicle began to move. He ignored them as they gave chase for a few meters.

He reached in his coat pocket and pulled his phone out. He dialed a number and waited for the other side to answer.

"Did they find him?" Van Der Haas spoke into the phone, his eyes staring outside. He was referring to Rafael Rabolini, the Vatican press secretary, who he knew was planning to meet Demetrious Mallas. No names were to be mentioned on the phone or online to avoid digital footprints. He knew government hackers and independent phishers and cyberpunks were on the lookout for keywords and phrases. Van Der Haas also relied on couriers to deliver messages and data by hand to hide messages and communicate freely. They also used burner phones, disposable SIM cards, and dead drops—leaving physical packages, information, or photographs in public places. Emails and SMS messages relied heavily on metaphors and codes to avoid interception.

"Yes, we did. He's still in the chic town," the voice at the other end of the line replied.

"Good. Find out what's he up to." Van Der Haas hung up. He knew "chic town" referred to Saint Moritz.

"Everything okay, sir?" The ponytailed driver, a giant of a man in a black suit, glanced back at the senator in the rearview mirror. He had rectangular eyes and a square nose below his widow's peak, with a short, thin scar running across the forehead.

"Everything is not okay. The Italians took the Greek and his friends to Venice. It's making things complicated."

"That's bad news, sir," the giant said.

Van Der Haas gazed out the car window. "The plan was simple: kidnap the pope, force the Vatican to comply with our demands, and that's it."

"What can I do for you, sir?" the giant asked.

Van Der Haas leaned back. "Be patient. When the time comes, I will let you know."

***

The helicopter circled above a section of Venice Marco Polo Airport before setting down. Nearby, planes whizzed and swooshed as they took off and landed on the different runways. Behind a fence, a chauffeur in a black suit stood outside a limousine. He greeted Cavallo as they approached.

The limo's minibar was filled with *Chinotto*. Cavallo handed bottles to everyone as the limousine sped out of the airport. Ayden still hoped for coffee.

"First to the water taxi. Then we take the gondola to my office," Cavallo said. "I would suggest you pull down your hoods so that nobody sees the blood stains." He studied their pants. "At least it's not obvious on your pants. The dark colors are concealing it."

Ayden began to feel impatient. He knew he shouldn't ask him anything. If Cavallo was trying to read him, he shouldn't make the assessment easy. In the espionage business, people didn't divulge information for free—they bartered, paid, or applied force. And if Cavallo was equally as talented as him, Ayden expected a deadlock. No doubt this whole affair with them being rescued by the Italians has something to do with the pope. But he was also wary of Cavallo, despite him being a savior. The Entity might be a church-inspired institution, but he would be naïve to think Vatican spies operated with decorum, as he had previously hinted to Cavallo. Their reputation conflicted with stories of both heroism and terror. Centuries ago, the agency, while still known as The Holy Alliance, was made up of Jesuit monks turned spies. Loyal to the pope, they had plotted to kill royals in several European countries, including England. They were also rumored to have helped Nazi officers escape to Latin America. The Entity had never bothered to confirm or deny the implications.

***

From the water taxi desk, they were escorted to a small dock. A plump man in a thick brown pullover stood behind the wheel of a speedboat as his partner helped them with their bags.

Saltwater sprayed on their faces and in their hair as the speedboat cut the water between centuries-old buildings. Feeling chilly, Ayden wrapped both arms around his uplifted knees while wondering where their rescuer was taking them.

The speedboat slowed down a distance away from the main ferry terminal and came to the side of a dock. The driver then edged nearer and tied up the craft.

Cavallo led them through a tide of tourists and carnival revelers around Doge's Palace and *Basilica Cattedrale Patriarcale di San Marco*. A flock of pigeons fluttered down into Saint Mark's Square, while another group flew across in a straight line, a few breaking into a zigzag, doubling back and then clustering about the building rooftops, ledges, and statues. Their cheerfulness was impervious to the silent melancholy amongst the human crowd. Everyone was feeling it — the unknown fate of the pope.

They passed an intersection at *Piazza di San Marco* and an egress underneath the *Procuratie Vecchie* arcade. Two masked ladies with period hairstyles stood nearby as tourists queued to take photos with them. Their masks and costumes brought Isabelle back to the time she was seven years old. At carnival in Paris, she remembered sitting on a pink carousel horse with a golden saddle as her parents watched her. She remembered every child's face on the different horses. They were all her friends, boys and girls. How she wished time could just freeze in that moment forever. She remembered seeing the men and women in masks performing an assortment of trickery and illusion. Magical. She even dreamt of following the carnival wherever they went. She would stare out at the window of her bedroom and imagine the pink horse coming to take her. Then it would gallop away with her to join the others.

***

The entourage snaked through a labyrinth of narrow passageways and alleys and emerged at a small lagoon. A black vessel with intricate designs and fancy upholstery rested on the side. Cavallo ushered them aboard. He removed a striped pullover and hat hidden under a seat, then put them on over his clothes. He raised the long oar and pushed the vessel away from the edge.

Winding around the canal, Cavallo steered the gondola across narrow corridors, tight corners, and under bridges. The vessel cruised past palazzi, canal-side hotels, cafes, and waterfront stores between the ancient buildings. It wasn't Ayden's first trip to Venice, yet each time he came it gave him a sensation of being lured into a surreal world. The city was frozen in time. He was always struck by a strange, unconscious sense of familiarity, a déjà vu moment that took him back centuries as a nobleman reveling in the carnival.

The gondola glided into an arch opening in an old building, and parked under a porch held by columns sheathed with moss and slime. A flight of stone steps led up from the water trickling against the edge of the wet stone. Beyond the platform edge, more stone stairs jutted from the walls leading to a faded metal door.

Cavallo removed his sunglasses as he led them up the stairs. The door opened into a broad room lit by a trail of spluttering electric torches. A guard in a thick black pullover, armed with a Beretta M12, stood at the end of the hallway.

"Never been to a nightclub in the daytime," Guy whispered to Ayden as they walked behind Cavallo.

"Neither have I," Cavallo responded, looking over his shoulder. "I'm taking you to my office."

The guard keyed in a password on the digital lock to open the door. He then stepped aside to let them pass.

***

Cavallo brought them into a dimly lit control room. A dozen people—men and women—sat behind arched counters with more than a dozen computer screens wrapped around the wall. Coffee mugs were everywhere.

They proceeded toward a small, glass-paneled conference room. Cavallo bade them sit as he took a seat opposite. He maintained a stiff posture while looking at everyone. "I'm reading your mind. Yes, this is about the pope," Cavallo began. "Firstly, I need to know who you people are. Nobody seems to know anything about you."

"You rescued us not knowing who we were? We could be dangerous people," Ayden said.

Cavallo leaned forward and clasped his hands into a ball on the table. "You can't be that dangerous...otherwise those men would be running away from you instead of chasing you."

The head of Vatican intelligence was a member of an old, aristocratic Italian family with its own coat of arms. Starting his career in the *Gendarmerie,* he was selected to join The Entity, and rose through the ranks. The demands of his job forced him to remain single, at least for now.

"We represent a private establishment," Ayden said. "How'd you find us?"

"An agent on the ground did. He was watching Rabolini when he stumbled upon you," Cavallo said. "He followed Rabolini to the Leaning Tower. After Rabolini vanished, my agent focused on you. When those masked men came to the ski dorm, he alerted us."

Ayden turned his head to the coffee machine on a trolley at the right side of the room.

"Help yourself. Don't let it be said Italians have bad manners," Cavallo said.

"Why did your agent follow Rabolini?" Ayden tore a sugar

packet and poured it into a mug. "You don't trust him?"

"We're investigating everyone, even the angels," Cavallo said. "If you expect me to answer your questions, you must answer mine."

"We're on the same side, that's all that matters," Ayden said.

"I don't know much about you people," Cavallo said. "Why did you meet with Rabolini?"

"To find out what happened to the pope," Ayden said.

"What've you learned?"

Ayden held back. "Nothing much. Anyway, if we find the pope before you do, we'll send him back to you. Gift wrapped."

"I'm not competing with you," Cavallo said. "I want to cooperate."

"We don't function that way," Ayden said.

"You're not a detective. So what are you? Are you one of those people involved in the kidnapping and ransom business?"

"There's no reward for us," Guy responded.

"You're doing it from the bottom of your heart?" Cavallo asked. "Do you represent a secret Catholic organization we don't know about?"

"We're not *Opus Dei.*"

"Of course you're not. If you were I would know." Cavallo smiled tightly.

"We represent an apolitical and non-religious secret society that hates to see the world in pain," Ayden said.

Cavallo raised a brow. "It sounds so noble…but very naïve. The world will not change. All we can do is build higher walls."

"I see pasta isn't the only thing Marco Polo brought back from China." Ayden's eyes focused on Cavallo.

"I was referring to a metaphoric wall," Cavallo said.

The coffee machine gurgled and hissed.

Ayden looked at the coffee machine and then back at Cavallo. "It's the coffee, isn't it? You probably drink more than you should.

That would explain your fervor."

"Who assigned you to find the pope and why?"

"Does it matter who and why?" Isabelle asked.

Cavallo raised his brows. "Yes, it does. We want to know your motive."

"There are many nations offering assistance to find the pope," Ayden said. "We're just doing our part."

"Those countries helping us have a motive, political reasons," Cavallo said. "What's your real reason?"

"We're nice people who want to help," Guy replied.

Cavallo tilted his head sideways. "You're doing this because you want to go to heaven?"

"Why don't you believe us?" Ayden asked.

"It's my business not to trust easily," Cavallo said. "In front of me is a Greek, an Austrian, and a Belgian — if all your identities are true — and you're telling me that you've come to be the savior of the pope. It's a little bit funny."

"The thief thinks everyone is a thief."

"You're unidentifiable," Cavallo said. "We checked with every intelligence agency in the world. Nobody knows who you are."

"Half a league onward, all in the valley of Death," Ayden said.

Cavallo leaned back. "What're you talking about?"

"*The Charge of the Light Brigade,* an elegy by Lord Alfred Tennyson. They don't question why. They just do. That's us. We do without questioning the reason."

"Sorry, what's the meaning of elegy?" Cavallo asked.

"A sad poem," Ayden said, trying to resist a sigh.

"Sad?"

"All the soldiers died because they followed orders," Ayden said.

"Ah, they had no tactics. *Stupido,*" Cavallo sneered. "If their tactics were good, that sad poem wouldn't have existed."

"The point is we do what we must for humanity," Ayden said. "I could ask you the same question. Would you die for the pope?"

Cavallo grinned. "Everybody is talking about humanity, spirituality, and that karma bullshit these days. An earthquake can take hundreds of thousands of innocent lives. A tsunami can swallow up thousands of people. I'm a Catholic soldier. You question my loyalty? Anyway, screw this discussion. The Swiss police want answers about Geneva."

"Ah, that would explain why you were able to enter Swiss territory like it was your backyard," Ayden said.

Cavallo nodded. "I told the Swiss police I'd send you along once I'm done with you," Cavallo said.

"So we're being detained." Guy folded his arms.

"Don't look so surprised," Cavallo said. "What did Rabolini tell you?"

"Nothing much," Ayden said. "He mentioned the name of the terrorist organization holding the pope—Sword. He said if the Vatican doesn't comply with their wishes the pope will be publicly executed."

"That's true," Cavallo said. "I don't want to see a religious war. Imagine two or three thousand Muslim suicide bombers retaliating across Europe in a single day."

"Did you talk to the Swiss Guard?"

Cavallo frowned. "Of course we did. Why?"

"The pope isn't a rabbit in a cage—baffling how he disappeared," Ayden said. "How good are the Swiss Guard, really? And aren't you supposed to be involved in his security too?"

"We've been thorough with our investigation," Cavallo said defensively. "What're you trying to imply?"

"There's a crack somewhere," Ayden said.

"What do you mean crack?"

"There might be traitors among you," Ayden said, walking back to the table.

An awkward silence filled the room.

"Take my phone number down," Cavallo said.

Ayden put down the cup and recorded Cavallo's number on his phone.

"I've booked you at the *Royal San Marco* for a couple of days. We will meet again before you go back to Geneva," Cavallo said.

"You're too kind," Ayden said sarcastically.

"My men will be watching you," Cavallo said.

"I feel shy when people watch me pee," Guy said.

Isabelle craned her neck back to look outside. "Your office is far from the Vatican. Why is that?"

"It's just one of our secret offices," Cavallo explained.

"Is it because you don't trust your own people?" Isabelle asked, rephrasing the question that Cavallo hadn't answered earlier when Ayden asked him.

"Those people outside were handpicked by me," Cavallo said. "I also deal with the other divisions secretly. Unfortunately, ever since the pope disappeared we have become paranoid." He fell into a momentary silence, and then said, "I hate to think one of us betrayed him."

Ayden smiled. "I don't think it should surprise you."

CHAPTER SEVEN

They left The Entity's secret office on the same gondola, escorted by one of Cavallo's men, a silver-haired agent. At the *Royal San Marco* they were assigned three rooms on the same floor. Ayden and Guy shared one room while Isabelle had her own. Silver Hair occupied the last one.

After cleaning themselves up, they decided to have brunch at a pizzeria. As they walked across *Piazza di San Marco,* accompanied by Silver Hair at a distance, a couple in pink and blue *Commedia dell' arte* costumes and masks invited the group to take a photo with them. They declined. Ayden's feet felt stapled to the ground trying to pass through the throng. Despite the dispirited mood, the tourist scene was always the same: people taking photos, strollers, and enthralled individuals throwing seeds to pigeons.

"They do this in Venice all day? Wear masks, take photos, eat ice cream, and feed pigeons?" Isabelle's eyes darted everywhere.

"You've never been here?" Ayden asked.

"No, never. Enchanting place, but I feel the mood is strange," Isabelle said. "They're upset about the pope, I feel."

"You can imagine how they'll react if the pope is killed," Ayden said.

They sat at a pizzeria overlooking a cobblestone square with a large tree in the center. Silver Hair sat a few tables away. A waitress arrived carrying a huge meat-lover, thin-crust pizza, while a second waiter brought a tray of juices. Ayden leaned forward and spoke in a low voice after they withdrew.

"We can't stay here. We have to go to Vatican City," Ayden said. "We've got to find a way to get rid of our babysitter."

"He's just sitting there, watching us. Not eating, not even drinking." Guy picked up a slice and sank into it as he cast his eyes in the direction of Silver Hair.

"Right," Ayden smirked.

"We sneak out to the train station tonight," Isabelle said. "And—"

"You think the hotel receptionist won't rat on us?" Ayden lifted a slice of pizza with both hands. He blew the heat away and took a bite. He shut his eyes for a few seconds as he tried to juggle a chew.

"*Monsieur*, I haven't finished talking and you interrupt me," Isabelle said. "We arrange with a gondolier to wait under our window."

"Now that's a thought." Guy crammed the remaining pizza into his mouth like it was on a conveyer belt.

Ayden's eyes narrowed at Silver Hair talking on his cell phone. "He looks agitated. Wonder what's up with him?"

The SIV agent hung up a moment later and approached.

"We must go now," Silver Hair said, looking troubled.

"But we haven't finished eating," Isabelle moaned.

"Please, we must go." Silver Hair's eyes scanned the environment rapidly.

"You look stressed, my friend. What's going on?" Ayden asked.

"Our office was attacked. Everyone is dead except Cavallo. I need your help to rescue him. He's hiding."

Ayden looked at Guy and Isabelle, then back at Silver Hair. "Okay."

Silver Hair leaned his weight on the gondola's paddle and

stroked the water. He took the narrow back routes, passing rear entrances, water garages, shops, and restaurants. Water gnawed between the brickwork and crumbling stucco of the buildings' foundations.

"Are you expecting backup?" Ayden asked.

"No, just us," Silver Hair replied.

The gondola went under the arch-shaped building entrance and rested by the side of the pillared porch. A body lay within the doorway. Silver Hair drew a Beretta from under his jacket. Ayden, Isabelle, and Guy did the same.

Silver Hair alighted from the gondola. He then ascended the steps, keeping his gun clamped with both hands. Reaching the top, he turned and signaled forthe others to come up.

The sound of automatic gunfire broke the silence. Silver Hair's body jerked and shook as bullets hit him, forcing him to fall backward. He rolled down the steps and lay sprawled.

"Dive!" Ayden shouted.

They turned and sprang into the water with a tremendous splash. Holding his breath, Ayden felt his skin shrink as he submerged. His clothes, wet and heavy, dragged him down. He swam with the others to a pillar column across the porch, and emerged behind it.

Two armed masked men in black fatigue clothes appeared. They descended the steps and crossed to the edge of the platform, inspecting the gondola.

"We can take them now," Isabelle said, wiping the beads of water off her face and eyelashes. Tiny drops of water trapped in the corners of her eyes magnified her green pupils.

"Save your bullets. I'll do it," Ayden said, gulping the air.

Guy raked a hand through his matted hair. "Make it quick, I'm freezing my ass off."

Ayden whipped out a suppressor from his jacket pocket and gave it a shake to remove the water before fastening it to the barrel of his gun. He moved to the other side of the pillar, aimed, and took both out with headshots.

The first man tumbled backward, the Heckler & Koch MP7 clattering out of his hands and dropping to the ground. The second man fell to his knees and rolled into the gondola as his weapon bounced into the water.

They swam to the platform's edge and pulled themselves up, shivering. Their clothing clung to them in the dry air. Seeing the MP7 on the ground, Guy picked it up, checked the magazine, and reloaded. He looked at Silver Hair's battered body in a quiet protest.

Isabelle made the sign of the cross as she stood beside Silver Hair's body, then picked up his Beretta and slipped it into her waistline. "If I don't make it, it was a pleasure working with both of you."

"Don't worry, be dead — be death," Ayden said.

Senses on alert, they raced up the steps and skittered across the hallway to the mangled door at the end. Ayden leveled his weapon as he led everyone inside.

The control room reeked of an invasive odor of sulfur. Bodies were everywhere, swathed in blood and shards of glass. A section of the ceiling had crumbled, dropping wooden beams on the floor. They slinked a narrow path amid the chaos of broken furniture, broken glass crunching under their shoes.

"They used grenades to get in," Guy said. "Can you smell it?"

Ayden nodded. "Watch out for surprises inside those cubicles."

Near a mix of private offices and cubicle workstations, he raised his hand to signal a cautionary stop. He sidled up the wall, eyes darting to both sides. Clear. They continued.

As they walked past a wrecked cubicle station, two arms coiled around Ayden's neck. He turned to find a semiconscious, bloodied man clinging on to him, and life. Guy rushed into the cubicle and held the man steady. He slipped his arm under the man's shoulder and led him out. Barely responsive, the man's face was bruised and soaked in blood. The light-haired, middle-aged individual wore a green V-neck sweater underneath a dark bullet-torn suit jacket.

"Can you talk?" Ayden noticed the severity of the man's injuries. Bullets had punctured his shoulder, abdomen, and thigh.

The man's eyes drifted in and out of focus.

"Who're you?" Ayden asked.

"Luca." He struggled to give his name. "I'm...one of... Cavallo's agents."

"Where is Cavallo?" Ayden asked.

Luca pointed to the door at the end of the corridor. "I show you."

Guy held Luca as they walked past the conference room to the end of the corridor. A door led them left to a well-lit, stone-tiled corridor. Isabelle closed the door partially and stood guard, peering through the gap.

Luca pointed to a stone tile on the ground. "Here."

Ayden knelt down and touched the surface of the tile. "Here?" Nothing looked out of the ordinary.

"Cavallo...inside," Luca said, breathlessly.

"It's a panic room. That's what he's trying to say," Guy said.

Ayden felt in his pocket for his phone. He pulled it out and touched a prompt to auto call Cavallo, who answered immediately.

"Right above you," Ayden said.

Ayden jolted sideways as the tiles opened upward to reveal a well-lit enclosure. Cavallo emerged by climbing a slim steel ladder. He looked at Luca with concern. "Luca?"

Luca didn't answer as he clung to Guy.

Cavallo turned to Ayden. "I need to get him to a hospital."

He looked around. "Where's Sergio?"

Ayden assumed he meant Silver Hair. "I'm sorry."

Cavallo pulled out his gun. "Ominous. Let's go."

Isabelle whistled softly and signaled with her fingers thats even armed men were approaching.

Ayden looked back at Cavallo. "Can the panic room fit all of us?"

"Yes, but we don't have time. This man needs the hospital." Cavallo looked at Luca again. "We can go this way." Cavallo pointed to the end of the corridor.

A tall, narrow crate stood against a wall. Cavallo dashed across and opened the crate's door and detached the back panel. The space behind led to a dim passage. Cavallo turned to Ayden. "Let's go."

"Take your man, we'll cover you," Ayden replied.

Ayden and Guy rushed back to Isabelle and stood pressed against the wall beside her.

"Where are they?" Ayden's eyes scanned the office space.

"Hiding," Isabelle said. "They—"

Two men popped up from behind a cubicle partition and released a blast of submachine gun fire. The projectiles ripped through the door and slammed it opened, scattering splinters through the corridor. Ayden pulled Isabelle back. When the conflagration halted briefly, Ayden leaned around the doorway and parried a torrent through the thin cubicle wall. The two attackers crumbled as bullets shattered flesh and bone.

Ayden drew back against the wall. He removed the magazine, checked the chamber, and reloaded. Suddenly, more bullets impacted around them, blowing holes in the door and walls.

"Too many of them," Ayden said, recoiling. "Let's go!"

"I'll stay," Isabelle responded, removing the other gun from her waistline.

"Don't be a fool. We fight another day," Ayden said.

"Go." She pushed Ayden and edged forward, firing a round to repel the unseen foes.

Ayden and Guy retreated to the other end of the corridor as projectiles whined in their ears.

The opening through the crate led to a bookstore's back entrance. After catching up with Cavallo and Luca, they walked into a bookstore furnished with scattered bathtubs and wooden boats full of books.

At the sight of a bleeding man and three others carrying automatic weapons, the quiet afternoon whipped into mayhem. Bookshelves overturned as customers clamored toward the exit facing the canal. Screams and shrieks came from the congested mass trying to pile into a gondola. The old gondolier at the rear struggled to balance the vessel from tipping.

Ayden and the others hurried toward the exit. "Get out of the gondola, all of you!" Ayden ordered, waving the pistol.

Customers scrambled back into the bookstore, pleading for mercy and chanting prayers under their breath. Others jumped into the water, agitating the gondola further.

Ayden hopped into the vessel's cabin as the gondolier protested.

"Don't move until I say," Ayden ordered, pointing the pistol at him.

Cavallo placed Luca's head on the cushion as Guy lowered the man's body onto the floorboard. Then they scrambled to position themselves on the starboard, weapons leveled at the entrance.

As the surging sounds of firefight drew closer, a familiar face darted toward them. Isabelle leaped into the vessel, almost flipping the craft.

Ayden turned to the gondolier. "Go now!" Facing the entrance again, he rested an elbow on the bow and fired at the attackers, forcing them back.

The gondolier paddled as fast as he could. Two heads popped out of the bookstore and sent a short, sharp burst of gunfire. Bullets peppered the water all around them, some whizzing past them, others causing small splashes and ripples. A few impacted the gondola, chipping away wood and creating holes. As water began to seep in, a bullet hit the gondolier's shoulder, knocking him overboard. The long wooden pole slipped from his hands and plunked into the water.

Ayden leaned over the side of the boat and grabbed the paddle, then reached out to grab the old man.

When the exchange ceased momentarily, Cavallo stood, took the paddle, and veered the leaking craft to an intersection, then turned into a narrow waterway.

Tiny waves lapped on both sides of the gondola as they moved along the canal. They reached a dead end with a fissure in the wall. By then, Luca was dead.

Cavallo looked at Ayden as he pointed to the gap in the wall. "You can go back to the hotel that way."

"And you?" Ayden asked.

"I must settle things." Cavallo looked at Luca, then at the gondolier lying on the floorboard pressing a scarf down onto his wound. He looked at the MP7 in Guy's hand. "I suggest you toss that into the water before you step out there."

Isabelle stepped forward and handed Silver Hair's Beretta to Cavallo. "It belonged to your agent, Sergio. You keep it."

Cavallo took the gun and reversed the vessel, then slowly disappeared behind a wall.

***

Floating on the still water, Cavallo pondered whether today's event was worth the sacrifice. The sadness he'd felt moments ago was overridden by a stoic attitude. He should plan his next step and regroup. Luca and the other agents had died as heroes. They would be remembered that way. His emotions should not distract him from the present situation. The mission was not over. Today was a setback, but tomorrow's destiny would not be decided now.

***

Ayden and the two other specialists emerged through the gap in the wall into a narrow alley. Thronging tourists meandered around glittering shops. No one gave a second look at their dripping attire — things happened in Venice. Maybe their gondola capsized.

Ayden's phone rang. He pulled the wet phone from his jacket pocket and answered.

"Demetrious."

"Rabolini," Ayden said, hiding his surprise.

"I'm calling you from a public phone in Rome. Something has come up. We need to meet again." Rabolini's voice resonated with stress. "Can you come to Rome?"

"Has something happened?"

"I can't talk now. Just meet me," Rabolini said.

Ayden hung up after getting the details and looked at the others. "Rabolini wants to meet in Rome. Wonder what's up."

"Anything to worry about?" Isabelle shuddered as the wetness and the cold clutched her.

"He didn't say, and I didn't ask," Ayden said. "The last thing I want is to make him distrust me. So I'll play along."

"Good point. *Allez*, we go. But first, I need a hot shower," Isabelle groaned.

Ayden sneezed, then snorted. "Me too. Bloody mommy, my cold's back. I need more aspirin."

***

Chief Inspector Guillaume sat at the table's edge in the squad room. He stared at the men and women in uniform as he lit a clove cigarette. Faces cringed at the smell permeating the enclosed space. He pointed to the blown-up photos of Ayden,

Isabelle, and Guy pinned on a board behind him. The grayscale image of Ayden showed his cheekbones starker, his eyes more hollow, his face gaunt.

Guillaume pointed to a young officer standing by the window. "Detective Kugler and I examined the bodies found at *Les Hauts de Rive*. The dead bodies, except for the hotel staff, had one thing in common — they all had the same signature tattoo on their right thumb's fingertip, a dagger with wings."

"Sword," said a plainclothes male detective sitting in the front row.

Guillaume nodded.

"We've also been informed by the Vatican's intelligence service the two hotel guests who didn't check out are in Venice, along with a third — the Greek who never checked in," Kugler said, pointing to their pictures on the board.

Heads turned to look at the photographs.

"Those people are not innocent bystanders," Guillaume added. "They're not the enemy either. But we don't know who they are. Initial investigation revealed nothing on them. They claimed to Vatican intelligence they want to help find the pope. The owner of *Les Hauts de Rive* stores the security camera footage in the cloud, so we know what happened that night.

"Demetrious, Borsok, and Duchamp are specialists. Who's behind them remains a mystery," Guillaume continued. "They entered Switzerland with fake passports. Borsok has been here for a year — undetected. He lives with his girlfriend. She told us she hasn't heard from him. He claims to be a cargo pilot, so she hardly sees him. They had that kind of relationship."

"They've survived several attempts to kill them," a blonde female officer sitting mid-row said. "My question is, how does Sword know every move they make?"

"Good question." Guillaume stared at Kugler and took another puff. "They're probably being tracked. As much as I hate to say this, we also suspect there's a traitor in our station. One of us — or more than one — could possibly be a Sword informant. It could be one of you in this room."

The room shrank at the suggestion.

"I was starting to enjoy the company of everyone in the station," said a muscular male cop with short-cropped hair sitting at the back. "Why do you think we have a traitor?"

"It shouldn't come as a surprise that an organization like Sword would be watching our every move," Guillaume said. "We should be more alert."

The room went abuzz with murmurs.

"It's a dirty word, I know. But Sword is a powerful organization. They're ten steps ahead of us. If we're going to win, we'll have to play by their rules," Guillaume said. "We're not dealing with a bunch of petty criminals here. So keep an ear to the ground, on the wall — everywhere. Watch your back. Let me know if you find out anything. Trust nobody. Dismissed."

The chief inspector walked down the corridor toward the elevator. An attractive young blonde with a short bob stood in the foyer. Clad in a brown parka and cream pants, she was speaking to a pale-faced, black-haired man in a sharp suit. Guillaume recognized the man: Robert Benzinger, the station's public relations manager. No doubt the woman beside him was a reporter. Why else would any female talk to an asshole like Benzinger? Guillaume stared at the carpeted floor as he sidestepped them toward the elevator.

"Chief Inspector, I'd like to you to meet Christa Braun from *Tribune de Genève*," Benzinger said.

Guillaume nodded at the reporter.

Christa smiled back. "Pleased to meet you, Inspector." She extended her hand, but wriggled and stepped back after being assailed by the cigarette's odor.

Guillaume noticed her reaction. "It's Chief Inspector."

"Sorry. Chief Inspector, I'd like to find out more about this case," Christa said, holding a pen and a notepad.

"What case?"

"The murders at *Les Hauts de Rive* and the incident on the train," Christa said.

"It's still a pending investigation, so I have nothing to say." Guillaume moved nearer to the elevator.

"I spoke to the hotel's owner, Bertrand. He's not too thrilled about what happened. Apart from the cost of repairs, his concern is the hotel's reputation. Not that I blame him. Anyway, he said some guests didn't check out: an Austrian and a Belgian. One other person, a Greek, didn't show up, but I know he's in the country. Care to elaborate?"

"How'd you find out about the Greek?" Guillaume asked.

"Ah, so we're getting somewhere. My sources at the airport told me," Christa said. "I've got sources everywhere, Chief."

"Please excuse me." Guillaume gave a contemptuous glance at Benzinger and stepped to the elevator and pressed the button. The doors parted. He stepped inside and turned around.

Christa stepped forward. "Inspector, one last question. Do—"

He wagged his fingers at Christa as the doors shut. *It's Chief Inspector, bitch.*

An overpowering smell of bacon and an occasional whiff of garlic clashed with the clinking of cutlery, tinkling glasses, and murmurs at the sandwich bar. Guillaume was not a stranger at the small eatery just down the road from the police station. He always received special treatment, like a few extra slices of everything on his plate. This was his secret abode, a place to think and reflect.

The fifty-four-year-old had a pessimistic outlook despite being a good cop. The last thirty-five years of his professional and personal life had been cyclonic. He'd married a twenty-seven-year-old Internet bride from Ukraine. Whatever she wanted, she got—a nice house, regular holidays, new clothes, jewelry. She brought him happiness, and regrets. Hidden cameras in the house confirmed his suspicions. Was he surprised she was unfaithful? Yet he kept her by his side. That was his personal life—nobody's damn business.

He groaned when Christa slid into the chair across the table. "What would it take to get rid of you?"

"Who killed who back at the hotel?" Christa asked.

"Zombies from hell," Guillaume said without looking up.

"Funny."

Guillaume scratched his right ear. "I've nothing more to say to you. Please leave."

A waiter approached and Christa ordered a glass of orange juice, then reverted to questioning Guillaume. "Does Switzerland have a new cult problem? Is the Mafia crossing in from Italy? Has this case been classified as an act of terrorism?"

"No comment," Guillaume said.

"I see Benzinger isn't doing a good PR job. Never say 'no comment' to a journalist; it makes you look more suspicious. So, tell me, what're you hiding?"

"Nothing. I'm just following procedures. Not the time to talk to the press. I'll let you know what we have when it's time."

The waiter arrived with Christa's orange juice.

"I don't have time, Chief, that's the whole problem. Think they've gone to Italy?" Christa stared at him over the rim of the glass as she took a sip of the juice.

Guillaume shrugged. "Who knows?"

Christa put down the glass and reached for her wallet in her bag. She took out one of her business cards and handed it to him. "If you're ready to talk, let me know. I know you won't call me, so expect to see me more often." She stood and exited.

Guillaume watched her go, then looked at the card. *Trouble.*

CHAPTER EIGHT

The sky was scaled with gray clouds, hinting at a looming storm, yet tourists continued to pour in at the famous Trevi Fountain. Photographers and coin throwers massed at the edges of Oceanus's domain. Ayden sat outside the café, back against the wall, waiting for Rabolini. He checked his watch. The Vatican press secretary should be here soon. He sneezed a few times quietly, each time pushing the mucus back into his nose. He asked for a napkin when a waiter walked past. He used it to blow his nose. He had developed a mild fever since Venice and it sent shivers through his pummeled body. The aspirin failed to do its job. Since he arrived yesterday, he'd done nothing but sleep.

In front of Ayden, the theater of life unfolded. A boy cried when his chocolate bar fell on the ground. Two policemen dragged a gypsy woman away after she stole from a tourist. A gaggle of nuns sang a hymn of hope to a crowd of onlookers. A gelato vendor tended to a group of customers huddling around his cart.

A bespectacled, bearded man in thick clothes with an ivy cap approached. Head bowed, eyes lowered, he sat beside Ayden.

"Ciao, Rabolini," Ayden said, staring at the space in front of him.

"How did you know it was me?"

"The way you walk. You didn't disguise it." Ayden picked

up the small cup of coffee and took a sip.

"I'll be more careful next time. You arrived today?"

"Yesterday."

"Where are you staying?"

"Some budget hotel." Ayden didn't want to give details.

"You sound like you have a cold."

"I do," Ayden said. "Come to the point, Rabolini."

Rabolini took a quick look around. "They tried to kill me."

"Who did?"

"Sword," Rabolini said. "A few nights ago an assassin found me at a friend's home. He stabbed my friend to death, thinking it was me. I managed to escape."

"I didn't read about it." Ayden put the cup down.

"Murder is so common here the newspapers don't bother to report everything," Rabolini said.

"Did you approach the authorities for protection?" Ayden asked.

"Who can I trust?"

"You can trust Cavallo."

"He has his fair share of problems, from what I hear."

Ayden sighed. "The last time we met, I asked you if the kidnappers gave any proof they have the pope. You mentioned a cross—"

Ayden jolted as small debris burst from the wall beside him.

"Sniper!" Ayden pulled Rabolini with him as he dived to the ground.

The crowd burst into laughter, amused at the spectacle. But the mirth switched to an infusion of fear and hysteria when a tourist dropped to the ground, blood streaming out of his temple. Panic rippled through the scattering crowd as bullets sparked the ground and pierced flesh. Frantic mothers rushed away with their crying children, lovers became separated, and people were stampeded in a throng of screams.

Ayden stayed close to the ground. His eyes searched for Rabolini. He was nowhere in sight. Another man fell in front of him, the life in him ebbing. An emotional convulsion took control of Ayden. Through a confluence of screams, groans, and moans from the strewn bodies, he crawled toward the ice cream cart, ignoring the agonizing scrapes on his elbows and knees. Crouching behind the cart, he held on to one of its wheels.

"Let go of the wheel," the ice cream vendor demanded, kicking Ayden in the ribs repeatedly.

Wrapping his arms around the ice cream seller's legs, Ayden pulled him down. After wrestling with Ayden, he managed to dislodge his grip and pulled himself up.

A bullet whizzed past. The ice cream man snapped back and fell to the ground. Blood oozed from his cheek and the back of his head. Ayden turned away.

Hunkered behind the cart, Ayden braced against the thumping projectiles. He reached into his jacket and yanked out his gun. He pushed the cart toward the corner of the building. Winding to a back alley where a van was unloading food supplies, he propelled himself forward as the bruises on his legs knotted the muscles. He glanced back. Three men were pounding after him.

The alley branched sharply to his left, and he followed it in time to dodge a bullet whining past his head. Pausing behind a large metal bin, Ayden shot back, managing to buy a gap of time as the assailants took cover.

Ayden's legs began to tire as his breathing rate increased. He knew he had to put more distance between him and his pursuers.

A bullet grazed him in the right shoulder. The flesh wound sent shafts of pain shooting through his arm. He tried to ignore it. Turning right onto a street, he ran as fast as he could along the pavement, not feeling the concrete under his shoes. He looked back once more and saw no one. He understood trouble could appear from anywhere — maybe the chasers knew a shorter route to cut him off.

Ayden reached an intersection and took the street where the traffic flowed in one direction. He zigzagged through the crowd.

A taxi dropped off a customer up ahead. He tried to push toward it. Reaching the taxi before it moved, he grabbed the door handle and jumped in.

The driver turned around, eyes wide open. "You're bleeding! What happened?"

"Drive!"

The taxi accelerated onto the crowded street. Ayden gave instructions where to go as he looked back through the rear window. No one was following. He leaned back in the seat and collected his breath.

***

Hotel Cisterna in Rome is a quaint, family-run establishment tucked in a quiet lane in Trastevere. Its obscurity — hidden in a quiet lane while blending with its ancient surroundings, surrounded by cafes, pizzerias, restaurants, and wine bars — made it the perfect location for members of the League of Invisible Knights to seek refuge. Not to mention, it was just a twenty-minute walk along the Tiber River to the Vatican.

Ayden sat on the edge of the bed in one of the hotel's rooms as Isabelle tended to the shoulder graze. The room was simple and basic, with an extra bed. A couple of paintings hung on the walls, while a working desk stood flush near a long window facing another building that stood between a narrow, cobblestone lane. The faded, wooden cupboard looked like it had been around since the eighties. The bathroom, complete with shower, was tolerable.

"It was like a passing black cloud before it started to rain bullets." Ayden recounted the Trevi fountain incident. "I shouldn't have agreed to meet Rabolini at a crowded place...so many unnecessary deaths."

"You didn't see Rabolini after that?" Guy asked as he sat opposite on the other bed.

"He vanished. I never got a chance to find out more from him about that night at *Borghese Park.* I don't think I'll see Rabolini again for some time, so I need to convince Mr. Somebody to reveal who the actual source at the Vatican is, because that person is going to know more. Otherwise, this assignment will never be resolved."

Ayden stood after Isabelle had strapped a bandage on his shoulder. He leaned against the window and pulled open the curtain a little. A group of teenage boys on scooters were catcalling a woman walking past. "Rabolini claimed an assassin tried to kill him. It was never reported in the news. The sniper tried to take out Rabolini before he shot at me. Why would anyone want Rabolini dead?"

Guy picked up Ayden's iPad on the bed. "Why, indeed."

"What're you doing with my iPad?" Ayden asked.

"Chill out, bro. Just doing a bit of research," Guy said. "Seen the crap on TV here? They're still rerunning *Charles in Charge.* Now how'd you expect me to put my time to good use? Seriously, I read something earlier, thought it might interest you."

"What?" Ayden asked.

"How I think the pope was kidnapped. Want to hear my theory?"

"Not you too," Ayden objected. "I'm sick of theories."

"Hear me out, man. Whatcha' gotta lose?" Guy insisted.

"Fine, tell me."

"I remembered a reporter asking at a press conference if the pope sneaks out at night to feed the homeless. The Vatican denied it, but it's the perfect time to nab him."

"Yeah, I read about it too, but I never took it seriously," Ayden said. "The story goes the pope dresses as a regular priest. Surely he would've been accompanied by the Swiss Guard and some SIV agents."

"What if they were ambushed?" Guy said. "What if an insider tipped off the kidnappers where the pope would be?"

"It makes no sense. Cavallo would've known. His people are also in charge of the pope's security," Isabelle reminded him as she handed Ayden two aspirin tablets and a glass of water.

"That's right." Ayden put the glass down on the bedside table after downing the tablets. His phone chimed inside his jacket hanging on a chair. He crossed over, unzipped the side seam, and removed the Android phone.

"Demetrious."

"Rabolini." Ayden turned on the speaker and sat at the edge of the bed again. "I tried looking for you."

"I saw you crawling toward the ice cream cart. I couldn't reach you. I managed to flee. Listen, Demetrious, I'm going to disappear. I can't handle this anymore. You won't hear from me again."

The call ended.

"Rabolini? Hello?" Ayden tried redialing, but there was no connection. "I'm going to try calling Cavallo." He tapped the screen and brought the phone to his ear again. "Not connected." Ayden looked out the window. "I feel like a headless chicken."

"Time to talk to the Swiss Guard commander," Guy said. "We might learn more."

Ayden grimaced. "What? Just walk into his office?"

"Every Wednesday he goes for lunch at a restaurant called *Aristocampo*. That should make our lives easier."

Ayden squinted. "How'd you find that out?"

"I had a chat with the hotel receptionist earlier asking for recommendations on where to eat. One of the places she suggested is this outlet, a favorite among some Vatican people, including the commander and his officers. Frei is about forty, married, and originally from Grinderwald, a small town. He's a former Swiss army captain—"

"You found out all that from a hotel receptionist?" Ayden asked in astonishment.

"No, I got the rest from Google," Guy said. "Not everything is a secret."

"You got to get your own iPad." Ayden looked out the window again. "You're assuming Frei's going to agree to talk to us. You mentioned he's never alone during lunch. It would make things more difficult for us. What if he's involved?"

Blankness crossed Isabelle's face. "You know, even if the Swiss Guard commander is involved, he's only going to repeat what he told Cavallo, who said he questioned everyone."

"For that reason, we'll have to flush him out. We'll tell him we know what happened, that we recorded the incident with the pope on a cell phone," Ayden said. "Isabelle, you'll give him a note with a number to call. If he bites, we've got something. If he doesn't, we walk away. How's that sound?"

"Nothing to lose." Guy said.

"I need to call Mr. Somebody and find out who's the Vatican source. He's not going to like it, but screw protocol." Ayden tapped a single digit number on the cell phone and stretched out his arm with the other hand to look at the screen. Moments later, Mr. Somebody appeared.

"What happened to you?" said Mr. Somebody, his voice and visual coming through the phone clearly. He was squatting down, tending to roses in a cottage garden.

"I just had an extraordinary day, that's all," Ayden replied.

"Sounds progressive. What do you need, Tanner?"

"A name. Need to know who the Vatican source is," Ayden said.

"I promised I wouldn't tell. That was the agreement," Mr. Somebody said.

"I wish it was that easy, but we're not making headway. I'm

not sure what Rabolini's game is."

"You're making this difficult, Tanner," Mr. Somebody reiterated. "Can't you work around it?"

"I'm afraid not. I have to know," Ayden said.

Mr. Somebody stuck his spade up in the earth and stood. "You're responsible for whatever happens. Cardinal Pasquino Bartolomeo, the pope's personal secretary."

Ayden ended the call. "We've got a name. He might be able to tell us more." He looked at Guy. "What other disguises do you have? Not the rabbi costumes again, please."

***

A sense of awe overwhelmed Ayden each time he visited Saint Peter's Square, a grand elliptical esplanade with majestic columns, statues, and sculptures. Wearing a monk's robe with the hood over his head, Ayden waited for Cardinal Bartolomeo at the central aisle of Bernini's colonnade facing the Basilica's west fountain. Despite the cold, he could feel the morning sun's rays. Its golden light strummed across the columns, friezes, and rooftop statues like a harp's melody in ascension.

According to Mr. Somebody, the pope's personal secretary had a daily habit of walking around the famous Egyptian obelisk as part of an exercise regime. The thought of Bartolomeo doing his morning walks around the obelisk reminded Ayden of his own exercise regime. Not that he felt weak, but he could feel his mood taking wild swings — those endorphins came in handy when he needed them. Especially since it helped him forget Maria…and he needed to forget.

Ayden caught sight of a short, bald man in a black sports suit and red sneakers. He meandered across the cobblestones toward him.

"Cardinal Bartolomeo?" Ayden greeted him, hands folded in the robe's sleeves as he walked beside him.

The cardinal paused and tried to peek under the hood.

"*Scusi?*"

"I'm Demetrious Mallas," Ayden said. "I work for the League of Invisible Knights."

The cardinal looked around suspiciously. "How did you find me? We should not be meeting."

"I asked Mr. Somebody for your name. We decided to break the protocol because we don't have a choice. Rabolini has disappeared."

"Disappeared?"

"He contacted me yesterday and said I'll never see him again. When was the last time you met him?" Ayden asked, sniffing. *Damn the mucus.*

"Hmmm… a few days ago." Bartolomeo moved again. "Why is he in hiding?"

"He claims Sword tried to kill him. I had destroyed Rabolini's cell phone. It had been hacked. That's how they got hold of every bit of information. Did you communicate with Rabolini at any time using your cellphone?"

"No. After I spoke to Mr. Somebody, I met Rabolini personally, and gave him instructions on what to do. No one could have connected us," Bartolomeo said. "If he's in trouble, why didn't he approach me?"

"I'm wondering the same thing," Ayden said. "I never got the full story from Rabolini. Perhaps you can tell me more. It's imperative you speak to me."

The cardinal cocked his head. "Mr. Somebody had approached me to offer his organization's services, but I told him not to reveal my identity."

A flock of pigeons swarmed over the square. The temperature remained cold even though the sun had risen over the Dome, its light penetrating the deep shadows of the columns.

"Do you want us to help you find the pope or not?"

Bartolomeo stared into empty space. "What do you wish to

know?"

Hoping to avoid sounding like a conspiracy theorist, Ayden hesitated asking the next question, but eventually conceded. "I'm at my wits' end, but rumor has it the pope goes out some nights secretly to feed the poor. This is the only possible theory to explain how he was kidnapped. So, my question is, is it true?"

"Yes, it's true. The pope puts on regular priest's attire so nobody knows it's him," Bartolomeo said.

Ayden pictured Guy in his mind and envisioned him saying *I told you so.* "Was he taken one of those nights?"

"Yes, he was."

"Who else knew about this?" Ayden came closer to Bartolomeo as the crowd increased.

"Some of the Swiss Guard and SIV agents. I was there, and so was Camerlengo Florentin, the executive director of the Vatican's operations. We were ambushed. They came in two vans. They killed everyone," Bartolomeo recounted. "Florentin and I pretended to be dead. I'm not proud of myself for failing to protect the pope."

"This incident was not reported to the media," Ayden said. "Why?"

"The security divisions were embarrassed," Bartolomeo explained. "They were not sure what to tell the public. So they withheld information and announced it a week later, after receiving the ultimatum from the kidnappers."

"Is that why you didn't tell Mr. Somebody about the incident?"

"I was sworn to secrecy."

"We need to know everything you know," Ayden said. "There should be no secrets between us. Rabolini mentioned a cross when I asked him if the kidnappers gave any proof they have the pope. I never got the details."

"Yes, the Pectoral Cross was exclusively designed by a

craftsman for the pope. He wears it most of the time. Thanks for reminding me, as I need to get it fixed," Bartolomeo said. "I've been so busy I forgot about it." He slapped his cheek. "Now, where is it? Ah, it's in my desk drawer. How careless I am."

"What's wrong with it?"

"The chain is made up of small, circular links. I noticed some of the links were dented," Bartolomeo said.

"Dented? Someone stepped on it?"

"Or something crushed it. I need to send it to the craftsman who designed it. He would know what to do."

"Were there other witnesses that night when the pope was taken?"

"No, the incident took place in a small lane when we were returning to the Apostolic Palace." He grabbed Ayden's arm. "Find the pope and bring him back alive."

"I will do my best. For your safety, this meeting never took place."

***

Aristocampo, with its yellow patina walls, stood on a cobblestone square in front of *Saint Maria della Scala* church. The temperature during the lunch hour flirted between hot and cold above a marble sky. Several *gendarmerie* officers stood around watching passersby. Tourists poked their heads into the little stores, while some stopped to take pictures.

Frei sat alone under a canopy twirling his pasta with a fork. Wearing a mauve winter jacket over a black thermal pullover, he was a tall, bony-face man with a monk's tonsure. Ayden and Guy, hiding their faces behind sunglasses, sat a few tables away.

A waitress approached their table. Neither could decide what they wanted to eat. The waitress finally decided for them both: *spaghetti alle vongole* with two bottles of *Chinotto.*

Guy nudged Ayden as Isabelle passed them. Wearing a black scarf over her head, she dropped a folded piece of paper on Frei's table and disappeared.

Frei put the fork down and picked up the paper. He unfolded it and read the message. He then picked up his cell phone and made the call.

"What does the video show?" Frei said in French, Ayden and Guy now seated opposite him.

"Before we answer your question, you answer a few of ours," Ayden said, trying to hold the reins.

"What kind of information?" Frei asked.

The waitress, seeing Ayden and Guy had shifted places, approached with their orders.

"You're in charge of the pope's security. We saw the pope being taken away by some men that night," Ayden said after the waitress excused herself.

"If you don't talk, the clip gets uploaded on YouTube," Guy blurted. "We also spoke to some of the cardinals who were there. We know there's a conspiracy to cover it up."

Frei grinned. "Who're you people?"

"Nobody, somebody," Ayden said.

Frei picked up his fork. "So you know. How much do you want for the video?"

The question excited Ayden, but he didn't show it.

"We want information," Ayden said.

"Why?" Frei asked.

"That's our business," Guy replied.

Frei looked at him. "And then what happens to me?"

"Maybe you should start talking now, or we'll go to the *gendarmerie* and the SIV," Ayden said.

Frei stared at the table, as if his head was too heavy to lift. "I tipped off the kidnappers when the pope would be out at night."

"Why did you do that?" Guy asked.

"I succumbed to temptation."

"What did they give you?"

INCOGNITO

"Five million American dollars."

"I guess the lesson from Judas didn't teach you anything," Ayden said.

Frei bowed in shame.

Ayden looked at his plate. Neither he nor Guy had touched their food.

"Where's the pope?" Guy asked.

"They never told me," Frei said, looking perplexed. "I'm sorry for what I did."

"Where's the five million?" Ayden asked.

"In a secret bank account set up for me."

"If you're sorry, why didn't you come forward?"

"I was afraid. I need not explain to you the psychology of a man in a situation like this. If I confessed to everything, I would be free of guilt, but not the shame."

"But you kept the money. Who else was involved?" Ayden asked.

"Camerlengo Florentin and a banker named Zanebono. He helped me hide the money."

"And who else?"

"Rabolini."

"Now we're getting somewhere," Ayden said.

"That night, your men were ambushed. How'd you manage to cover up their deaths?" Guy asked.

"We came up with excuses—training accident was one of them," Frei said. "Now what?"

Ayden looked at Guy, then back at Frei. "You know Mauro Cavallo?"

"Yes."

"Confess to him."

***

Camerlengo Florentin stepped out of Dolce Maniera bakery at Via Barletta, carrying takeaway in a brown paper bag. He walked to his car, parked just outside the shop. Seeing him, Bartolomeo rushed up and grabbed the driver's door just as it was about to close.

"Florentin, we need to meet—it's urgent." Bartolomeo stared at the lanky individual with an owl-shaped set of eyes.

"What is it?" Florentin asked, confused.

"Not here. Let's talk somewhere else," Bartolomeo said.

"Meet me at the library in two hours," Florentin said.

Underneath the fresco ceiling of the Vatican Apostolic Library, Florentin sat at the end of a long wooden table with a large tome open, taking notes. As Bartolomeo approached, Florentin looked up.

Bartolomeo pulled out one of the chairs and sat down opposite Florentin. Just as he was about to say something, someone passed them. He gestured Florentin to come closer.

"Have you seen Rabolini?" Bartolomeo asked.

Florentin leaned forward. "No. Why?"

"I have some news about him," Bartolomeo said. "He's in hiding, did you know that?"

"Who told you this?" Florentin said.

"A special group of people to find the pope. Today I met one of them. His name is Demetrious Mallas."

"Mallas?"

"Yes, he works for a covert division of Anonymous. A representative had contacted me to offer their services."

"Why didn't you tell me this earlier?"

"I wasn't sure if you would agree with my decision," Bartolomeo said. "But now I am compelled to tell you in case I'm implicated for something I didn't do. It's important another person in the Vatican knows."

"I see."

Bartolomeo reached into his pocket for his wallet. He removed the white card with Ayden's number on it and handed it to Florentin. "In case anything happens to me, call him—Demetrious Mallas. He'll know what to do."

Florentin looked at the card. "It's blank."

"It's written in invisible ink. You have to heat it to see it," Bartolomeo said.

Florentin tapped Bartolomeo's hand. "It's good you came to me. We all love the pope."

***

Florentin stepped off the train at Varenna. He looked over his shoulder a few times as he rushed down the slope toward the ferry terminal. Adorned in old clothes, a pair of thick sunglasses, and a woolen ivy cap, he waited for the next ride to Bellagio across the lake. From there, he would grab a cab and head to Van Der Haas's rented bungalow.

In his mind, he rehearsed what he wanted to say to Van Der Haas. He no longer wished to be associated with the man and his organization. He had done his part. The tides were changing, he could feel it. Sword may be a large organization, but somehow good always wins. Demetrious Mallas represented good. It would not be easy to convince the pompous Dutchman he wanted out. The senator was a smart man, and seemed to believe he was invincible.

Once upon a time, Cardinal Florentin had been the most decent man on the planet. Circumstances changed him. He had entered the clergy and risen through the ranks. Somewhere along the line, money—more than Jesus—attracted him. It began as gifts, simple ones: fresh cannoli, a gold pen, a handmade winter scarf. And then some cash. He resisted the last one. But his givers insisted after they felt blessed by his touch. The gifts increased. His quality of friends changed. The fishmonger, butcher, confectionary maker, florist, tailor, carpenter, and people in the poor man's clinic were replaced by businessmen, bankers, and politicians.

The surveillance cameras on top of the red brick pillars at the gate shifted down and zoomed at the taxi outside the three-story Bellagio villa on a quiet road. It was presently occupied by Van Der Haas, who was renting it for a couple of weeks while on vacation.

Florentin lowered the window and leaned out to show his face. Seconds later, the opaque metal gate opened with a crank.

The taxi stopped under the porch. Florentin exited and climbed the short flight of steps. The door opened before he could press the doorbell. A giant with blond hair, wearing a brown flannel suit, stood before him. He stepped aside to let Florentin in.

Inside, a grand, ornate foyer led to a long hallway next to a spiral staircase extending through the second level. Footsteps were heard coming down the spiral. An average-sized man with hay-colored, combed-back hair appeared.

Van Der Haas, in a purple turtleneck pullover and black flannel trousers, stood at the bottom of the stairs and stared at Florentin with vacant eyes, then gestured him to the door beside the stairs.

"Hope you're enjoying your holiday in Lake Como," Florentin said as he entered the spacious living room. He sat on the leather sofa. The closed French windows overlooked a dreaded winter garden of rotten leaves and dried up grass.

"I didn't come here for a holiday. I came here to check on my investments. So come to the point, what brings you?" Van Der Haas stepped over to the fireplace and knelt down in front of the hearth. He picked up two pieces of wood on the side and threw them into the space.

Florentin cleared his throat. "Cardinal Bartolomeo is in contact with Demetrious Mallas."

"I see."

"I knew sooner or later he would reach the Vatican doors if

we failed to stop him," Florentin said.

"By the way, my agents told me the Swiss Guard commander was approached by two men. They reported seeing a white man and a black man with him." Van Der Haas stood and stared at the painting above the mantelpiece. He placed his hand on the ledge.

Florentin adjusted his glasses. "Demetrious went to see Frei? I'm worried."

Van Der Haas knelt down again and tendered the burning wood pieces. "Worried?"

"Yes, it's getting too close, Van Der Haas. I don't want to be implicated in the kidnapping," Florentin said.

"It's too late to be good. You took money from us," Van Der Haas said.

"I'll return the money, and then leave me alone." He removed the white card with Ayden's number on it and left it on the table. "That's the phone number for Demetrious Mallas. You know what to do."

Van Der Haas looked at the card. "A blank card?"

"It uses invisible ink. The number will be revealed when you heat it up," Florentine said.

Van Der Haas then turned to Florentin with scornful eyes. "Thank you and goodbye."

"Goodbye."

***

Florentin boarded the train from Varenna station to Rome. He went through several carriages before finding a seat to his liking. The carriage was clean, unlike some. Tossing his bag in the rack above, he settled in by the window. Resting his head on the glass window, he began to lapse into memories. His smile reflected in the window as he recalled his childhood in Florence, his career in the Church, and the sacrifices he'd had to make... like Lucina, his one and true love. What would life have been if he had chosen her instead? The last he heard, she was married.

How he had hoped to bump into her by chance during the few days in Florence, just to say hello. Their eyes would talk more than words.

The intercom announced the next train station as it stopped at the platform, the words partially drowned out by loud voices, the clatter of shoes stomping, and luggage being dragged by passengers embarking and disembarking.

The front door between the carriages slid open. A bearded man in a carpenter's jacket and a ski hat boarded and settled opposite Florentin.

"It's a lovely day, wouldn't you agree?" the bearded man said in a raspy voice, making himself comfortable.

"Yes, by the grace of God," Florentin said, not looking at the other passenger.

"Ah, you're a religious man." He looked straight at Florentin. "I'm from Naples."

"It's a wonderful place." Florentin faked a yawn and covered his mouth.

The bearded man continued to ramble about his city, his family, and work. Florentin was infuriated, but he didn't show it. He thought about getting up and moving to another seat, but that would be too obvious and rude. The man was a carpenter, he learned, recently married to a woman from Vatican City. She had refused to move to Florence, thus forcing him to relocate. He had spent three days in Florence to arrange for his personal belongings to be sent to his new home, her home. Florentin pretended to be interested in the man's rambling, issuing a fake smile from time to time.

The train slowed down as it neared the next station, much to Florentin's relief. The passengers readied and headed toward the exits.

"It's warm in here," the bearded man said. "Are you feeling the same?"

"I'm fine," Florentin said.

The bearded man unbuttoned his jacket and slipped his hand inside. The train stopped and the passengers began to disembark. The bearded man looked at his watch. "It's 3 p.m. now. In one minute it will be 3:01 p.m."

Florentin acknowledged with a nod. "Yes."

The bearded man smiled. "A minute can make all the difference in a man's life. Wouldn't you agree, Florentin?"

"*Scusi*?" Florentin didn't recall mentioning his name to the man.

"A message from Van Der Haas — *ciao*." The bearded man swiftly removed a long blade from his jacket and plunged it deep into Florentin's chest with an overhand thrust.

Florentin gasped once as he collapsed forward. He tried to defy mortality as his mind desperately searched for a memory... of when he and Lucina enjoyed a picnic under the breezy, tall cypress trees in the country, their love shrouded by nature. If only he could freeze that moment forever. He felt his heart rate slowing down. The pieces of the memory began to crumble. Then it vanished, as blankness erased all.

KHALED TALIB

PART TWO

Chapter Nine

Sitting in her cubicle amidst the tapping keyboards, ringing phones, and buzzing intercoms, Christa ran through the nebulous details on her notepad. Exhausted from over thinking, she tossed her notepad at the computer screen, leaned back, and chewed her plastic pen. The appearance of a familiar face jolted her back to her senses.

A dark-haired, bespectacled man in his fifties wearing office attire appeared in front of her cubicle. "My office — now," said Theo Robinson, the newspaper's editor.

Robinson shut the door behind her and stepped behind his desk. "You're going to Rome to meet Demetrious Mallas. He just called me."

"Demetrious Mallas called you?" Christa asked, surprised.

"Yes, he wants to break his silence. He said he will tell us what he knows. He will be accompanied by the two others, the Belgian woman and the Austrian," Robinson said.

"What a development," Christa said. "Did he say anything else?"

Robinson took a silver pen out of his shirt pocket and fiddled with it. "No, it was a quick call. I gave him your cell phone number. He'll call you to arrange where to meet. I've booked you at the Hyatt. Bring back some cannoli."

Christa's eyes sparkled. "Sure." She thought of Chief

Inspector Guillaume. *Here's an opportunity to negotiate with him.* If the chief knew Demetrious Mallas had contacted the newspaper, Guillaume might have a change of heart about dealing with her. She also needed him to verify whatever Mallas was going to tell her.

***

Christa entered the sandwich bar and sat down in front of Guillaume. "I've got some updates." She called a waiter over.

Guillaume lowered the sandwich in his hands and looked up. "What's that high frequency sound? Ah, it's a mosquito."

Christa flinched. "I'm seeing Demetrious Mallas. He called the newspaper."

Guillaume looked at her attentively.

"Got your interest, I see." Christa beamed.

"He contacted your office?"

Christa leaned back. "He spoke to my editor, Theo Robinson, who told me to go to Italy to meet him."

The waiter came over. Christa ordered a glass of orange juice…again.

"The reason you're telling me?"

"I am hoping to form an alliance with you. Once I interview Mallas, I need to verify the facts. You, my newfound friend, can help me with that."

Guillaume drank some of his coffee. "Did your boss explain why Mallas agreed to meet you? I find it all too sudden."

Christa smiled. "I did a story about the hotel murders, got a byline for it. Mallas is probably a fan of my newspaper."

"Give me some time to find out what's going on," Guillaume said.

"There's no need. Look, Chief, it's easy. I take the flight to Rome, talk to him, come back, then I talk to you," Christa said.

"It makes no sense," Guillaume said. "Why would he want to talk to a newspaper? I suggest you delay your trip."

The waiter arrived with Christa's orange juice. She took a sip of it. "You don't sound enthusiastic, Chief. Why is that?"

"I want you to be careful," Guillaume said. "I know you crave a story, but—"

"Do you have something to hide? I've got a job to do and I can't sit around and wait for the Swiss police to feed me with crumbs, you know. Here's an opportunity for me to find out the truth. And you know how it is with the newspapers—if I don't deliver, I might end up here serving you every day for the rest of my life."

Guillaume leaned forward. "Give me a few days. I've got contacts in Italy. Let me make a few calls and—"

Christa stood. "You do that, Chief. You've got my business card. Call me sometime."

"You don't understand, you—"

Christa waved her fingers at him. *"Arrivederci."*

***

Ayden's cold and runny nose were gone. The aspirin had done its magic. Even the tuna sandwich he was eating felt tastier.

Guy sat down on the next bed beside him, resting his back against the wall. Skimming through an Italian newspaper's headlines on Ayden's iPad, one headline caught his attention.

Camerlengo Stabbed to Death

"Yo, check this out." Guy raised the iPad in front of Ayden.

"What is it?" Ayden asked.

"The camerlengo is dead. He was stabbed to death," Guy narrated.

Ayden glanced at the article. It had a photo of Florentin sprawled on the train seat with blood everywhere. He rushed to the side table and picked up his cell phone.

"What's poppin'?" Guy asked.

"Poppin'? What do you mean?"

"You know, what's happenin'?"

"Need to get hold of Frei," he said, urgently thumbing the screen. "He's probably next. We need him alive to testify. I wonder if he spoke to Cavallo. Damn that Italian! Where is he?" Ayden put the phone to his ear and waited for Frei to answer. The call went straight to voicemail. He hung up. Then, a message popped up. "Now what?" Ayden opened the mail and read the message aloud:

> This is Christa Braun from Tribune de Genève.
> Please call me. I'm in Rome.
> My number is +41-22-754837.

"How did a reporter from *Tribune de Genève* get my burner number?" Ayden said.

"Getting sloppy, man," Guy said.

"I'm going to call her." Ayden pressed the number on the screen and waited to be connected. The line buzzed twice before a woman's voice answered. "Christa Braun?"

"*Oui.*"

"I'm Demetrious Mallas, returning your call. How'd you get my number?"

"Bonjour Demetrious, thank you for calling me back. I'm doing a follow-up story about the incident at *Les Hauts de Rive.* I've been talking to the Swiss police. You might find some of the information useful, especially since it is connected to the pope. I also hope to learn something new from you."

"What do you know about the pope?" Ayden kept the tone of his voice disinterested.

"I can tell you more when we meet."

"You still haven't told me how you got my number."

"Cardinal Bartolomeo gave it to me. He's one of my Vatican

sources."

"I see," Ayden said, shaking his fist. He'd cautioned Bartolomeo not to tell anyone about their meeting.

"Let's meet tomorrow. Do you know *Sant'Ivo alla Sapienza?*"

"Never been there, but I'll find the place," Ayden said.

"It's an old church. Say 5.30 p.m.?"

"I'd rather meet you at your hotel," Ayden said.

"Me too, but I don't want prying eyes."

"I'll see you at the old church then." Ayden hung up, then looked at Guy and Isabelle. "Says she got my number from Bartolomeo. I don't feel good about this — something is amiss. How do I even know if she's a real reporter?"

"One way to find out, call the newspaper," Guy said.

Ayden checked the newspaper's number on his phone and put the phone on speaker mode. Background music played as he waited to be connected.

"News desk," a man's voice answered.

"I'm looking for reporter Christa Braun," Ayden said.

"She's gone to Rome on assignment. Would you like to leave a—"

Ayden hung up. "What am I supposed to believe?"

***

The taxi driver pointed straight ahead to the dome of *Sant'Ivo alla Sapienza* underneath a golden sky as the transport came nearer. The sun began to set over the city, the temperature outside dropping. Ayden couldn't feel his fingers as he collected his change after stepping out. He cursed under his breath when the driver pulled away after shortchanging him ten lire.

As he neared the entrance of the building, Ayden scrolled Christa's cell phone number and called her. The same female voice answered.

"Hello, Christa, you here yet?" Ayden asked. He could hear the woman's breathing at the other end of the line.

"I'm inside, waiting for you."

Ayden hung up, then took out a wireless walkie-talkie earpiece from his jacket pocket and stuck it into his ear. "Everybody in position?"

"I'm in position." Guy's voice was first, followed by Isabelle.

"Do you see her inside?"

"No. It's too quiet," Guy replied.

"She claims she's here," Ayden said.

"I've got you covered," Guy said.

"Watching," Isabelle responded.

Ayden entered through a large, unassuming doorway into the old church. The portico opened to a row of pillared arches cloistering the side wings of the old church, a spire on its dome. A tile path between the green patches took him to the courtyard. He stood at the center, turning a full circle to see the surroundings, feeling assured Guy and Isabelle had his back.

"I see you," Guy said. "I don't see anybody else."

"I can feel her watching us," Isabelle said unnervingly.

"I know what you mean," Ayden said.

A ghost wind blew, moaning through gaps in windows, frames, and siding. The heavy entrance door slammed shut with a huge echo. "Someone closed the entrance door, I'm going to check." Ayden ran back to the door and tried to pull it open. It was locked from outside. "Someone locked us in."

"I still see nothing," Guy responded.

"Me neither," Isabelle said.

Ayden drew his gun and fastened the suppressor, eyes roving around the environment. A grating sound, the resonance of boots stomping on concrete, alerted him. "I hear something," he reported.

He felt a sudden, sharp pain slicing the back of his neck, leaving a painful trough. He clasped the back of his neck, then lowered his hand and saw blood on his fingers. "I've been hit."

Ayden glanced across the aisle. He recognized the form peering from behind a pillar—Satan's Nanny. She wore the same costume with the black hat over her piping straight hair. But there was something else: a blade in the sheath strapped to her right leg. And her face, something about it looked different from the last time. She had a white mask on.

"Shit! It's the crazy woman." Ayden ducked as Satan's Nanny fired her suppressor-equipped weapon once more. The metallic splatter missed him by inches. Stress heat flooded his body. He sprang right to the nearest pillar and hid behind the wall, which deflected the second bullet.

"What crazy woman? I can't see anything," Guy said. "Isabelle, any visual?"

"Zero visual," she replied.

"She's wearing all black. I've seen her before, at the airport," Ayden said.

"It's the crazy woman from the hotel," Isabelle said.

"Watch it, people," Guy warned.

"I can hear something upstairs," Isabelle said.

"Careful," Guy said.

"She's got a ballistic mask on. Bet she's wearing a bulletproof suit too," Ayden said.

Flattening himself against the wall, Ayden gave a quick peer and fired back at Satan's Nanny. The bullet missed her face by inches.

"Did you get her?" Guy asked.

"No time to talk!" Ayden cried into the wireless gear.

Satan's Nanny marched toward Ayden, gun pointed in his direction. Ayden scuttled further down—pillar to pillar—until he reached the final pillar. Near the stairs leading to the right side of the building he braced himself, realizing he would be exposed briefly.

The thumping of Satan's Nanny's boots grew louder behind

him. He recoiled against the wall as a tall, thin man in a black coat appeared around the corner. The man pointed an *SWD Cobray* at Ayden. At that moment, Isabelle crept up behind him and sliced his throat. Blood cascaded down the assailant's neck as he stood frozen for a few seconds before tumbling down the stairs, sprawled in his own blood.

Ayden looked at Isabelle, pointing back with his thumb. "She's right behind me."

"Can't see her," she replied, crouching back behind the corner.

A bullet whizzed from the right and the pillar's edge disintegrated into powdery splinters. Ayden shifted further in.

The muffled sound of a semiautomatic erupted. It was followed by a cry — then a loud thud. Ayden peeked around and looked at the courtyard. Another accomplice of Satan's Nanny had fallen from the second floor of the annexed building on the other side of the courtyard.

"Got one," Guy said.

"Where're you?" Ayden's eyes wandered to the balcony.

"Right above you," Guy said.

Ayden looked at the rooftop of the other annexed building facing him. Guy lay on the textured rooftop, clutching his weapon.

Zipping bullets tore the roof's edges, forcing Guy to roll back. "Almost got me — I'm not camping here no more."

Ayden turned and looked up at the second floor at the other end of the courtyard. A gun in a familiar black-gloved hand protruded from behind a pillar. Satan's Nanny peeked out, her white mask partially exposed.

"Second floor, third pillar from your left, other side of the building," Ayden said. "I'm going up. Isabelle, cover me."

Isabelle descended slowly, then spurted toward him. They dashed toward the stairs at the other side of the building. Ayden led the way as they hurried to the second floor. Midway they halted, seeing a body sprawled at the top of the stairs. It was a blonde woman with a ponytail in winter clothes. The frozen face, eyes wide open and mouth agape, stared at them.

"Who's she?" Isabelle whispered.

Ayden searched the woman's pockets for identification. He found a wallet and opened it. The press card identified her as Christa Braun.

"They killed the real reporter," Ayden said, leaving the wallet on the steps.

"I still don't see the bitch," Guy said.

The sound of a weapon reloading along the corridor broke their conversation.

"I hear something," Ayden slid his eyes across the annexed building.

Guy had come down from the roof and was now standing on the opposite balcony, partially hiding behind a pillar.

Ayden looked back at Isabelle two steps below him, then peered around the wall. Satan's Nanny, pinned behind the pillar, turned sideways and raised her gun at arm's length at him.

Ayden fired a shot. On impact, her gun's barrel exploded with a spark flash. Dropping the weapon on the floor, Satan's Nanny slipped her other hand into her side pocket and removed a stun grenade. She unpinned it and tossed it across the floor toward Ayden.

Ayden spun back, grabbed Isabelle, and scrambled down the stairs as the device exploded. At the bottom, he turned, aimed the gun at the stairs, and waited.

"Did you get her?" Guy asked.

"No, I missed. She threw a stun grenade at me," Ayden replied.

"Watch out!" Isabelle cried.

Before Ayden could react, Satan's Nanny plunged down the stairs, knocking both of them down. Their guns slid across the floor. Isabelle lay semiconscious while Ayden grappled with Satan's Nanny for the knife as she pinned him down.

"I see her," Guy exclaimed over the earpiece. "On my way!"

Those were the last words Ayden heard before his earpiece came off.

The hat and wig Satan's Nanny was wearing dropped and bounced on the floor, revealing a ballistic face mask that also covered the back of her head.

Guy rushed toward them. Dropping his weapon on the ground, he grabbed Satan's Nanny by the neck and pulled her backward. As he tried to dislodge the knife in her hand, she wrapped one arm around Guy's calf and pulled him down. She then raised the blade and plunged its tip into the side of Guy's calf before yanking it out.

Guy roared with pain.

Ayden lunged forward and threw his weight onto her. The knife dropped from her fingers and clanked on the floor. Using a wrestler's maneuver, Ayden wrapped one arm around her neck and the other around her leg. As he attempted to lock his hands, she turned sideways to prevent the cradle.

Guy slithered sideways. Grabbing the knife, he turned around the floor, rolled over once, and stabbed Satan's Nanny in the back of her calf. "Feel that banger, bitch!"

The scream of pain converted to rage as Satan's Nanny swung her fist into Guy's face. The knife dropped from his hand as the blow threw him back.

Seeing Satan's Nanny trying to grab the knife, Isabelle dragged herself across the floor toward her gun. She picked up the weapon, lifted her torso off the ground, and pointed it at Satan's Nanny.

"Hey bitch!" Isabelle yelled.

Satan's Nanny mechanically looked at Isabelle.

"Die!" Isabelle fired through the mask's eyehole.

Jolting backward, Satan's Nanny writhed in pain, then went still.

Isabelle raised herself up slowly on one elbow, massaging the bump at the back of her head. She approached Guy. "I need to stitch that up, that wound is crazy."

"I should've fished some other part of the lake that day when Mr. Somebody visited me in Norway," Guy whined, slurring through his words as he tried to resist the pain.

"He would still have found you," Isabelle replied. "Now keep still, I can be clumsy." Using her knife, she sliced a few pieces of her inner clothing and wrapped Guy's leg tightly. She then turned to Ayden, who had dragged himself against a pillar. He swiped his neck wound again with his hand. The bleeding continued.

"Want me to look at it?" Isabelle asked.

"I'll be fine, just a scratch," he said, waving his hand. He crawled to Satan's Nanny's body. He reached out to remove the mask: a bloodied face stared frozen in that moment of death, mouth agape and salivating. But what shocked him more was the face behind the mask. Satan's Nanny wasn't a woman. The phantom was a bald-headed man.

"That explains her strength — a man."

"I'm just glad the thing is dead, man or woman," Guy said.

Ayden stared at the face. "Let's hope *it* doesn't have a twin."

Back at the hotel, Isabelle placed two pillows under Guy's leg as he lay in bed. She took out a medical kit from her bag and began to work.

Ayden's phone chimed. Cavallo.

"Demetrious."

"Didn't think I'd hear from you again," Ayden asked.

"I've been trying to regroup since Venice," Cavallo said. "Florentin is dead."

"I read about it. And we almost got killed this evening at

Sant'Ivo alla Sapienza," Ayden said, watching Isabelle stitching Guy's wound.

"My sources briefed me, and Frei called me. He confessed that he collaborated with Sword to kidnap the pope."

"Yes, I know. I encouraged him to contact you," Ayden said.

"You met him?"

"Yes, over lunch. Well, we sort of imposed ourselves," Ayden said.

"We arranged to meet him, but he didn't show up, and he didn't return my calls. My agents visited his office. They were told he didn't show up for work for several days now."

"You must find him. Did he mention the banker?"

"Zanebono? Yes, he did. He's my priority. I'm planning something. I need your help."

"Tell me when and where. By the way, I also learned from Bartolomeo how your men and the Swiss Guard were ambushed that night."

There was a deafening silence.

Cavallo sighed. "Yes, they were. I didn't want to tell you because—"

"Your secret is safe with me," Ayden said. "We're not infallible."

"I owe you a big favor," Cavallo said.

"No, you don't. Who would I tell, anyway?"

"You're too philosophical, Demetrious," Cavallo said. "Don't think too much."

"That's always been my problem."

CHAPTER TEN

Doney Restaurant was a high-end restaurant located under a refurbished building along Via Veneto in Rome. The interior of the restaurant shimmered with gold accents and mirrors. But it didn't impress Zanebono as much as the cozy outdoor terrace under the canopy. A regular visitor, he would have reserved a table outside if it had been summer. However, he was in no mood to picture in his mind what the street looked like in summer. Even the food tasted different today. But it wasn't the chef's fault—it was Rabolini's. The man had vanished with fifty million dollars of Sword's money after hacking into the secret bank account.

Amidst the clink of glasses and murmurs of satisfaction from the customers, Zanebono sat at the window table near the decorative fire place. He could see a faint reflection of himself in the glass. He unbuttoned his jacket and loosened the tie. From his vantage point, he could even see everyone who entered or left the restaurant. He looked up from his plate occasionally as he dined, and gave the silent hello to faces he recognized. Some people approached him and chatted briefly before going back to their table or exiting.

He stared at the window for a moment. Just as he was about to take another bite of the fettuccine, his eyes caught sight of a man in leather on a black sports bike pulling up. He was expecting the man.

The man removed his sunglasses and black helmet. His face was hardly visible because of the dark bangs and dense beard. He walked toward the entrance of the restaurant. Zanebono felt his heart plummet as the man approached his table.

"Have you heard from Rabolini?" the man asked.

Zanebono looked around, then lowered his fork. "No."

"Now listen to me very carefully. You're going to help us get our money back."

A waiter approached to take the man's order. He waved him away without shifting his attention from Zanebono.

"I don't know where Rabolini is," Zanebono said.

"You don't have to worry about Rabolini anymore. We'll take care of him. You worry about putting the money back into the account," the man said.

"I don't have that kind of money," Zanebono said.

The man smiled. "But you do—you work in a bank."

"You want me to rob the bank?" Zanebono whispered, glaring at him.

The man smiled. "It's easier than turning eggs into gold."

"What if I get caught?"

The man grinned. "You missed the point of our conversation. You have already been caught. It's just whose punishment is harsher."

"Give me time to work this out," Zanebono quivered.

"We don't have much time," the man said, then looked at Zanebono's plate. "Wish I had time for lunch, but I have to get back to—ah, you're not supposed to know anything. So final warning, help us to help yourself." He stood up and walked briskly out the door.

Zanebono watched the man put on his helmet, slam his foot down to kick-start the bike, and roar away.

"God save me," Zanebono said. "If you still accept me as part of your flock."

INCOGNITO

***

The van parked along the side of the road half a mile from the bank. Inside, two agents sat in front of a bank of monitors, running their hands over the console, touching buttons, and flipping switches to set different zoom levels on the screen. They watched the scene outside the bank through Ayden's and Isabelle's camera specs. One of the agents dragged a clip under a horizontal bar and tapped it to enlarge the screen.

Cavallo placed his hand on the agent's shoulder. "Do you see the banker?"

"Not yet." The agent handed Cavallo an earpiece with a mic.

"Demetrious, Camille, can you hear me?" Cavallo said, adjusting the headpiece.

"I can hear you," Ayden replied.

"*Oui,*" Isabelle said.

"Okay, standby. Once we see the banker, we'll let you know," Cavallo said.

"Copy that," Ayden said.

Banca Nazionale del Lavoro was located at Via Vittorio Veneto, a picturesque street with tree-lined pavements bordering cafes, hotels, offices and government buildings. The trees' branches were bare now, but in summer they provided a welcome shade. The day began like any other day. Groomed tellers with smiles greeted customers with deposits, transactions, loans, and requests for miscellaneous services. Security kept a watchful eye, with more than three dozen cameras installed inside and out. At 10:15 a.m. the bank alarm went off, sending a swarm of people rushing out of the building as if a bee hive had been sprayed.

Smartly clad in a *gendarmerie* police uniform, Ayden stood in front of a police line manning the crowd as official vehicles converged. The bank's entrance and the surrounding area had been sealed off. Traffic on all sides was halted. In neighboring buildings, the occupants were ordered to evacuate. Onlookers stayed clear down both sides of the road behind erected barriers. Reporters and their camera crews jockeyed for the best spots from which to report the episode.

Ayden's specs zoomed in for a closer look at the bank's entrance. Zanebono, in a cream suit with gold-rimmed glasses, was the last staff member to emerge. A police escort of two rushed him down one side of the street. They removed the road barricade to let him through, where he was joined by other bank employees in front of a Sky TG24 News van.

"That's him—Zanebono," the agent said, pointing at the screen.

Cavallo spoke into the mic. "Demetrious, I've a visual. A plump man with brown hair wearing a cream suit and gold-plated spectacles. Do you see him?"

"I see him. Camille, I'm going to stand in front of the banker, so you can recognize him," Ayden said, walking toward Zanebono.

Isabelle, masquerading as a nun, ploughed through the crowd, pushing through a forest of elbows and shoulders until she stood behind the banker. She slipped her hand into her side pocket and slowly removed a retractable pen. She then squeezed tightly beside Zanebono, pretending she'd been nudged by the crowd. At that moment, she pressed the top of the pen and stabbed the nub into Zanebono's hand.

"*Scusi, scusi,*" Isabelle apologized in Italian to Zanebono for the abruptness.

Zanebono smiled back, raising his palm. He gave Isabelle a quick glance and then looked back at the scene. Moments later, his eyelids started to close and his body swayed.

Isabelle grabbed the banker with the help of another bystander just before he fell.

Ayden stepped forward. "What happened?"

"I don't know," Isabelle replied. "He just fainted."

"Everybody please make space for the man," Ayden said,

kneeling beside Zanebono.

A senior *gendarmerie* officer, arms behind his back, approached. "What's going on here?" he asked.

"This gentleman just fainted." Ayden pointed to paramedics approaching with a gurney. The officer turned away without saying another word.

"Please make way! Please make way!" Ayden advised the onlookers as he lifted the police barrier.

The crowd drew back. The paramedics lifted Zanebono onto the gurney. Then one of them placed an oxygen mask over his face. They exited the perimeter and proceeded to the awaiting ambulance. The paramedics lifted the patient into the ambulance, and the siren wailed as the ambulance eased away.

***

Zanebono stirred in the dimly-lit office. Sitting in a chair innocuously, he felt two hands on his shoulders preventing him from slumping forward. He lifted his head to see a man staring at him from behind a desk. The smell of cigars sunk deep everywhere: curtains, carpets, sofas, and oak-paneled walls. It was suffocating, claustrophobic. Sweat dripped down Zanebono's cheeks, his back, and down his sleeves as he sat, unsure how he ended up in this place.

Cavallo rested his arms on the maroon chair. "Julius Zanebono."

Zanebono's heavily-lidded eyes struggled to stay open. "Who're you? How did I end up here?"

"You've been behaving badly, Zanebono," Cavallo said. "I want information. We can do this decently or violently."

"What kind of information?" Zanebono looked up to see another unknown face holding him. The banker looked back at Cavallo. "You're Mafia?"

"No, but we are as brutal," Cavallo said. "Now tell me, where's Rabolini?"

Zanebono moaned and shook his head. "I don't know."

"Don't test me."

He looked straight into Cavallo's eyes. "I seriously don't know."

The man is not lying...so far, Cavallo thought. "Where's the pope?"

"I don't know. I had nothing to do with that," Zanebono protested.

Cavallo snapped his fingers. The man holding Zanebono hit him on the head. The banker cried out, sagging in the chair.

"There's no need for violence if you cooperate," Cavallo said.

Zanebono sat up straight. "I know little."

"Let me try again. Where is the pope?" Cavallo asked.

"Sword kidnapped him," Zanebono said.

"I know that part," Cavallo said.

"I don't know where he is," Zanebono replied.

"Are you a member of Sword?"

"No, I'm their banker and bookkeeper," Zanebono said. "My role was to create a secret bank account. I'm not involved in their clandestine activities."

"Who do you report to?"

"The camerlengo and Rabolini," Zanebono said.

Cavallo gave him a pensive look. "Florentin is dead. Why was he killed?"

"He wanted out, he got nervous." Zanebono pursed his lips.

"Who told you?"

"Someone from Sword. They threatened me with the same fate. They also enquired about Rabolini."

"Why is Rabolini in hiding?"

"He stole all the money in the secret account I created for Sword. He got someone to hack into the bank."

Cavallo stood and went around Zanebono as the other man continued to place his hands on the banker's shoulders. "How much was in the secret account?"

"Fifty million American dollars," Zanebono said in a furtive, shaking voice.

"How did Rabolini know about the money?"

"I told him during a conversation. But I didn't expect him to steal it."

"Didn't Sword suspect you might be conspiring with Rabolini?"

Zanebono sighed. "Sword has already paid me for setting up the secret account. I didn't see the need to steal from them. However, I'm living on borrowed time. I pleaded with them to give me some time to recover the losses."

"How will you do that?"

"Tomorrow night a group of professionals will break into the bank's fault and steal one hundred million dollars. They will then give me half of the money, and they'll keep the other half. I will then return the money to Sword."

"I see you don't mind the extra headache. What if the crime leads back to you?"

"I'm a desperate man. It's better to be in jail than dead."

Cavallo looked at his men. They nodded back at him to indicate they understood what must be done to prevent the bank robbery.

"No guarantee you won't be dead in prison either. Who in Sword do you deal with?"

"I don't know, they're people with no names, no faces."

"Did you give Frei five million American dollars?"

Zanebono's eyes widened. "How did you know about Frei?"

"Answer me: yes or no?'

"Yes."

"Sword told you to pay him?"

"Yes."

Cavallo walked back to his desk and picked up his cell

phone. "Thank you. I've got it all on record now," he said, raising the phone.

Two men approached and lifted Zanebono. One of them cuffed him as the other placed a hood over his head.

"Hey, what're you doing?" Zanebono struggled.

"We're sending you somewhere safe for now. The bank robbery is not going to happen the way you want it. But as far as Sword is concerned, it happened," Cavallo said.

"What do you mean?" Zanebono said.

"You don't have to know the details."

Zanebono continued to protest and struggle as they dragged him out. When the door shut, the room lights were turned on.

A man in a vest approached Cavallo and patted him on the back. "You should've played in *The Godfather*, Cavallo."

Pietro Bianchi was an Italian movie director and actor. The entire scene had been played out in his studio. The Entity chief needed a place to interrogate the banker, so he'd contacted his old school chum, Pietro, requesting help. Pietro also supplied the costumes worn by Ayden and Isabelle for Zanebono's kidnapping, as well as the ambulance and its crew.

"Thanks for lending me your studio, Pietro. I didn't want everyone in the agency to know what I was doing. Let's keep this between us," Cavallo said.

"We're all good at keeping secrets down here. In fact, this whole day never happened," Pietro said. "Where are you going to keep this banker?"

"I know some trusted people among the *gendarmerie*. For now, they'll hide him somewhere. Then we'll make sure the bank robbery doesn't happen, maybe leak it to the press."

"You must have a reason," Pietro said.

"I do." Cavallo smiled at him. He pointed to the phone in his hand. "It's all here…the conversation."

Pietro slapped Cavallo on the shoulder. "If you ever decide

to change jobs, you know where to come. We're always on the lookout for new actors."

Cavallo smiled. "I might take you up on your offer someday."

***

Midnight. The car was parked at the side of the Sant'Angelo Bridge over the Tiber just after midnight. Four men emerged in dark overcoats and went around the back of the car. The giant opened the trunk. Frei, wearing only his underwear, was inside, his legs and feet bound and mouth gagged. His terrified eyes and muffled screams were ignored by the captors.

The giant and two other men lifted him out of the trunk and carried him to the baluster wall near one of the angel statues lining the bridge. The giant and another held Frei, while a third man went to get a rope from the trunk and gave it to the fourth man. The fourth man proceeded to climb the wall and fasten the rope around the angel's neck. Then he took the other end of the rope and made a noose.

The freezing weather had no effect on Frei as a panic attack oscillated his body temperature.

They finally put the noose around his neck and raised him over the wall. Fear drilled into his nerve cells. He stared below at the river and tried to scream behind his gag. Thoughts rushed his mind like water from a broken faucet. Suddenly, the river below appeared calm as the moon lit a path.

The next morning, the front page of the *Corriere della Sella* reported the Swiss Guard commander's body was found hanging over Sant'Angelo Bridge. Police classified the case as murder.

CHAPTER ELEVEN

A dozen sailing boats bobbed up and down in a cluster on the calm lake as Ayden sat leaning against a whitewashed stone wall under an awning. He was familiar with many cafes in Lago Bracciano, a lake area of volcanic origin about thirty kilometers northwest of Rome. He tried to imagine how he would paint the scene. Should he go for oil, acrylics, or watercolor?

His mind brought him back to the present as he waited for Cavallo, who chose to meet here because of its discreet location. On the train, which departed from Rome's main terminal, Ayden read the news about Frei on his cell phone. Damn. They were too late to save him. If only he could have gotten through to Cavallo earlier. Then again, the Vatican head of intelligence had his hands full. Understandably, there was only so much he could do. Moreover, Ayden was an outsider who officially didn't exist. Even if he and Guy had dragged Frei to the police station that day when they met, would he have been safer in custody…or his death expedited?

Ayden's view was suddenly blocked by two men in dark shades. The first, he recognized. Cavallo stood in a quilted hooded jacket with a stand collar. The other person wore a long leather coat. Cavallo had mentioned he was bringing someone: Detective Kugler from Geneva.

Cavallo sat against the wall beside Ayden, while Kugler

placed himself on a chair in front of them, back facing the lake.

"Nice place you chose to meet," Ayden said. "Quiet, meditative, relaxing—the kind you read about in glossy magazines. Above all, it's far from prying eyes."

Cavallo looked at the man he'd brought along. "Demetrious, this is Detective Eglin Kugler, as I mentioned on the phone. Eglin, this is Demetrious Mallas."

They shook hands.

"Good to have the trust of the Swiss police. I remember Cavallo was going to send me back to Geneva for questioning," Ayden said.

"Pleasure to meet you, Mallas, if that's your real name," Kugler said.

"Why shouldn't it be?" Ayden asked.

"We ran a background check on you with the Greeks. Nothing came up. About that trust, well, let's work towards it."

"Fair enough," Ayden said.

Cavallo scanned the area, then looked at Ayden. "Did you hear about Frei?"

Ayden nodded. "What of Rabolini?"

"Nowhere to be found," Cavallo said.

"The more I think of what happened at the Trevi fountain, the more I believe Rabolini set me up," Ayden said. "Yet he claims people are trying to kill him." He looked at Kugler. "Tell me more about the Swiss reporter."

"Christa Braun kept pestering the chief inspector for information," Kugler said. "He tried to convince her not to go to Rome until he investigated further. She refused to listen." Kugler handed his business card to Ayden.

"Thanks." Ayden took a moment to read the card. "The person impersonating Christa Braun claimed she got my number from Cardinal Bartolomeo. I wasn't sure what to believe." He slipped the card into his wallet.

"We've been watching her boss, Theo Robinson. We suspect he sent her to Rome knowing she wouldn't come back," Kugler said. "Christa Braun was a persistent reporter. He must've felt threatened by her."

A waiter took Cavallo and Kugler's orders: one coffee black with milk, the other cream caramel macchiato.

"Her own boss had her murdered? Talk about one-sided company loyalty," Ayden said. "What proof do you have against Robinson?"

"Nothing," Kugler said. "When Christa Braun became obsessed with the murders at *Les Hauts de Rive*, we think Robinson felt it was time for her to go. His columns are usually focused on anti-migrant policies. We know he's been meeting with some people in the Netherlands — fascists. We've been working closely with Interpol. Their agents have shown us photos of Robinson meeting with some anti-Islam provocateurs."

Ayden scratched his right sideburn. "Speculation."

"We can't touch Robinson yet."

Ayden pursed his lips. "Tell me more about Robinson's background."

"He was born in Geneva. He graduated in journalism from one of the Swiss universities, married with two kids," Kugler said. "He's been involved in fascist activities since his youth, and was detained several times for being involved in protests and riots. He attended several meetings of the Order of the Solar Temple, but then decided it was not his cup of tea. He has received several journalism awards. The man has no bad habits, no debts, no hobbies."

"Interesting," Ayden said.

"What's on your mind?" Kugler asked.

"I was wondering if I could talk to him," Ayden said.

"I'd appreciate it if you did not interfere in our investigation," Kugler replied.

Ayden nodded somberly. "I understand." He stared at a boat moving out on the lake, its sails up. "Does Rabolini have family? They might be able to tell me something."

"He has a brother," Cavallo said. He paused for a moment, then said, "He's an old man. I don't think you'll get much from him."

Ayden looked at Cavallo. "Give me a chance."

Cavallo looked at Kugler, then back at Ayden. "His brother lives in Lugano."

Ayden smiled. "*Merci beaucoup.*"

***

The speakers at Roma Terminal Station announced the Lugano train on the outbound track was scheduled to depart soon. The guard blew the whistle once over the sounds of people and machines that filled the air.

Three days had passed since Ayden's meeting with Cavallo and Kugler. He still didn't have an idea how to approach Rabolini's brother without panicking him. The blue train crept away from the platform onto the tracks, and accelerated until it was travelling at a constant speed. They shared a sleeper room, and Isabelle insisted the window curtains be kept open even though the light outside was glaring.

Ayden had climbed on the top bunk after removing his jacket and boots, while Guy had dragged himself onto the lower bunk.

"How's the leg?" Ayden asked, looking down.

"Bearable," Guy said.

"Which hotel are we staying in at Lugano? You didn't tell us." Isabelle lolled on the pillow of the top bunk opposite of the train's couchette.

"I've checked us in at Hotel Gabbani, it's a three-star," Ayden replied.

"Okay, whatever. Wake me up when we've reached there." Isabelle turned onto her side and shut her eyes.

Ayden looked out at the passing view as the train chattered along the track. His mind began to wonder about the Swiss reporter, Christa Braun. Clearly Theo Robinson, her editor, wanted her out of the way. If they could win over a newspaper editor, who else was on their list? The colorful flashes became increasingly gloomy outside, and finally impinged on his thoughts. *Maria.* He tried everything to get her out his mind. The festering scene just kept playing over and over again.

He started thinking about Cavallo and the conversation they had when they first met. The soldier of Christ seemed surprised the three of them were willing to die for the pope, even though only one of them was a member of the faith. Cavallo didn't know Isabelle shared the same faith as him, but Ayden understood how his mind worked. He lived in a world carved into denominations instead of one nation. He functioned for God's sake, whereas he, Ayden, would do things for humanity. For Cavallo it was God's will above everything else, and if God chose to destroy humanity, so be it.

The train came to a halt an hour and a half into the journey. Ayden looked at Isabelle. Her chest heaved rhythmically as she slept. He bent over the top bunk and looked below. Guy's nose orchestrated whizzing sounds.

Ayden slid down from the bunk to the floor, put on his boots and jacket, and stepped out. He trudged down the aisle to the bistro. A woman got up from the stool and left. Seeing his opportunity, Ayden stepped up to take the seat. He ordered a tuna sandwich and a cup of coffee, black.

"Why did the train stop?" he asked the young staff member wearing a bowtie behind the counter.

"Didn't you hear the announcement?" said a male passenger beside him.

"I must've fallen asleep," Ayden said.

"Technical problem, they said, nothing serious," the

passenger said, raising his glass of beer.

"Where are we exactly?" Ayden asked, looking out the windows to a green fuzz of pine forest on both sides.

"We're somewhere in Arezzo," the staff member said.

Another announcement came through indicating the train would resume its journey shortly.

The passenger beside Ayden pointed a finger upward. "There you go."

By the time Ayden returned to his compartment, the train had resumed its journey. He noticed Isabelle's bed was empty, while Guy was still asleep. He checked the bathroom. She was not inside. She hadn't passed him when he left the bistro either.

Ayden stepped out again and proceeded down the aisle.

The hum of a helicopter alerted him, its silhouette moving past the carriage windows. *Something is wrong.*

Ayden ran to the back of the train, exited, and climbed up the ladder to the roof. A few feet away, a dark-haired man lay with his arm over a motionless Isabelle. Hair flaring in the wind, Ayden removed his gun from underneath his jacket and crawled forward along the length toward them.

The helicopter hovered above, swaying from side to side, trying to center itself over the train. The man reached for his weapon inside his jacket and fired at Ayden. The bullets missed by inches over Ayden's head. The man then placed his gun against Isabelle's head, making it clear what would happen should Ayden retaliate.

"Take the risk or not?" Ayden muttered, fearing his aim wouldn't be accurate considering Isabelle was too close to the man. Against his better judgment, he pulled the trigger. The man's right eye bulged as the bullet lanced through, killing him instantly.

Ayden crawled toward Isabelle rapidly on the assumption she was still alive. She may have been drugged. When he reached her, he felt her neck pulse. She was alive. Placing his hands on her hips, he held on to her as the train crossed a giant bridge straddling the large void of a canyon.

As the helicopter pulled up, Ayden fired repeatedly at its tail rotor. It swirled, tipped its nose to the ground, and crashed into the canyon with a loud blast, sending debris in various directions as black smoke billowed into the sky. The remaining bulk of the machine bounced on the rocks, and lay strewn on the ground after a second explosion.

***

A chirping sparrow sat on the hotel room's window ledge, alerting Ayden to the morning. Preening, the sparrow was joined by another as the bright, low winter sun poured in. Tucked under a flannel blanket, Ayden stirred, opening an eye. Yesterday's incident on the train was still fresh in his mind. After making their way back to Rome, Ayden contacted Cavallo, who picked them up at the station. The Vatican intelligence chief then arranged their stay at *Donna Camilla Savelli,* formerly a 17th-century convent in the Trastevere district. Two of Cavallo's men had also checked in to watch over them. The hotel management had been instructed to shut down all the rooms on the top floor for "repair work."

Ayden looked at Isabelle on the other bed with a blanket over her. She was awake. "Hello."

"*Allo.*" Isabelle propped an extra pillow under her.

"Feeling better?" Ayden asked.

Isabelle gave a half-smile. "*Comme ci, comme ça,*" she said, revealing that she was neither good nor bad.

"Cavallo had a doctor come over yesterday while you were asleep. You'll be fine," Ayden said.

"What do you remember? How did you end up on the train's roof?" Guy asked, drinking coffee on the extra bed.

"I went to the toilet. The flush was not working. There was

also no water. I desperately needed to go. So I went outside to use the public one. When I stepped out, someone pushed me back in. I saw a hand clasping my nose and mouth with a piece of cloth. Then everything went black. How did they know we were on the train?"

"Only two people knew: Cavallo and Kugler—and I am damn sure it wasn't Cavallo," Ayden said.

"You think Kugler betrayed us?" Isabelle winced.

"If Cavallo trusted Kugler, we should trust him. It's someone else…someone that Kugler overly trusted on the Swiss side." Ayden looked at the two birds outside the window. "I hope you've got your gun under the blanket. Who knows what's next?"

CHAPTER TWELVE

The Apostolic Palace had more than a thousand rooms, comprising several apartments, museums, administrative offices, the Vatican Library, and a number of private and public chapels. It also boasted the famous Sistine Chapel and the Raphael's Rooms, a series of papal apartments famous for their frescoes. They were painted by the Prince of Painters, Raffaello Sanzio da Urbino (Raphael) in the 16th century after being commissioned by Pope Julius II.

At precisely 9 a.m. the twenty cardinals arrived at the palace, the tension carried in their bodies keeping them warm on that extra cold morning. They pounded the marble corridor with arched walls toward the assigned room where the small consistory would be held. Here, they discussed the affairs of the state and the pope.

They came to an abrupt stop at a tall wooden door. The two Swiss Guards came to attention and stepped aside to let them enter. They walked into a massive room with a massive chandelier illuminating the ancient frescoes and paintings on the four walls.

A bony-framed man in his forties with dark hair sat at the end of a long table with an embroidered runner. Cardinal Gustavo Altimari did not stir from his seat when the rest entered. It was he who had initiated the session to declare *Sede Vacante,* a Latin term to describe the Holy See's vacancy even though the pope was not yet dead. Had it been the case, a conclave meeting of the College of Cardinals would convene to elect a new pope. The procedure for choosing the new leader had been practiced for about a thousand years. Altimari was about to break tradition. Everyone at the table would have to decide whether Pope Gregoire got to live or not.

Altimari had a motive for the meeting. He wanted to be the next camerlengo. The moment was now. Under normal circumstances, until a new pope had been elected, the camerlengo served as acting head of State of the Vatican City. But Florentin's violent death had sparked fears that whoever replaced him would suffer the same fate. Altimari understood that a crisis represented danger and opportunity at the same time. The protocols of appointment in this context would be bypassed. The man was ambitious. His confrontational and brash style had earned him enemies, but he also knew one thing: desperate people cast desperate votes.

A more senior cardinal led everyone in a short prayer after everyone had taken their places. When the prayer ended, all eyes turned to Altimari.

"Brothers, it's imperative that we stand as one mind. May I remind you that time is not on our side. If we don't comply with the kidnappers' demand, things can get uglier," Altimari said.

"What do you propose?" asked a cardinal sitting in the middle of the table.

"We set a deadline. If by that time the pope isn't found, we'll convene to elect a new Bishop of Rome," Altimari said.

"Is this the best you can come up with, Altimari?" Another cardinal posed the question.

"How much longer do you want to wait? Have you not seen the faces of the people? They're in disarray," Altimari replied. "Appointing a new pope would resolve our present problem. It'll serve as a distraction. Let's appoint a charismatic personality, someone with energy who can bring everyone together.

Moreover, it'll send a message to the terrorist group that we're not easily intimidated."

"May I remind you what the kidnappers intend to do to the pope if we don't comply?" said another sitting at the far end.

"The risk we must take. The foundation of this institution was not built on a cushion," Altimari replied.

"So we sacrifice Pope Gregoire? Let him die? Is that what you're saying? We're not yet ready to destroy the ring."

"Pope Gregoire shall die a martyr," Altimari said.

"Did you just hear yourself?" a bespectacled cardinal cried. "This is murder! Replacing the pope won't resolve the problem. Have you not been watching the news? The world thinks the Muslims kidnapped the pope. If you abandon the pope now, you'll go down in history being responsible for the modern crusade!"

Altimari folded his arms. "There won't be another crusade. Even if we agree to the kidnappers' demand, what guarantees do we have the pope will be returned to us alive? The Vatican shouldn't yield to terrorists' demands."

"It's your neck, Altimari," another cardinal said. "If they kill the pope, we'll hold you responsible."

The room went silent.

"Brothers, let us stand together as we look forward to the future. Trust me on this matter," Altimari said. "There's something else I would like to discuss. Would anyone object to me becoming the new camerlengo?"

The cardinals looked pointedly at Altimari.

***

The Dutch newspaper, *De Telegraf*, reported that if the pope was not found by March 14, the Conclave would convene to appoint a new pope. Cardinal Gustavo Altimari had been chosen to replace the late Camerlengo Florentin as head of the Office of the Chamberlain. Tucked at the bottom of the newspaper page, a smaller article reported a man with a gunshot wound had fallen off a train bound for Lugano. The man's body was discovered with no identification. In the same area, a helicopter had crashed. Police gave no further details.

Van Der Haas read the article as he sat behind the polished desk at his office in The Hague. The interior's walls were laden with copies of 17th and 18th century paintings. The pleasant décor didn't subdue his irate mood as he continued reading the story. He knew of the plan to capture one of the Invisible Knights and threaten the rest to back off until the Vatican officially announced their alterations to the Vatican II doctrine on March 14. Then, it would no longer matter if the captured Invisible Knight was dead or alive. But he hadn't expected the mission to botch. It was supposed to be an easy task. He had received a tip from a mole in the Geneva police station that the Knights were making their way to Lugano by train. He saw an opportunity to act. The Dutch senator was also not prepared to let Rabolini go. A virus like him could infect his campaign. Others were depending on him to complete the assignment.

Van Der Haas pressed an intercom button. Moments later, there was a knock at the door. Van Der Haas bid the person to enter. The giant with the blond hair appeared. He sat opposite the senator, resting both arms on the hand rest.

Van Der Haas looked at him. "Assemble everyone. I'm calling an urgent meeting."

***

Rabolini must die. Rabolini must die. The phrase crept into Van Der Haas's mind above the helicopter's swishing blades as it slowly descended on the French Alps. He pushed the collective down to start a slow descent, sweeping the powdery snow. In the distance, smoke twirled from a cabin's chimney. Snowmobiles parked near the stack of chopped wood underneath the frosted window signaled the presence of the others. Likeminded individuals with a shared belief: *Islam and its God is incompatible with our civilization.*

Van Der Haas zipped up his thick white jacket, adjusted his sunglasses, and pulled up the hood, and then clasped his gloved hands together. Not that his hands felt cold, but seeing his plan set in motion elated him. Inside the snow-capped log cabin on the mountaintop, surrounded by a forest with a partially frozen stream running behind it, Europe's destiny would be fulfilled.

As the blades slowed down and stopped, he alighted and trudged toward the cabin. The door of the cabin opened. The giant, in thick winter clothes with a long knife strapped to his thigh, greeted him. He stepped aside to allow Van Der Haas in. The door closed to the encapsulating smell of burning wood in the rustic fireplace.

Van Der Haas removed his sunglasses, gloves, and then jacket. To his left, a ladder rested against the wall beneath the loft opening. A wall-mounted ski rack held several pairs of skis and poles on the opposite wall next to the window looking out to the forest. A trophy bear's head stood out among the other decorative items placed above the fireplace. Underneath the ceiling where the beams crossed, a set of unpolished leather sofas rested on a black and white abstract carpet. Eight men sat around a wooden table having coffee near the open kitchen. Another window above the stove and sink overlooked the frozen stream.

The giant took the jacket and hung it on the wall. The eight men stood as the Dutch senator approached. He knew each of them by reputation. They were politicians, senators, ministers, bankers, and industrialists—members of Sword, a guerrilla force created by NATO and the CIA after the Second World War to thwart a potential Russian invasion. Today, Sword had a new purpose after being abandoned by their makers.

Once upon a time, the network had been established with the support of several Western governments, which also formed similar networks. During the Second World War, anti-Nazi resistance movements faced difficulty in receiving supplies throughout Europe. Sword networks, with support from partisans, managed to avoid such problems by stockpiling weapons in secret caches in advance. Volunteers were also trained and ready for action as saboteurs and espionage agents when called upon. The program remained a secret until the CIA admitted in the late '90s it had a hand in its creation, together with several European partners. However, the networks were abandoned after the Soviet threat was reduced.

Refusing to disband, Sword echelons had resorted to domestic acts of terrorism. The secret army used their hidden caches of weapons and explosives to carry out political violence, resulting in the deaths of many civilians. Today was a different era. Russia, once upon a time the foe, was now a friend.

Van Der Haas took his place at the head of the table, and placed his gloves and sunglasses near the edge. The giant stepped out, wind whistling through the room when the door opened.

"Gentlemen, thank you for coming," Van Der Haas said, holding the coffee pot and a clean mug. "I'm not going to beat around the bush — our funds in the Italian bank's secret account are missing."

The men around the table scrutinized Van Der Haas in disdainful silence.

"Missing? How?" said an old bespectacled man in a beige wool pullover with an unmistakably German accent.

"Rabolini stole it," Van Der Haas said bluntly.

"When did this happen?" the bespectacled man asked.

"Some weeks ago," Van Der Haas said.

"You only chose to tell us now?" said a broad-faced man with thick red hair in a black V-neck vest over a long sleeved shirt. He had a Russian accent.

"I thought I could recover it," Van Der Haas said.

"What's Rabolini going to do next?" the Russian asked.

"Nobody knows Russia is involved, if that's what you're worried about. We'll find Rabolini. We'll take care of it," Van Der Haas reassured.

The door opened again. The giant entered with small pieces of wood in his hands. He knelt down in front of the fireplace and kindled the fire by putting the smaller pieces of wood on a larger chunk. The crackling flame grew and consumed the smaller pieces. He stood, crossed the room to the ladder, and ascended.

"How much do you want?" the Russian asked.

"Twenty million," Van Der Haas said.

The Russian sighed and folded his arms on the table. "I'll talk to my people. Of course, we like everything to go smoothly, but we understand when circumstances go against us. In this case, Russia will expect a big favor in return."

The room froze.

"What kind of favor?" Van Der Haas asked.

The Russian shrugged. "I don't know, but when the time comes, we will call upon you."

"Since we're all here, you might as well know the next phase of the operation is about to be launched," Van Der Haas said.

"What exactly are you planning?" the German asked.

"We plan to create a series of terror attacks." Van Der Haas picked up the coffee mug and drank from it. "I trust you read the newspapers. They're planning to appoint a new pope. The Vatican has refused to yield. So we thought we'd make some noise to scare them."

"How does this plan fit my country's agenda?" the Russian asked.

Van Der Haas smiled as he put the mug down. "We plan to create a fictitious terrorist group in Turkey showing the world they have the pope. A video clip will be uploaded on YouTube threatening to chop the pope's head off if the terrorists' demands aren't met. The Turks will earn a minus point in their bid to join the European Union for failing to uncover the plot. NATO might even be pressured to abandon Turkey. Let's not forget boycotts and sanctions. That will serve Russia well, no?"

"You think the European governments will abandon Turkey? They helped Germany with the refugee problem," said the German. "You need to convince us harder."

"Don't worry about Germany or any other European government," Van Der Haas said. "When the people of Europe and the world see the video, they'll run amok in the streets. Even non-Catholic Europeans will react out of solidarity because it appeals to their bigotry. The governments will feel the heat. What do you think they'll do next? I don't think this will help Turkey's relationship with the Americans either, especially when the Catholic lobby flexes their muscles. This would put Turkey in a desperate situation."

The sound of wood crackling amplified as the room became silent. All eyes stared at Van Der Haas. "It's ugly, but it's effective. You will appreciate this strategy of chaos when you see the results. With sufficient publicity and political posturing, there'll be a climactic alignment in policy," Van Der Haas said.

"Well, Van Der Haas, good luck. If you fail…it's your neck," the Russian warned. "I'll contact you to arrange for the money to be sent to you, but please don't lose it again. And make sure you find Rabolini."

Van Der Haas clasped his hands together and cracked his knuckles. "Thank you for trusting me…again."

***

Ayden's cell phone chimed as he sat in the hotel room. The call came from a private number.

Ayden recognized the voice. "Rabolini." He put the phone on speaker mode. "This is indeed a surprise. I didn't expect to hear from you again."

Guy and Isabelle perked up to listen.

"I know where the pope is."

The words sounded unbelievable. Ayden looked at Guy and Isabelle. Their faces reflected cynicism.

"Is he in Italy?" Ayden asked.

"Yes."

"Then call the police," Ayden said. "Why tell us?"

"Don't you want to rescue him?"

"Of course we do, but the Italian police should be informed," Ayden said, refusing to entertain his lies. "If there's going to be trouble, they have the manpower to handle it."

"It's not that simple," Rabolini said.

Ayden looked at Guy and Isabelle again. "Why is that?"

"They have me. You must come alone," Rabolini said. "If you don't, they'll send a photo of the pope missing a finger to the *gendarmerie*. And they'll kill me."

"What do they want from me?"

"They want you to back off," Rabolini said. "Please come... please save me."

"When and where?" Ayden asked.

"Tonight at eleven. At the Colosseum's hypogeum."

The line went dead.

"You believe that piece of shit?" Isabelle looked at Ayden.

"Not a single word," Ayden said. "I'm not going alone."

***

Stars swept over the sky's horizon as Ayden waited in the hypogeum underneath the Colosseum's platform. He had arranged to meet Cavallo here, but he was nowhere to be seen. He knew Italians weren't exactly punctual, but he expected The Entity chief to be different since he was in the intelligence business.

Ayden waited behind a pillar and scanned every section of the basement. The amphitheater's night lights glowed over the network of tunnels and cages. The past echoes of raging madness swathed the Flavian enclosure with the sound of spectators cheering and jeering, animals roaring, swords clanking, and shields crashing.

A shadow crept over the ground in front of him. Cavallo, in a long overcoat, appeared from behind a pillar.

"Cavallo?"

"*Si*." Cavallo stepped closer. "Is Rabolini here yet?" He moved toward Ayden.

"No," Ayden replied.

The lights went out, leaving them in pitch darkness. Cavallo pushed Ayden behind a pillar as a bullet zinged past. Rebounding, Cavallo raised both hands. Ayden looked up to see a black form throwing a rope down.

"Climb up," Cavallo said.

They squatted on top of the pillar after climbing up. A dozen of Cavallo's men in black fatigues crouched along the tops of many pillars like a murder of ravens. They quickly donned night vision goggles and activated the infrared screens. One of the men handed goggles to Cavallo and Ayden. Then, on a signal from Cavallo, they slid to the ground and crept behind the pillars. They stabbed, strangled, and slit the throats of everyone who'd come to kill them. It happened fast.

One of Cavallo's men looked up and raised his thumb, signaling all was clear.

"Rabolini is not here," one of the men said after Cavallo and Ayden had descended.

"He knew you wouldn't come alone. He thought he could get us both," Cavallo said, looking at Ayden as he removed his goggles.

Ayden sighed. "I guess he doesn't need me alive anymore."

CHAPTER THIRTEEN

On that morning, while Altimari was having a briefing with his young male secretary in his new office, the phone on his desk interrupted them. Altimari raised his finger to give the signal for silence as he answered the call. The voice at the other end of the line sounded robotic.

"Don't think we don't know what you're doing," the voice said.

"Who is this?" Altimari asked.

"I'm the voice of reason. If you appoint a new pope on March 14, then expect an unpleasant response from us."

"We're not afraid of your threats," Altimari said into the phone as he stared at his secretary, who looked equally perplexed.

"I don't think you understand what we'll do, Altimari. My suggestion is that you comply or the problem will not go away. The Vatican will blame you. Then you'll ask yourself the question, was it worth it?"

"Yes, it's worth it."

"We're planning to release a video. Islamic terrorists of Turkish origin are holding the pope hostage. They're demanding terms. The Vatican will then cut ties with Turkey."

"This is different from the previous terms."

"The previous terms stand. We still insist you amend the *Nostra Aetate*."

"If I refuse?"

"Then you won't get to enjoy this year's Christmas at the Vatican."

"I'm not afraid," Altimari said.

"You don't have to be...you won't even know when it happens. And it won't stop with you."

Altimari held his breath, then said, "What do you want me to do?"

"Wait for the news on television, then organize the press conference and denounce Turkey. And remember, things will happen around you, but at least you get to live." The line went dead.

***

The sun's light bounced off the television screen as its rays sneaked their way through the small holes of the hotel room's curtain. Ayden ignored the glare as he watched a Vatican representative speak during a live transmission of the press conference.

"Pope Gregoire the Seventeenth has been kidnapped by a Turkish Islamic terrorist organization. They're demanding the release of Islamic militants held in Western prisons, including those in Israeli jails."

The subsequent footage showed a masked gunman with two accomplices standing in front of a large flag with Arabic inscriptions on it. A leader read a declaration in Turkish and then in Arabic. The pope, in a blue jumpsuit, sat on the floor with his cotton white head hanging, shoulders slumped.

Within an hour, violent riots erupted worldwide. Catholics set fires, stoned businesses, and fought with Muslims and the police. Governments from the Philippines, South America, parts of the United States, and Europe called out the military to enforce order. A day later, the Vatican held another press conference with Cardinal Altimari, the new camerlengo, announcing the

Church's plan to cut diplomatic ties with Turkey. He had called for an emergency meeting to inform them about the call he'd received.

"We're holding the Turkish government responsible. With immediate effect, we're severing ties with Turkey," Altimari said, sitting at the dais, littered with microphones, along with several cardinals as he faced rows of journalists and their camera crews' snouted-cameras.

A murmur ran through the crowd.

"The Vatican's decision to sever ties with Turkey seems drastic. Are you alleging that Turkey is sponsoring terrorism?" The question came from an Al Jazeera reporter.

"All you have to do is look at the country's history," Altimari said. "Some of the terrorists supply lines pass directly through Turkey. Explain that."

A murmur spread among the crowd.

A CNN reporter raised her hand. "Do you believe Islam is to blame?"

Altimari leaned toward another official to his right and they began to whisper. He then sat up straight and looked at the reporter. "Islam is a religion that promotes peace. But radical elements exist in the Middle East. Until the governments of those majority-Muslim populated countries take stringent steps to curb the problem, we don't wish to associate ourselves with countries like Turkey."

"How do you intend to meet the demands of the terrorists?" a reporter from the *Guardian* asked.

"The demands of the kidnappers are beyond our control. As you know, the Vatican is not a member of the United Nations. Our special observer status does not qualify us to steer decisions," Altimari said. "We don't expect the world powers to heed the call of the terrorists. We will pray for a solution. In the meantime, we ask the faithful to stay calm." There...message sent. Whoever was watching him in the news should be happy. He had complied. The bravado crumpled.

"Pray for a solution?" the Guardian reporter smiled. "What if God doesn't answer you on time?"

The crowd burst out laughing.

"We don't choose our path all the time. Please refer to John 16:33 of the New Testament, where God talks about fate," Altimari replied, ignoring their laughter. "There is always a solution to a problem."

"So what you're really saying is that the Vatican is willing to negotiate with terrorists," a German newspaper journalist said.

"We're not negotiating with terrorists. But the pope must come home alive," Altimari said.

"Do you think the deaths of the previous camerlengo and the Swiss Guard commander were committed by the same terrorist group?" an *RT* journalist asked. "Nobody officially claimed their killings."

"We won't rule that out," Altimari replied. "The investigation is ongoing."

A *Washington Post* reporter raised his hand. "Do you think some Vatican officials may be involved in the pope's kidnapping?"

Altimari banged his fist on the table. "Are you suggesting the Church of Christ conspired with terrorists to kidnap the servant of the servants of God?"

"Given the Church's history of scandals, should anyone even be surprised?" the reporter retorted. "Perhaps there's an inside man."

"And why would such a man exist?" Altimari growled.

"Many reasons—money, politics," the reporter said.

The room fell silent.

"This press conference is over." Altimari stood and left the long table, accompanied by his entourage.

Ayden picked up the remote control and switched off the TV.

Somehow, the coffee tasted bitter today. He wondered whether his stress hormone receptors had interfered with his taste buds.

***

Cavallo ploughed the engine dinghy through the choppy swells at 3:00 a.m. toward one of the Tremiti islands in the Adriatic Sea. A revolving lighthouse beacon perched on a cliff sweeping clockwise increased his sense of urgency. Somewhere in his mind, he felt that he had little power. He was only one man and needed help. He needed the voice of unity. He would start with the country's deputy prime minister, Fabio Tucci, one of the most trusted men in the country. He was on a three-day vacation on one of the islands, Cavallo had learned, but decided to impose on him as the matter could not wait. Someone like Tucci could be the voice of reason. The world needed to hear the truth. Enough of the lies.

Cavallo maneuvered between the rocky inlets under the blank night sky. As he came nearer the cove, he cut the engine and scrambled out. He trudged through the water as he pulled the boat onto the sand. Wearing a neoprene beanie and jacket, he unzipped a small pouch hanging from a thick lanyard around his neck, took out night vision goggles, and slid them over his eyes. He switched on the equipment, illuminating the landscape in a greenish tint. Small wood and stone houses dotting the hills became visible. Not a soul in sight. At that hour, in this cold, only the trees and bushes danced to the tune of the howling winds.

He started up the beach until he reached a flight of wooden stairs leading up. He climbed them, and kept walking uphill toward the cliffs, breathing in the earth's scent. As he climbed higher, the sound of waves crashing against the cliff masked the thoughts in his mind.

The stone cottage came into view, perched on a cliff with a fence around it. He opened the picket fence gate and walked up to the front door. There was no doorbell. He jiggled the knob. The door was locked. He removed the hat and goggles, then took his phone from the small bag. He entered the minister's number by memory and hit the call button. It rang for a long time before a disgruntled, sleepy voice answered.

"Do you know the time?" Tucci said.

"Yes, Minister, but it's urgent," Cavallo said.

"What do you want?"

"I'll explain if you let me in," Cavallo said.

"What?"

"I'm standing outside your door."

The door swung opened with a dim light spilling out. A groggily fifty-something face with thick black hair in disarray stood there. With a sweater over his pajama top, he stepped aside and gestured Cavallo in.

"How did you find me?" Tucci asked, shutting the door.

"Do you even have to ask? I came here to ask for your help," Cavallo said, standing in the middle of the cold living room filled with rustic furniture and a dead fireplace littered with ashes.

Tucci, eyes-half closed, put his finger to his lips. He turned and walked up the short stairs, then tiptoed back downstairs. "Okay, she's asleep."

"Your wife?" Cavallo unzipped his jacket.

Tucci smiled. "My wife thinks I've gone on a fishing trip."

"That's between you and God," Cavallo said.

"Give me a break. Don't preach," Tucci said.

"You've read my reports. I'm thinking of organizing a joint press conference with the Turks. The world needs to know about this deception. This is serious, Tucci. The media is giving the impression the Muslims kidnapped the pope. We must intervene," Cavallo said.

Tucci pulled a face. "The Vatican won't like us interfering."

"People want blood. They believe the lies in the news," Cavallo said. "My sources told me the Vatican held that recent press conference with the new camerlengo thinking they could get the pope back if they reduce Islam's reputation. Two things: I don't believe they'll spare the pope, and I also don't agree with their decision to amend the Second Vatican Council's decision on Islam. There's a lot of paranoia these days. This so-called Islamophobia has gotten worse. We need to defuse the tension. Can I count on you?"

"We had a private meeting with all the owners of the leading Italian newspapers. We told them our concerns, and asked them to tone down their language. They said that's our problem, not theirs," Tucci said.

"I have a plan: when the world sees our faces on television together with the Turks, they'll begin to understand. We can fix the past by correcting the future," Cavallo said.

"You're going to Istanbul?"

"Yes."

"You expect me to tag along?"

"You don't have to. We'll do a teleconference," Cavallo said. "I'll go, and then we'll connect with you via satellite."

"I need the prime minister's permission." Tucci rubbed his eyes.

"I'll take care of the rest." Cavallo went to the door and turned the knob gently.

***

Ayden was looking outside the hotel room window when his phone on the table rang.

"I need you to accompany me to Istanbul," Cavallo said.

"What for?" Ayden asked.

"We need to fix the situation. I received a call from my Turkish counterpart through the embassy earlier. I've been informed that no such terrorist organization exists, otherwise their intelligence office would've advised us. This is Sword's doing. The Turks believe they are trying — "

"To disparage Turkey's effort to enter the European Union," Ayden said.

"Yes, and possibly more," Cavallo replied. "I need to see the Turkish foreign minister immediately. We must arrange a joint press conference. Some of our trusted officers from the *gendarmerie* and the Italian government have agreed to participate in the conference via satellite interviews. I will go with you alone since nobody knows who we are. If anyone from the Italian ministries were to fly there, the press would find out. They must not know our plans until the press conference is confirmed."

"I'll start packing," Ayden said, then hung up.

***

The ambulance sliced through the VIP gates at Rome's *Ciampino Airport* that afternoon and halted at the tarmac. It had special clearances, the paperwork endorsed by the respective authorities in question. The Turkish "patients" on stretcher beds were accompanied by a "doctor" and several "nurses" right from the ambulance onto the aircraft.

The plane moved gradually around the tarmac and taxied down the cleared runway. As it accelerated, lights on the edges winked in rhythm. The floorboard trembled and the wheels roared before ascending.

"Okay, you can stop pretending to be sick now," Cavallo said, looking down at Ayden.

Ayden unbuckled himself and removed the false cast on his neck. A tall, brunette flight attendant approached carrying a glass of orange juice. She bumped into Ayden and it spilled on him.

"I'm so sorry. Let me clean this up for you." The flight attendant fussed over him.

Ayden handed his jacket to her and watched her walk down the aisle toward the lavatory.

"Who's meeting us in Istanbul?" Ayden wondered.

"Turkey's intelligence chief, Osman Huseyn."

***

Huseyn, in a black winter jacket over a black shirt and a pair of jeans, stood grimly at the bottom of the air stairs on the glazed tarmac at Ataturk's airport. The head of Turkish intelligence was a medium height, broad, fifty-something Turk with short-cropped hair and a brush moustache that almost covered his lips. More than a dozen field operatives huddled around him. Three white cars and a black, twelve-seat Mercedes Sprinter van parked near the plane.

"That's Huseyn?" Ayden whispered to Cavallo as he descended the steps.

"That's him." Cavallo pulled up his collar and bent his head against the chilly winds ripping across the wet tarmac.

"*Merhaba.*" Huseyn greeted a welcome in a raspy voice, shaking Cavallo's hand. He then turned to Ayden.

"Salam." Ayden smiled.

Huseyn gestured to the awaiting van with polarized windows. Some of the agents got into the van after them, filling up the remaining seats. The van moved, with the convoy trailing them.

Ayden, sitting on an aisle seat, whispered across to Cavallo. "This van is ballistic." He knocked the glass window to indicate its thickness. "Bulletproof glass."

Cavallo tapped the glass on his side. "We have a few too, just a different model."

The Turkish intelligence chief, sitting in front of them, craned his neck halfway. "Gentlemen, we'll send you first to your hotel. Then tomorrow we meet for a brief discussion with the foreign minister."

"Sounds good," Cavallo said.

By chance, Ayden saw his reflection in the rearview mirror. His intense blue eyes gazed at the sullenness. The last few days had made him less invincible, as a dull emptiness grew inside him. *Not now, Maria.*

The van rolled along the waterfront artery as nondescript buildings loomed into view on the left side, with a few tankers anchored on the Marmara Sea on the other. The Oriental city resembled a souvenir glass ball rising above water through the tinted windows.

Ayden closed his eyes, picturing the scene in silhouette, like the cover of a romance novel. On the layers of hills, towering minarets were accentuated above their domed mosques, straddling a parallel world between ancient and present. The grand old palaces, villas, and mansions flanked one side of the waterfront as ferries taxied to and from their docks along the Bosphorus.

The van hit a pothole as it snaked around narrow, steep lanes into the heart of the old city, Sultanahmet. It brought Ayden back to his senses.

"Tomorrow morning the driver will come and pick you up. Be ready by ten. *Inshallah* we will meet the foreign minister," Huseyn added, affirming God's will. "You'll meet with him to discuss the best way to handle the press conference."

Ayden smiled at Huseyn. "*Inshallah.*"

***

Ayden and Cavallo met for breakfast on the glass-paneled rooftop of *Hotel Spectra*, located in the corner of Hippodrome Square in Sultan Ahmet. The view from the rooftop offered glimpses of the light blue sea, the Obelisk of Theodosius, first erected by Pharaoh Thutmose III, and the Blue Mosque in Hippodrome Square. They were the first guests to show up for breakfast.

"What do you think about Islam?" Ayden asked, tearing the pita bread and dipping it into a small plate of mezze.

Cavallo didn't say a word. He was engrossed in fattening up the pita bread with halloumi cheese, olives, tomato, and salad.

"Did you hear me?" Ayden looked at Cavallo.

Cavallo looked up. "Sorry, what?"

"What do you think about Islam?"

"Islam? I know it as much as any European, from the Crusades. The Arabs reached as far as Toulouse and left a legacy in Sicily. I know about Vatican II and how its followers are described as 'People of God.' Do yourself a favor, don't listen to the newspapers. Journalists are immoral people. They'll publish anything to sell the newspaper. One day they pretend to be angels, tomorrow they work with the devil. The Vatican doctrine acknowledges Islam and its devotees as one of the respected Abrahamic faiths. There's an entire chapter in the Quran dedicated to Mary, the mother of Jesus. I'm not a theologian, but I've read a little. Why do you ask?"

"Interesting," Ayden said. "So which religion is the truth? Surely God didn't create the world without a system. My question is, which is the right one?"

"I respect all religions," Cavallo said. "And I hope they respect me. If I go to some country, I'll drive the way they drive."

"I was just curious," Ayden said. "I don't know what it feels like to believe in a god."

"A god or God? Anyway, to answer your question about Islam, I like the fact Islam forbids drinking. That law could do wonders in many non-religious societies. I like the fact married Muslim women don't have to take their husband's family name in Islam. That guarantees their individuality. Women have rights in Islam, contrary to the lies you read in the newspapers. Did you know Napoleon took elements of *Sharia* law and superimposed it into French laws? I'm not sure if there's any need for me to convert. They believe in the same God as I do. I don't think God is going to send a person to hell for some slight variation. He might penalize you, but to burn you forever...well, that's a bit harsh."

"Well, this is how you perceive things to be," Ayden said.

"Too much philosophical talk in the morning, Demetrious," Cavallo said, sipping his drink.

"Last question, if I may?" Ayden leveled his eyes at Cavallo. "Go ahead."

"If a man doesn't believe in God, but does a lot of good for humanity, is there room for him in Heaven?"

Cavallo put down the cup. "Doing good and being good are two different things. Some people have an ulterior motive for doing charity work. Others do it from their heart."

"So if a man is genuinely goodhearted but he thinks God doesn't exist, he still goes to Hell?"

"God is merciful. He will judge people differently," Cavallo said.

Ayden stared at a green olive on his plate. "I wonder how He will judge me…if He exists."

The thoughts continued to linger in his mind for a while. *Religion. Who's right and who's wrong?* Or should he rephrase the question: *who's more arrogant?* But he didn't really care about the answers. He was not searching for them. He was merely pondering. He classified the disbelievers into two groups: those who lost faith because God never came through for them, and those who felt that if God does exist, so do little green men from outer space. He belonged to the second group. For that reason, he had never been angry with God, nor had he ever felt forsaken. The believers were also classified into two departments: the zealots and the moderates. The former seemed to think he was God's judge and jury on Earth while the other preferred not to bother since God had a stockpile of lightning bolts He could use anytime to incinerate a sinner. *And why are there so many religions and denominations?* The thoughts evaporated after he paused to take a sip of the orange juice in the small glass. Cavallo was right…one should never mix breakfast with philosophy.

The van arrived at 10 a.m. with four escorting agents, whose instructions were not to say where they were being taken. It wasn't until they reached a hilltop area that Cavallo knew where they were.

"An old café," Cavallo whispered to Ayden.

"Something different," Ayden said, looking around. "I like old. I could sit here for hours and—" He paused just as he was about to say *paint*. Too much information.

CHAPTER FOURTEEN

Pierre Loti Café, named after a French naval officer and writer, sat on a hilltop park overlooking Eyup's Islamic district and the Golden Horn estuary. In the café's open area, a deck below, wrought-iron tables with checkered tablecloths and wooden chairs lined the stone-tiled pathway in front of a leafy wall. More tables rested near the baluster along the steep edge, with tourists soaking up the view while drinking apple tea and coffee underneath slim trees with rustling leaves.

Ayden and Cavallo, accompanied by several agents, headed toward the park's stairway between the leafy walls, which led to the café.

Upon entering the café, they walked across the dining room toward a subsection with a separate door. Ozgur Abdul Hakim, the foreign minister, sat on a divan against the wall in a corner of an Oriental room plastered with old paintings and Arabesque-framed mirrors. His suit jacket rested on an extra poof beside him, his loosened tie hanging on his white, long-sleeved shirt. A brass tray laden with smaller plates of mezze sat in front of him. Huseyn, in a pullover, sat beside him.

"My friends." Ozgur didn't bother standing up. He gestured for Ayden and Cavallo to sit with them. They were formally introduced to each other.

Ayden greeted the minister as he sat in front of him.

The bodyguards kept their distance, their eyes roving everywhere.

"Thank you for coming." Ozgur looked at Cavallo, then at Ayden, then back at Cavallo. "As I understand from Huseyn, Italy is prepared to lend a supporting voice. We were dismayed by the Vatican's response."

Cavallo nodded. "Yes, my government is prepared to counter the Vatican's position on the matter. We have a recorded confession from a banker to prove a conspiracy to kidnap the pope. This will help clarify a lot of things."

"It's good to know Italy is our friend," the minister said. "Turkey's friendly relationship with the papacy dates back to the time of the Ottoman Empire. Prior to that, it was not so good, but this is a new world we live in. We have already celebrated our 55th anniversary of diplomatic relations between Turkey and the Vatican. We aim to work harder to build this relationship."

Ayden knew the relationship between Turkey and the Vatican had never been smooth, even though there was a golden moment during the Ottoman Empire under the brief leadership of Sultan Abdul Hamid II in the 19th century. In recent times, one of the pope's predecessors had accused the Muslim state of being responsible for the 1915 Armenian genocide, which Turkey denied ever took place. It didn't help that several European countries, including Germany, had officially approved a motion to describe the killings as "genocide." Media reports of secret cables sent from the American embassy to the Holy See also revealed one of the cardinals speaking out against allowing a Muslim state to join the EU. The Vatican foreign minister responded by telling US diplomats that the comments were personal rather than the official Vatican position. Since then, both sides had adopted a "path of reconciliation" in building better diplomatic relations.

At the larger political picture, the political and diplomatic relationship between Vatican, Europe, and the rest of the Middle

East had always been bumpy. Remarks by a previous pope about how Christian minorities were ill-treated in the Arab world, and quoting a Byzantine emperor as saying how some of the Prophet Muhammad's teachings of Islam were "evil and inhuman," had caused the Grand Sheikh of the Al Azhar University to suspend dialogue with the Vatican.

Ayden had often discussed the Middle East with Maria, who had schooled him that the Western media was biased against the Middle East and the prevailing religion stemming from the Crusades. She described how Western journalists would exaggerate the narrative to suit their storyline. More often than not these communal incidences happened in the rural villages among the ignorant lot on both sides, whereas the tolerance level was higher in the cities.

They also discussed whether or not religion and politics should be separated from governing a country. They both unequivocally agreed to keep them apart, but they also saw the hypocrisy of their country's judicial system, because many of the laws were taken from the scriptures. And the irony of it all was that some were even taken from the Quran. Napoleon Bonaparte, for example, had relied heavily on Islam's *Sharia law* to produce the French Civil Code. And yet, everyone was talking about Islam like it was inspired by the devil. He remembered what Cavallo said earlier during breakfast back at the hotel: the Quran had devoted an entire chapter to Mary, the mother of Jesus. If this religion preached hatred, why would it even bother praising a Jewish mother?

"This is not about religion or politics. This is about preventing more bloodshed," Cavallo interrupted Ayden's thoughts.

The minister nodded. "It's imperative we resolve the matter quickly. People should not die for lies. We politicians are often guilty of such acts. Moreover, this malicious attempt to defame my country will hurt our efforts to join the European Union. We have friends in Europe, and we cannot afford to jeopardize all that we've built. The Vatican's support is but a blessing."

"Let me clarify something, sir. You don't have the support of the Vatican. But you have the support of some trusted people," Cavallo said. "We're lending our voices to Turkey."

"That's good enough. You can imagine if these conspirators had succeeded." The foreign minister paused to catch his breath. "It'd make my country an international pariah for abetting a terrorist organization, which in reality doesn't even exist. The pressure would force NATO to discredit us."

"Has NATO said anything?" Cavallo asked.

"Prior to meeting you, I had a secret meeting with NATO officials with my generals. They want answers, especially the Americans. It doesn't help us at a time when we are trying to acquire American weapons, missiles, and equipment like UAV drones. As it is, the United States doesn't want to export them to us. They fear we will use them against those Kurdish groups that offer strategic support for American interests. With the pope's kidnapping and Turkey being blamed for it, imagine how much lower the trust level will be."

"The Americans think Turkey is collaborating with Sword?" Ayden asked.

The foreigner minister shifted his gaze to Ayden. "No, but it's the excuse they use to prolong our request. We also can't afford economic boycotts and sanctions."

Ayden listened attentively, then said, "It puzzles me that both of you are members of NATO, and yet there is that trust problem. The irony."

"This is politics." The foreign minister flipped his hand to show his palm. "It's crazy for anyone to actually believe that a sovereign nation would kidnap the pope. He is more popular than any world leader."

"Many countries have blood on their hands for invading Iraq

and supporting the invasion," Ayden said.

"God sees all, knows all," the minister said.

"Holding the press conference will only fix the problem short term. I am not expecting this problem to go away that easily," Ayden said.

Huseyn gave an equally bemused look as the foreign minister, curious to know what Ayden's next sentence would be.

"There's always a counter reprisal, and another after that. Even if we chop off the head of the snake, it's not the end of the snake family. More will come."

"What do you suggest we do?" the minister said.

"For now, we will deal with the problems as they appear," Ayden said. "I have a question that has been bothering me for a while."

"What is it?" the minister asked.

"Who stands to benefit if Turkey gets hurt? Surely not Sword," Ayden said. "Why did Sword pick Turkey to set up this ruse? Why not pick Afghanistan or one of the Arab countries? Who would gain from seeing Turkey's downfall?"

"We have many enemies, both external and internal," the minister said.

"I know you do," Ayden said. "I believe Sword is being aided by a country, and I wouldn't be surprised if that country is — "

A loud burst of automatic gunfire erupted outside. Four agents rushed up to the minister. Two of them grabbed him on each side as the others led them toward the door.

"Follow me," Huseyn ordered Ayden and Cavallo.

Ayden and Cavallo reached for their weapons as they accompanied the agents guarding the minister. They ran through the kitchen entrance, and then headed out the back door toward a white Mercedes Sprinter in the parking lot.

A shot rang in the air.

"Move," Cavallo said as he ran toward the van.

Ayden looked back as he ran. Five masked men in black coveralls emerged with semiautomatic weapons. Two Turkish secret service agents, hunkering behind a parked car, responded. A bullet hit one of them in the arm, causing him to drop his weapon. The other agent waved at the van driver to pick them up.

They jumped into the van. The minister sat in the middle row, flanked by two agents. The sound of gunfire heightened. The Mercedes Sprinter screeched toward the battered parked car. It pulled up beside the wounded man, shielding him and his partner from the fray as the other side of the van absorbed the impact of the bullets.

An agent with light curly hair sitting near the side door jumped out of the van and scooped up the gun on the ground. He slipped it behind his back, then wrapped his arms around the incapacitated operative, hauling him into the van with the help of another.

They placed the wounded associate on the back seat as the van rolled toward the exit. The curly-haired agent knelt on the floorboard and removed a dagger strapped to his ankle. He began to cut the wounded colleague's jacket. Then, grabbing underneath the wounded man's arm, the curly haired agent wrapped his fingers around the brachial artery below the armpit to suppress the bleeding.

As the van veered down the slope, four more attackers emerged from behind bushes, blocking its pathway. The driver stamped his foot on the accelerator. The vehicle shot forward as its windshield, radiator, and lights took the brunt of submachine gun chatter. Curses erupted in Italian and Turkish inside the van. A masked terrorist, shouldering an RPG, stepped forward and aimed the antitank weapon at them.

In a brazen maneuver to circumvent the trajectory, the driver swerved sideways, almost tilting the vehicle onto its side. The grenade flew past and hit one of the other groups of attackers behind the van. The explosion splattered them into chunks as a shining ball of flames erupted in the air.

The incendiary sent a shockwave to the van, its front and back wheels bucking like a bronco horse trying to dislodge its rider. The four other attackers behind them had splintered in various directions as shrapnel dispersed at high velocity, flames scorching ferns and trees on the side of the road. Fire spread rapidly through the tangled greenery.

"Get us out of here," the minister yelled, slapping the back of the front seat.

The repetitive thuds on the Mercedes Sprinter's armor managed to breach the van's defenses, as a series of bullets shattered the windshield after surpassing the initial flex layers.

Ayden stared at Cavallo in disbelief.

"They're using high-caliber bullets," Cavallo said.

Another masked individual lay prone on the road with an eye behind the scope of a Barrett M82A1. He hammered the windshield consecutively with shots from the rifle's twenty-inch barrel.

A bullet pierced the driver's chest and passed through the cushion seat, its tip protruding. The driver fell sideways, sending the van swerving. A golden-haired agent clambered into the driver's seat and relied on the wheels' run-flat system to steer down the slope. The sound of alloy grinding the road indicated bullets had torn through the tires' rubber.

The new driver jammed on the brakes when a burning tree fell in front of the van. It squelched and skidded to an abrupt stop at the hill's edge.

Seeing an opportune moment, the attackers launched a frenzied assault.

The new driver extracted a *Sarsilmaz* submachine gun from underneath his seat and stuffed the muzzle into the cracked windshield. The spewing bullets cut down some of the attackers, causing others to rush for cover. Using both legs, he then kicked at the windshield, sending the glass flying out. He put the van into drive, but it wouldn't move.

"The van can't withstand the pounding," Cavallo shouted over the nonstop trouncing. "We must move!"

They fought until their ammo ran out. The other side continued to pound without relenting. Suddenly the Turks inside the van gave out an elated scream. Turkish Special Forces, supported by SWAT and regular police, had arrived. The hundred member *Bordo Bereliler* commando unit jumped out of their light armored vehicles and led the counterattack.

The firefight reached an end in minutes, capped by the sound of a final bullet casing from a tactical officer's semiautomatic weapon bouncing off the ground.

Huseyn motioned to check on the wounded agent. "He's going to be all right?" He looked at the curly haired agent.

"The bleeding stopped."

"How did we survive that?" Ayden asked Cavallo as he jumped out of the wreck.

"God is watching over us," Cavallo replied.

Ayden was about to say something sarcastic, but he restrained himself. "Right you are," he finally said.

The bodyguards rushed the minister into another vehicle as more field operatives appeared. Arrests were made, weapons confiscated. Ambulances arrived in droves. Traumatized tourists and employees rushed toward medics pleading for help. The scene left bullet-riddled walls, smashed glass, dented metal grills, and tables and chairs strewn about. Charred trees, bushes, and shrubs remained as firefighters worked to quell flame remnants.

A tall agent approached. "We caught one. He's wounded, but he'll live."

"Nationality?"

"German," the tall agent said. He pointed to two paramedics tending to a man lying on a stretcher.

"I want to talk to him," Huseyn said. He slipped his gun back inside his jacket and , looked at Ayden and Cavallo. "How'd they know we were here?"

"I'm asking myself the same question," Ayden replied, looking at Cavallo.

Cavallo bit his lips. "I told my deputy prime minister about my plan. He was supposed to tell the prime minister."

Ayden groaned. "This calls for a sheesha to clear my head."

The tall agent slipped his hand into his jacket pocket and retrieved a device the size of a cigarette packet. It emitted a static sound after he turned it on. A series of numbers came into display on the screen underneath a navigating arrow. The static grew louder when he moved. He walked toward the man on the stretcher. He then turned to Huseyn and nodded.

"What did he just do?" Ayden gazed at the device in the tall man's hand.

"Portable bomb detector, Chinese made. He was checking to see if that man was wearing a suicide vest."

Huseyn stood above the man as the two paramedics continued to wrap his wounds with bandages. "I'm giving you a chance to speak to me now. Turkish prison can be a scary place. If you cooperate, your life becomes easier. Understand?"

The man nodded.

"Did Sword send you?"

"Yes."

"Why did you try to kill us?"

"Orders."

"Whose orders?"

"I don't know, just orders. I'm a foot soldier. Kill him and him." He shifted his eyes to Ayden and Cavallo.

Huseyn looked at the two men, then back at the German.

"How'd you get weapons?" Huseyn asked.

"We arrived as normal tourists, and then we bought the weapons from the PKK," the German replied.

Huseyn looked at Ayden. "Partiya Karkeren Kurdistan is a Kurdish Communist party."

Ayden nodded. "I know who they are."

"Where's the pope?" Cavallo asked the German.

"I'm just a foot soldier. I know nothing."

Huseyn waved for the medics to take the man away. They watched the medics put him into the ambulance, accompanied by two agents.

Huseyn's cell phone rang. He paid extra attention to the call after answering. He kept shaking his head. "You have to leave Istanbul now," Huseyn said after disconnecting the call.

"Leave? Why?" Ayden asked, disappointed.

"The press conference has been postponed indefinitely," Huseyn said. "Our ambassador to the Vatican and his family have been kidnapped by Sword. They'll kill them if you open your mouth. You're not to speak to the media."

Cavallo folded his arms. He looked at Ayden, then back at Huseyn. "This is not going as planned."

"One more thing," Huseyn said, looking at Cavallo. "They found your deputy prime minister dead in a cottage on some island. He was shot in the head. The woman with him also didn't survive. It's in the news now."

"Tucci? God rest his soul," Cavallo said.

"All to pot," Ayden said, referring to the mess of the situation.

Cavallo hit his hands together. "It's my fault!"

"As a precaution, I don't suggest you fly back into Italy. We can arrange another way back," Huseyn said. "If you don't mind the smell of fish."

The fishing trawler bobbed about on the choppy waters of the Mediterranean Sea, maintaining nine knots as it headed toward

Italy. The transport was the best Huseyn could arrange to thwart tracking.

"I'll never order another tuna pizza ever," Ayden said, standing on deck staring at sailors pulling a net through the water. "Damn fucking squib."

Chapter Fifteen

Cardinal Bartolomeo spouted like a geyser after walking an extra lap around the Obelisk that morning. He had never missed a day in the last twenty years, rain or shine. The morning walk was a wonder cure for his panic attacks, a psychological undertone he had managed to smother of his abusive father and memories of a male schoolteacher who had molested him. The daily walks made him forget.

Bartolomeo stopped after the tenth round. Panting, he looked at the statues. He could've sworn one of them moved. Time for an eye checkup. Statues didn't move. He didn't feel dizzy, so it had to be his eyes. The statue appeared to take an archer's stance. How could this be? He shifted his eyes elsewhere to check his vision, and then glanced back at the statue. *No, it's not possible.*

The archer swiftly pulled the arrow back on the bowstring and released. Bartolomeo looked aghast as the arrow whizzed toward him.

Staggering sideways, Bartolomeo's fingers tensed as shock conquered his thoughts. His mouth pulled into a grimace as his eyes slowly lowered to the thin stick in his throat. His eyes then followed the crowd around him. They stood frozen. The guitarist stopped playing. Screams erupted, blending with the shrill crescendo of police whistles.

***

Islamic Terrorist Kills Cardinal with Arrow!

The front page of *La Repubblica* screamed the headline. The rest of the newspapers merely insinuated "Islamic terrorists" who had kidnapped the pope were probably behind the latest heinous act. The news postulated the kidnapping of the pope and the series of murders as being part of a campaign to terrorize Italy.

Broadcast news stations invited experts to offer insights, opinions, and analysis of the situation. Anti-government stalwarts were also quoted as insisting NATO sack Turkey from the alliance. Protests, riots, and violence broke out again around the world as anti-Islam sentiments burgeoned across Europe. Political factions and parties fed the frenzy of discrimination and prejudice against the faithful, inciting Islamophobia to fuel the hate. They came out of the woodwork, hosting indoor and outdoor events, seminars, and conferences. Street protests lampooned the religion, carrying flags, banners, and picket signboards with inflammatory slogans, while satirical magazines and liberal newspapers featured no-holds-barred articles promulgating the climate of fear.

That was the main news occupying the Italian newspapers two days after Ayden returned from Turkey. Yet, not a single journalist even bothered to decipher the truth. The wire services and several cable and satellite television channels showed the leaders of several Middle Eastern countries, including the Grand Sheikh of the Al Azhar University in Egypt—Sunni Islam's leading seat of learning—urging all sides to remain calm after condemning the killings and acts of terrorism. In a separate press statement, the Islamic body highlighted that killing of innocent civilians violated the tolerant teachings of the faith.

Sitting in the hotel room surrounded by the others, Ayden read a biased op-ed piece about the current situation on his iPad. "This is a major cock up," he said.

"And we're not even close to finding the pope," Guy said.

Ayden looked up. "That makes me feel guilty."

***

The squeaky clump of Van Der Haas's sneaker-clad feet maintained a tempo with his regulated breath as he jogged alongside a tree-studded quay with boats darting that early hour in Leiden, a province located about an hour's drive from Amsterdam. He kept an apartment here, as he visited it regularly to escape his other life. Here, amidst centuries-old edifices connected by canals, he could be himself. He felt more relaxed, far away from the madness.

He could feel his heart pounding against his sports jacket and felt perspiration break out on his forehead. He kept his eyes focused ahead...he felt driven, all doubt as to the madness of his ambition banished from his mind. Two bodyguards jogged ahead of him and two behind.

The sudden ring of the phone in his pants broke his concentration. He slowed down and answered the call. The bodyguards scanned the area more intently.

"What is it?" Van Der Haas answered, panting a stream of vapor into the air.

"Rabolini—we know where he is," the voice said.

Van Der Haas paused. "Where is he?"

"We got a tip off he's hiding in a monastery south of Italy."

"You've done well. There's no need for you to do anything else. Leave it to me." Van Der Haas hung up and continued jogging, feeling exceptionally good.

***

Streaks of lightning crossed the sky as Rabolini pulled open the heavy oak door that led into the small church. The interior of the sanctuary smelled of musty wood and candle wax. Several monks sat scattered around oak pews in the otherwise empty environment.

He walked down the aisle and stood in front of the altar. He lit a candle, then knelt, took out his rosary, and prayed. He

INCOGNITO

looked at the statue of Jesus on the cross and at the statue of Mary nearby. He felt both statues smiling at him, and he smiled back. A sign that they understood the reasons for his actions. He was their soldier, not the Vatican's, which had lost its purity with its history of scandals. It gave him the right to fight back as none were innocent, especially Florentin, the Swiss Guard commander, and the others who lurked in the dark. Even if it was not Sword, they would have conspired with others. Those who chose to turn a blind eye, like Bartholomeo, deserved their fate too. Why didn't he sacrifice his life for the pope that night? Stealing Sword's money was justified. His conscience was clear. No sin should befall him for stealing the money in the secret bank account. But he would have to find a way to disburse the money, preferably to charity organizations. He would do it when he was ready, and when he felt it was safe to do so. He did not betray the organization. Van Der Haas deserved to be robbed for his menacing ways. He needn't worry about him and the rest anymore.

And Demetrious and Cavallo should have died at the Hypogeum that night. They were an obstacle to his plan. They wouldn't understand what he was trying to do. For now, this monastery on a high mountain would serve as his place of refuge. It was just him and God.

***

The ancient monastery with an imposing belfry clung precariously on the wind-battered mountain spur, silent and austere, void of distraction. Access to the hermitage required a strenuous climb up a long ladder lashed together along the precipice as clouds of mist blew across the cliffs, covering the view now and then.

The giant, in a monastic tunic, felt his knees smack the rock, but he had been trained to endure pain. An eagle screeched as it flew past. The giant tilted his head to follow its flight. The eagle landed on a jagged edge and cocked its head to the side, blinking without shutting its eyes, as if aware of the intruder's motive. Was the eagle a "surveillance camera" for the monastery? He chuckled under his breath. Too good to be true. Besides, it didn't appear to be wearing a mini-camera on its neck. In any case, the giant didn't care. Van Der Haas had assigned him to find Rabolini, and nothing was going to stop him. Investigation had led him to this private abode. He expected the place to be well guarded. Rabolini could afford to buy bodyguards now. Even so, the giant was not worried. He could take them on — whoever, whatever, whenever. God had blessed him with the strength of ten men. He may have been stripped of his championship titles, but at least he had his freedom. For that he was thankful to God; also for his good health, and for using Van Der Haas to save him from a life in prison. For that, his loyalty to Van Der Haas was unquestionable.

The giant reached the top as the dismal afternoon turned to darkness early. The path opened up into a grassy clearing. Pulling the monk's hood over his head, he walked across the narrow, stone-laid path toward the monastery's gate, which lay underneath a stone archway with boundary walls. He unhooked the latch and walked through.

A small chapter house carved out of stone stood in the east wall. Tiny lights flickered inside its interior. A monk of equal stature stood outside the door sweeping away the snow.

The giant hid his right arm inside his robe while the other arm slipped into the empty sleeve opening. Then he approached the monk.

"I am looking for Brother Rabolini. I understand he is here," the giant said in Italian.

The monk looked up. "No such person here. Who're you?"

"I was told he was here," the giant said. "I must give him a letter from our Order. It concerns the pope's disappearance."

"You're mistaken, Brother. As I told you, there's no such person here by that name," the monk said.

"Perhaps you're mistaken. I should enquire inside." The giant stepped forward.

The monk dropped the broom and pulled out a gun. "The mistake is yours, Brother. Perhaps the bullet from my gun should look inside you instead." He pressed the muzzle against the giant's belly.

The giant grunted. "Why does a man of peace keep a gun in his robe? It's so strange."

"Why not? Jesus carried a sword," the monk replied.

"You're not a real monk," the giant said, slipping his right hand into his pocket and wrapped his index finger around his gun's trigger.

The monk sneered. "Nor are you."

The giant pulled the trigger. The bullet ripped through the fabric and into the guard. The force of the close-range shot sent him reeling backward and he fell to the ground. He jerked once, his breathing a heaving, strenuous pant. Then it stopped.

The giant picked up the extra gun and kept it.

Burning torches illuminated the giant's path along the cloister in the quadrangle. Snow covered a lawn swathed in compost plant debris and wilted flowers. Several monks passed him, prayer books clutched to their chests. As their eyes exchanged gazes, they bowed to each other. Hearing no subsequent footsteps, the intruder pulled out the suppressed gun and spun. He ducked to the side as they were about to lunge at him with knives and fired at them. Their blood flowed onto the snow after they collapsed on the ground.

The giant darted along the colonnade to the rear of the monastery. He then trudged across the snow-covered courtyard that led to the monks' dormitories behind a cemetery. Crows from the snow-covered rooftop swooped across, landing on the old tombstones. He was taken by surprise when another man in a robe loomed out of the snow with a knife. Turning his body swiftly, the man swung a leg back to bring his heel above the giant's ankle. He jumped, knees hitting his chest, to deflect the sweep. As the bodyguard tried to get up, the giant kicked his chin, sending him sprawling backward onto the ground. He then fired two bullets through the man's chest.

The giant glanced back and then slipped up two flights of stairs to the second level. Reaching the corridor's end, he stopped in front of the last door. He rapped the door twice and then ducked beside the wall, expecting an unwelcoming reaction.

A shotgun blast came through the door and the giant faked a screech of pain. A moment later, the door creaked open. Rabolini, in a robe, peered out.

The giant clinched the shotgun tightly and elbowed Rabolini's face, forcing him to stagger backward. Holding the barrel with both hands, the giant rushed inside and swung the stock across Rabolini's head, dropping him. The giant then plunged a syringe into Rabolini's shoulder and carried him outside.

With Rabolini over his shoulder, the giant retraced his steps toward the mountain's edge as shouts of alarm rang behind him. Reaching the gate, he looked back. A dozen armed monks rushed toward him. He knew they wouldn't shoot for fear of hitting Rabolini.

He dragged Rabolini to the edge and dropped him on the ground, then threw off his robe and adjusted the parachute rig on his black jumpsuit. He next slid the goggles strapped around his neck over his eyes and lifted Rabolini again, strapping him into the harness, and pulled the parachute chord as he leapt off the cliff.

***

Cavallo's phone number flashed repeatedly on Ayden's phone. He answered.

INCOGNITO

"Meet me at Saint Peter's Square, now," Cavallo said.

The taxi driver stopped outside the gates of Saint Peter's Square. Ayden stepped out to a cacophony of screams and snaked his way through the crowd toward the Obelisk. A handful of *gendarmerie* policemen tried to subdue the massive, hysterical crowd. Their communications via walkie-talkie were hampered by the loud emergency sirens of police and other emergency vehicles. People were trampled in the crush and chaos, running toward the scene. Newspaper reporters, broadcast journalists, and camera crews pushed through the turmoil to make their way toward the Basilica.

A woman screamed as she pointed at the Obelisk, her eyes transfixed to a grotesque sight. A noose hung around Rabolini's neck, the notch end fastened around the iron cross at the tip of the Obelisk. His eyes bulged and his tongue stuck out. A placard hanging from a string around his neck bore a message: *Allah is Great!*

A hand tapped Ayden on the shoulder, and he turned to find Cavallo. Ayden pointed to the sign. "It's a lie; you know that, right?" he said. "Tell them it's a lie. Go to the press and correct this madness," Ayden said, feeling pressure building behind his eyes.

"You think the newspapers are the panacea for this problem? Listen to the crowd—the newspapers love this kind of day," Cavallo responded.

"Death to Muslims!" a young man bellowed in Italian. The crowd echoed his angry sentiments.

The crowd's frenzied screaming and chanting seemed to fuel the madness of the moment.

Ayden grinded his teeth and clenched his jaw. Cavallo was right. There was nothing anyone could do...for now.

By the time Ayden got back to the hotel, Isabelle and Guy already knew what had happened. The news about Rabolini was sensationally televised. The footage eventually showed several firemen bringing down his body from the Obelisk. The news also reported religious violence had erupted in various parts of the world between Muslims and Catholics.

"The world has gone crazy." Isabelle switched off the TV with the remote control, bringing the room to silence.

"A car bomb just went off at the Swiss Guard's barracks. *Al Jamiyah al Akbar* has claimed responsibility," Guy said, staring at the iPad. "Thirty people were killed, including a dozen Swiss Guards and their family members."

Ayden sighed. "Should I be worried for tomorrow?"

***

The *Tribune de Geneva's* office was located along Rue des Rois. Kugler, in undercover mode, sat in the front passenger seat of his car a few meters away from its building on the quiet road. The building entrance faced one of the side gates of *Cimetiere de Plainpalais*. From his car's side mirror Kugler could see everyone stepping in and out of the building. He expected Robinson to appear soon. Yesterday he'd made an anonymous call to the newspaper editor, threatening to blackmail him with evidence that could implicate him in Christa Braun's murder. The chief editor had taken the bait and agreed to meet.

When Kugler had first visited the newspaper office with Guillaume, he had observed Robinson closely. The detective noticed Robinson kept a classic silver pen in his shirt pocket. An idea struck him. Switch the pen with a GPS tracker and monitor the chief editor's movements.

Kugler didn't share the plan with anyone. Not even Guillaume knew. It was best not to share such information given the present situation in the office. He'd learned his lesson after informing a close group of supposedly trusted colleagues about Ayden's plan to visit Lugano. In any case, hiding information from fellow police officers was not uncommon. It was an old trick

INCOGNITO

to hide details so if it was ever brought up the culprit would be exposed, because how else would the person know unless he was responsible for the act? If his plan worked out, he would be one-up over Guillaume. He'd never forgotten how the chief inspector rebuffed him for failing to spot the tattoos on the cold, dead thumbs. Even though Guillaume never brought it up again and did not patronize him about the way he worked, Kugler knew he must put it behind him to make him completely forget the incident. Even though his career so far had been impressive, he was not about to let the oversight hinder Guillaume's judgment of his handling of the case.

Robinson came into sight and stood on the pavement just inches away from the crosswalk leading to the cemetery gate. Kugler picked up the two boxes of pizza lying on the driver's seat and exited the vehicle. He walked briskly toward Robinson. As he came closer, he crashed into him. Both fell. The pizza boxes flew into the air before hitting the ground.

"Are you okay, sir? I'm so sorry. I didn't see you," Kugler said, partly resting on Robinson, a palm on his chest.

"Yes, yes, I am fine. Now get off me," Robinson said, annoyed.

"Sorry sir, I'm so sorry," Kugler reiterated as he got up. He looked at the ground and pointed to the silver pen. "That's your pen, sir? You must've dropped it."

Robinson stood and adjusted himself, then picked up the pen and stuck it into his shirt under his jacket. He then stepped away from Kugler.

"The customer isn't going to be happy. Must go back to the outlet and return with replacements." Kugler picked up the boxes and returned to his car.

Kugler sat in the driver's seat and reached in his trousers pocket for the silver pen. He smiled to himself.

***

Theo Robinson's disguise didn't fool Kugler as he watched

him from an adjacent window several floors above in a room at Hilton The Hague. He knew Robinson never stayed at the same hotel when he visited The Hague. Stalking Robinson the last few months had not been easy. He moved like a sewer rat along the pipelines. Good thing he'd managed to switch the pens; the newspaper editor could now be easily tracked.

Wearing a wool hat and a long winter coat, Robinson stood on the pavement under three flags where a large drain ran under the road a short distant away from the hotel. The street was ghostly quiet. Weather like this, it would have to be important for anyone to want to go out.

Kugler zoomed his infrared camera onto Robinson's face. The lens focused so close it even showed the vapor emitting from Robinson's mouth.

A Lexus approached and stopped beside Robinson. He stepped forward and opened the front passenger door. The driver's face could not be seen through the tinted car windows.

Kugler shifted the lens on the driver's windshield and took some more pictures. He then looked at the LCD screen on the back of the camera. He swiped the images for the best shot. He nodded to himself as he looked at the image.

CHAPTER SIXTEEN

Ping! The text message on Ayden's smart phone read:

Take the train to Bellagio. Stay at Hotel Fioroni.
Reservations under Demingo Calidad.
Bring everybody. See you there.
 Cavallo.

Ayden looked up. "It's Cavallo. He wants us to meet him in Bellagio."

"Why so far? Can't we just meet here?" Guy said.

"I'm sure Cavallo has his reasons."

It was past eight in the morning when they arrived at the small train station in Varenna. From there, they headed to the ferry terminal to take them to Bellagio. Hotel Fioroni, a family-run establishment, was about a fifteen-minute walk from the promenade. The shops along the promenade were still closed, except for *Bar Caffe Rossi* serving breakfast daily.

Ayden relied on his phone's GPS mode to guide them to the hotel. Wearing their thick winter clothes, they climbed a series of steps to a back lane, which later turned to a quiet, inclined road.

They strolled along the shady pavement next to a low-rise building, its ground floor occupied by a hair salon with a large glass front. On the opposite side of the road, a few homes hid behind walls with ivy and wild flowers topped by stone urns above the gate pillars. They passed more buildings on the left side, older ones with slits in between leading to garden paths overlooking the blue lake and boats.

The stone walls running along the right side became taller, and lessened when the road widened up to a cemetery, a florist, and a few pottery shops. The GPS indicated *Hotel Fioroni* was located around the corner from the petrol station.

The elderly female receptionist acknowledged that a reservation under the name Demingo Calidad had been paid for. They were given separate rooms, each a superior double room with an extra bed prepared. The rooms were cozy and had sufficient amenities as well as balconies.

Ayden opened the glass door to the sound of chirping birds as he stepped out onto the balcony which overlooked a hilly green slope with homes dotting the expanse. If he had his art tools he would paint an impression. His thoughts were interrupted by a text message.

Meet tomorrow at Villa Balbianello in Lenno @ 10:30 a.m. Do the tour.

Ayden contacted his sidekicks to assemble in his room.

The doorbell of his room rang, followed by a knock. He opened the door and let Isabelle and Guy in.

"Cavallo wants us to tour some villa called *Balbianello*," Ayden said. "No details, as usual."

"I know that villa!" Guy exclaimed, resting against the headboard. "Hell, I'm going, leg injury or not."

"What are you so excited about?" Ayden asked, surprised by Guy's sudden burst of enthusiasm.

"That's the James Bond villa," Guy said, beaming. "They made one of the movies with a scene at the villa. Cool to take a few photos there."

"Don't know what you're talking about. I'm not a big fan of that wanker," Ayden said.

Breakfast the next morning took place in a converted basement, with small windows featuring little curtains and pots of flowers.

"What time is Cavallo expecting us?" Isabelle smeared jam inside her croissant. She had her long brown hair tied up into a loose knot on the back of her head.

"Half past ten. We have time," Ayden said.

The majestic villa, with manicured gardens and tree-lined paths pruned in candelabra style, was located on a small peninsula above the lake and had been built in the late 18th century. It had changed hands several times. The last owner was Guido Monzino, a wealthy explorer and mountaineer, who led the first Italian expedition to Mount Everest.

The ferry churned through the smooth waters of the lake. Above, the sun was shining and the warm glow lit up a string of villages, towns, and private homes dotting the mountainous landscape. Upon arriving at the villa, they signed up for a guided tour. They were instructed, along with the other visitors, to wait for the guide at the porch of arches located between the main building and the loggia.

A chestnut-haired female guide named Francesca arrived. After a brief introduction about the building's history, she led the group into the villa's various rooms, elaborating in detail on how the owner had collected items from around the world to decorate his home: tapestries, antique furniture, Oriental carpets and boiseries, Ming porcelains, Mayan and Aztec objects.

The house tour continued to the owner's private museum. They entered a room lined with world flags around its slanted ceiling, its walls surrounded by built-in glass cabinets, black and white photographs, and maps. An old dog-hauled sledge rested in the middle of the carpeted room between two tabletop display cases.

"Good thing I came." Guy put his arm around Ayden. He pointed to a picture of Monzino's Everest campaign on the wall. "Impressive. Wish I had the kind of moola to live that kind of adventure life."

Ayden rolled his eyes. "Aren't you living it already?"

"Without the tension," Guy qualified.

The tour ended in the garden. They converged near the baluster overlooking the lake. Guy stopped a passing tourist and handed over his phone to take a picture of them with the lake's backdrop.

"Ah, serenity," Guy said.

Ayden smiled. "I can't promise you it will last once I hear what Cavallo has to say."

"I was almost there, man. You had to remind me, didn't you?" Guy said.

"I need to go to the toilet," Ayden said afterward.

"Me too," Guy said, limping beside him.

They proceeded to the porch. The guide Francesca was standing there. She smiled at Ayden.

"Hope you enjoyed the tour," she said, hands behind her back.

"I did, very much," Ayden said. "Could you tell us where the toilet is?"

"Follow me." She led them to an area inside the villa and pointed to the toilet door at the far end.

Francesca was still there when they came out. As Guy walked ahead, the guide held Ayden back. "Follow me, he's waiting for you." She led him into the library and moved to a section of the bookshelves. Standing in front of it, she pushed, and it opened to a flight of steps down to an underground passageway. They descended into a tight hall before emerging through a closet into a lavish bedroom.

Cavallo, in a black double-breasted zipper jacket, jeans, and boots, stood facing a window with a lake view, hands behind his back. He turned and gave Ayden a casual salute. The guide stepped into the closet again and vanished.

"Why are we meeting here? Trying to get away from it all?" Ayden sat at the edge of the bed, his eyes roving around the room, admiring the decor.

Cavallo heaved a sigh. "No, I've got another office somewhere nearby."

"You're like God — you're everywhere, but when I need you, you're not there," Ayden said.

"But I appear when least you expect it." Cavallo stuck his hands in his pockets. "I've got some updates."

"What?"

"Kugler called me. Robinson was seen in The Hague again. We now know who he's been dealing with," Cavallo said.

"Brilliant," Ayden said.

"Robinson has been friendly with the far right Dutch senator, Willem Van Der Haas," Cavallo said.

"The name doesn't ring a bell. Am I supposed to be shocked?" Ayden asked.

"Yes, you should be. He is anti-migrant, anti-Muslim."

"Okay, how'd Kugler get this info?"

"He has photographs of Robinson getting into a car driven by Luuk Zeghers, a former national boxer who is now Van Der Haas's bodyguard," Cavallo said. "This giant of a man killed someone in a bar fight, but got away easy with manslaughter. Van Der Haas, for whatever reason, paid for the man's legal bills."

"Will they arrest the senator now?" Ayden wondered.

Cavallo sank his heel into the carpet. "They need more proof. A photograph proves nothing in this instance, although we now know conclusively Robinson is in touch with Van Der Haas."

"You need more proof? Since when does anyone care about following procedures in such a situation?" Ayden said.

"We're dealing with a man who can influence the masses across Europe. We have to tread carefully. Detaining a senator of that caliber is like accidentally pressing a nuclear button," Cavallo explained.

"I understand," Ayden said.

"If it's any consolation, the Swiss police have the right to question Robinson whenever they want since Christa Braun was murdered. They can use that as a pretext to learn more about his relationship with Van Der Haas."

"You brought me all the way here to tell me this? You could've called me," Ayden said.

"I'm arranging a helicopter ride to Geneva for all of you tomorrow. The Swiss still want to talk to you. They want to know who you are and what you know."

"I'm not saying anything to them," Ayden said.

"Let me sink this into your head, Demetrious. You're now moving freely because we allow you to do so," Cavallo said. "Sure, there's been some hiccups, people are trying to kill you, and we've been breathing down your neck even though you and your friends are impeding an investigation. But imagine if the authorities of the neighboring countries turn against you. That will make your assignment tougher."

"Sounds like a threat, mate," Ayden said.

"I see you've forgotten how we rescued you on the Swiss mountain," Cavallo said. "We're simply asking you to play along."

Ayden met Guy and Isabelle under a walnut tree.

"Where did you go with that pretty tour guide?" Guy asked as Ayden approached.

"Tell you later. Let's get out of here," Ayden said.

They disembarked the ferry at Bellagio. Ayden suggested *Bar Caffe Rossi* for lunch. They sat outside on the portico with the view of the lake and ferry terminal. To their right, the shop selling souvenirs and knick-knacks was packed with tourists.

A waitress appeared from inside. With a remote, she lowered the motorized, retractable canopy as the sun's rays encroached. She then approached them and took their orders. Ayden didn't say a word about his encounter with Cavallo during lunch. Their conversation revolved around other things until after dessert, when the crowd had subsided.

"I met Cavallo just now. He said the Swiss authorities might know who the mastermind is. He's a Dutch senator named Van Der Haas."

"Van Der Haas," Isabelle said. "I've read about him. He's a fascist."

"We have to leave for Geneva." Ayden lingered over the cup of cappuccino. "We have to be nice to the Swiss police or else things can get nasty for us. They also want to know who we are. So we'll tell them what we've been trained to say — absolute bollocks."

They took a ferry to Como. Meandering round, they ended up at a flea market near the ancient walls. Isabelle suddenly tugged Ayden's hand.

Ayden looked at her uptightness. "What's wrong?"

"We're being followed. Those two men." Isabelle tilted her head to the left at two men in front of a lingerie stall. "I saw them get off the ferry with us."

Ayden sneaked a surreptitious glance. "You're right. We're being followed. Unless they've got some kind of a fetish of looking at women's underwear." He began to trot.

Skirting out of the area, they hurried toward the Piazza Cavour near the waterfront, swerving and evading passersby and bystanders. They dashed past a tobacco shop and a string of canopied cafes at the piazza. Running across a crosswalk, the ground made progress difficult with its uneven path. The soles of Ayden's boots almost gave way, while Guy limped furiously trying to keep pace.

The two pursuers were joined by three others. Guy picked up a stone and hurled it at them, throwing one of them off balance.

"Six minutes to reach the ferry terminal," Ayden warned, checking his watch.

They rushed into the fenced platform and pushed to the foot of the gangway.

"They still chasing us?" Isabelle glanced back.

"I can't see, it's too crowded," Ayden said.

The ticket master stood in front of the ferry with his deckhands, ready to release the mooring ropes. Ayden handed three return tickets to him. The officer looked at them, then at the tickets, and back at them. "*Tre?*" He indicated three with his fingers.

Agitated, Ayden raised three fingers. "*Si, tre.*"

The ticket master showed two fingers. "*No tre, due.*"

It suddenly occurred to Ayden Guy was not with them.

"Shit! Where's Guy?" Ayden's eyes scanned the dock.

"Thought he was behind us," Isabelle said.

"Let's get onboard, there's no time," Ayden said halfheartedly.

As they crossed the space between the dock's edge and ferry, Ayden's phone chimed a message from an unknown sender.

We have your friend.
We will contact you again.
Have a nice day.

"Assholes. They've got Guy."

***

Ayden found Cavallo on his bed back in the hotel room, back against the wall, arms folded, legs stretched out. He had texted

INCOGNITO

Cavallo about Guy. "That was fast. How did you get in? No, don't bother answering." Ayden shut the door.

"The Apostolic Palace was bombed," Cavallo said. "The *gendarmerie* inspector general was killed in the explosion, along with many others. As usual, the Muslims did it. Tell me what happened at Como and how you lost Guy."

Ayden's cell phone rang. He swiped the phone to answer the unlisted number. A familiar voice whispered through. Guy.

"Demetrius?"

Ayden turned on the phone's speaker for Cavallo to hear.

"Where are you? Whose phone are you using?"

"One of theirs. They destroyed mine. Listen, they want to make an exchange," Guy said.

"What kind of exchange?" Ayden asked, realizing others were listening in, because Guy had called him by his fake Greek name.

"My life for Cavallo's."

"Why?" Ayden stared at Cavallo. The Entity head didn't react.

"I don't know. They didn't say," Guy said.

"Have to talk to Cavallo. I don't know where he is," Ayden lied. "How much time are they giving me?"

"Two days. We'll meet at the Gardens of the Vatican City. 10 a.m. Cavallo must come alone," Guy said.

"You okay?" Ayden asked.

"Leg's bleeding again, but I'll live."

"Know where you are?"

"No. But there's lots of skeletons hanging on—"

The line went dead.

Ayden sat at the edge of the bed. He kicked his shoes off and wriggled his toes in his socks. "Can you trace the call?"

Cavallo nodded. "Maybe. I'm not sure what kind of technology you use, but we have our ways."

"I'm making coffee. Want a cup?"

"Sure."

Ayden went to the table beside the refrigerator. He picked up the half-filled kettle and plugged the cord into the wall socket, then pressed the on switch. When the ready light turned on, he prepared two cups. Meanwhile, Cavallo started making a few calls, trying to trace the unlisted number.

"My people are trying to trace the call now," Cavallo said, taking the cup from Ayden.

They drank another cup of coffee while waiting. Half an hour later, Cavallo received a call.

"He called you from a prepaid SIM card," Cavallo said, after hanging up. "It's registered with *TIM Italia,* one of our phone companies. This is strange."

"What's strange?" Ayden asked, putting his coffee cup down on the bedside table.

Cavallo winced. "The call came from under the Basilica, in the *Necropolis.*"

"He's underground in the Scavi?"

"He's probably in one of the underground areas off limits to tourists," Cavallo said. "Archaeologists are still doing work down there, and they don't want the public to know yet. If your friend is down there, we need backup."

"How many men do you have left?"

Cavallo smiled. "Enough."

"Good. I hate going in dark places alone."

Chapter Seventeen

Thousands of candles filled Saint Peter's Square as people gathered to pray and sing hymns. The crowd was hoping for answers from the heavens.

Disguised in monks' robes with the hoods pulled over their eyes, Ayden, Cavallo, and seven of SIV's elite men moved toward the front of the Basilica.

One of the Swiss Guards raised his palm hand as they approached the entrance. "Stop. Where are you going?" he asked.

Two of Cavallo's men pulled out Tasers from under their robes and administered sufficient voltage to incapacitate the guards. The shooters lurched forward and plunged syringes into their necks, then shed their robes to reveal the non-ceremonial blue uniform worn by the Swiss Guards before taking up their posts.

Cavallo descended the stairs to the vestibule, with several of his men carrying the two unconscious soldiers. Ayden followed closely as the SIV head of intelligence brought them to a double airlock glass door. They went through the second glass door and entered a confined, climate-controlled space. Here they disrobed, revealing tactical attire underneath their robes, as well as a range of assault weapons.

Cavallo unzipped his breast pocket and took out a piece of paper. "An archeologist drew this map for me. There is another layer under the Scavi that is out of bounds to visitors. Excavation is taking place slowly because of weak soil," Cavallo explained, showing Ayden the map.

"Lead the way," Ayden said.

The two sleeping Swiss Guards were left against a wall, mouths gagged, hands and feet restricted with zip ties. Cavallo pulled a Beretta 92S out of his hip holster as he held the map in front of him. The path led them into a narrow passageway constructed of ancient red bricks. Ayden had never visited the Scavi, but he knew the history of the narrow pathways underneath the Basilica, once the ancient streets of Rome.

They turned on their shoulder-mounted flashlights as they ventured deeper. The air turned dry as the scent of earth and bone lingered in the decrepit environment. Darkness echoed their steps. Mausoleums jutted as they snaked through the Scavi's tight passageways. They turned into a constricted corner and entered a small room. A double-decker tomb with sculptural friezes rested between two alcoves.

Cavallo stepped forward and touched the tomb, feeling its sides. He ran his fingers from top to bottom. "Here," Cavallo told Ayden. "This feels like fiberglass — a fake tomb. The archeologist told me one of the popes created an escape route in case he ever came under threat. According to the map, a tunnel runs below it." Cavallo pushed the cover aside with ease. A ladder was extended through a lit hole. He led the way as they descended.

The hole led to a tight corridor with a low ceiling with modern spotlights lining one side of the wall. They walked for some distance before pausing at an intersection. Cavallo studied the map again. "This way," he said, turning right.

They exited onto a bridge above a duct. A dim overhead light illuminated the final leg of the journey. They stopped in front of pa dried up fountain hidden in a recess, in the shape of a young maiden taking a bath. "Dead end," Cavallo said, looking at Ayden.

Ayden stepped forward and began to feel around the statue with his fingers. An inward push caused the statue to swing open to a crypt holding an assembly of stone coffins.

"That was lucky," Cavallo said.

"It wasn't luck, just something I learned in the movies," Ayden said.

They crept through the space and approached the first sarcophagus. The cover bore a reclining couple. Another sarcophagus lay behind it. There were two more on the opposite side. Cavallo stood in front of the first sarcophagus and studied it. He felt its surface. "The lid is also made of fiberglass." Cavallo lifted it.

The coffin's interior revealed a steel staircase reaching twenty feet below.

Cavallo slipped the pistol back into its holder and removed a *Socimi* 821 submachine gun fastened on his chest rig. He looked at his men. "Ready?"

Wearing face masks, two of the men climbed into the sarcophagus and scrambled down.

A report of gunfire exchange erupted. Then, one of the agents appeared at the bottom of the stairs. Looking up, he gave the clear sign.

They landed inside a depository for bones of the dead, bodies strewn on the stone floor. Ayden felt trepidation staring at the bones, which formed pillars beside three doors with iron-framed peepholes on both sides of the wall. Skulls, leg bones, pelvises, and vertebrae were stacked to make columns and arches. Smaller pieces were used for floral designs. Some of the fallen pieces presumably had been dislodged by the ricochets during the firefight earlier.

"There's a family inside here," one of Cavallo's special agents said, peeping through a cell window.

Cavallo approached. "It's the Turkish ambassador and his family. Find the keys — get them out."

Another special agent pointed at the opposite door. "The Austrian is here, too."

Ayden found the keys after searching one of the bodies and handed it to one of the agents. After several attempts the agent managed to open the door. Inside the cell, they found a disheveled young couple with two young girls.

Guy appeared a moment later, hanging onto the agent's shoulder.

Ayden looked at his injured leg. "We need to get you to the hospital," Ayden said, then turned to the family. "You must be the Turkish ambassador," he said, addressing the man.

The diplomat nodded as his wife held her children closer.

"You're safe now," Ayden said.

"Thank you," the ambassador said, helping his wife and kids up.

One of Cavallo's men approached and whispered in his ear.

"Some people are coming," Cavallo said. "Mr. Ambassador, you and your family stay here. Demetrious, take your friend to his cell and stay there." He turned to one of his men. "Remove those skeletons on the walls and climb up in their place."

Ayden left Guy's cell door ajar half inch and stood peering through the gap as Guy leaned in the corner behind him. Outside, shoes clanged on the stairs and the sound echoed off the bare walls. Fifteen men had descended, heavily armed. They noticed the disturbance, and some inspected the dead. A few began moving toward the door where the Turkish family was. One of them peeped inside.

Ayden closed the gap slowly and rolled over onto his back facing the door, legs pressed against it. Clasping a submachine gun in both hands, he waited.

Outside, voices grew louder, angrier. Footsteps came nearer.

Ayden tilted the weapon up, aiming the muzzle at the peephole. Shadow movements under the door indicated a presence in front of the door. An eye looked through the peephole. Ayden fired.

Blood splatter striped right down to the threshold. Ayden then rolled sideways to avoid a burst of automatic reprisal. The impact forced the door to open wider. The metal barrels rattled a cacophonous clang, passing through the door and bouncing against the wall.

The shooting stopped.

The silence was interrupted by Cavallo's voice. "This one is still alive."

Ayden helped Guy out of the cell. They approached Cavallo, who was kneeling beside a wounded foe.

"You're not going to make it," Cavallo said to the man. "Do the right thing. God will forgive your sins. Where's the pope?"

"Doctor...get me a doctor." The bearded militant moved his head sideways, eyes half shut. Blood dripped from his nose and mouth, coating his beard.

"Tell us where the pope is."

The man raised his arm, took a deep breath, and held it for several seconds before exhaling. His arm dropped as his eyes stared, wide open.

PART THREE

Chapter Eighteen

The newly appointed inspector general of the *gendarmerie*, Leonardo De Felice, occupied a temporary office at a section of the Apostolic Palace. The recent bombing had forced the authorities to reshuffle office space and official positions. The room contained minimal furniture. The most distinguishable feature was an ornate cornice running around the ceiling. Its white walls and wood flooring resembled a ballet studio, if it had mirrors round the room.

De Felice, in a dark blue suit, sat behind a wood desk with basic stationary and a telephone. A uniform hung in a transparent plastic bag on a wooden hanger in the room's corner. In his late fifties, the new inspector general had a round face with thin, light hair.

"I hope this nonsense ends soon," De Felice said. Ayden and Cavallo sat opposite him. "I don't like that new camerlengo. Forgive my language, but Altimari is a brash son of a bitch. But I'm happy to hear the Turkish family is safe." He looked at Ayden. "Cavallo's mother and mine are cousins. Did he tell you that?"

"No, he didn't, but it's good to know at least there's someone we can trust," Ayden said.

"Yes, Cavallo briefs me and a few others regularly. I'm now in a better position to assist. I hate talking bad about the dead, but the old inspector general was hopeless. He didn't care to find the pope. The man wasn't that religious, so he didn't care. His death was a blessing in disguise."

"Could be," Ayden said.

De Felice's desk phone rang. He answered the call and listened attentively. "Altimari is dead," he said after hanging up.

"What happened?" Ayden asked.

"They found him in his bedroom dead after self-flagellating. It seems he suffered a heart attack. I dread the day we find out the pope is dead. We must find him." He looked at Cavallo, then at Ayden. "Whatever you need, I'm just a phone call away."

***

Kugler pulled up in front of *Hotel Royal,* located in the southeastern France region of Evian. The Belle Époque-styled resort, surrounded by snow-filled parks and illustrious gardens, overlooked the sludgy Lake Geneva. The three other detectives that had traveled with him, including a representative from the French side, jumped out of the vehicle before the engine was cut. Holding a paper-sized brown envelope, Kugler emerged under a grayness that spread across the sky like a sharkskin and led the troop into the hotel's cream-colored interior. He admired the grand architecture, its chandelier, and elegant silence. He couldn't wait to see the surprised look on Robinson's face when they met. To his left, some guests were talking near the curved stairs near the entrance. In front of him, through the row of arches with a few plant stands dotting the floor, a porter brought a newspaper to an old man sitting on a sofa.

Kugler approached the registration desk beside the old-fashioned glass elevator. A pleasant female receptionist in a black blazer greeted him. He flipped open his badge case. "Do you have a guest by the name of Theo Robinson?"

The receptionist's smiled vanished as she looked at the badge. Her eyes then met Kugler's and the men behind him with bewilderment. She turned to a senior manager in a severe gray suit and a maroon tie standing at the end of counter talking to another staff member. Having already noticed Kugler, he approached with a concerned look. "Good morning, sir. How may I help you?"

"I'm looking for your hotel guest named Theo Robinson," Kugler said.

The manager tapped his spectacles as his fingers reached down to the keyboard and began typing with one hand. He shook his head and looked up at Kugler. "I'm sorry, sir, there is no such guest in this hotel."

Kugler removed a photograph from the envelope and showed the manager. "This man is not a guest at your hotel? Are you sure?"

The manager held the photograph and examined the picture. "This man is registered as Francois Voclain." He frowned. "In fact, he's in the breakfast room right this moment."

"Show us the way," Kugler instructed.

The manager bowed stiffly. "Certainly."

Just then Robinson emerged from the dining room. The manager, still standing behind the counter, pointed at Robinson. "That's him."

Kugler and the troop turned behind to see Robinson in casual winter attire walking past them. "Theo Robinson."

Robinson paused and stared at Kugler.

"Remember me? The pizza boy outside your office," Kugler said, then flashed his badge at him.

Robinson's eyes widened. Then he darted off, pushing a few guests as he headed toward the exit.

"Such a waste of time," Kugler sighed, closing his eyes.

The agents gave chase as Kugler waited in the foyer. Minutes later they returned, with two of the agents holding Robinson under his arms. Kugler took a few steps toward Robinson.

"You're going back to Geneva with us," Kugler said. "We

have some questions for you."

"What's this about?" Robinson said.

"The murder of Christa Braun, and your relationship with Willem Van Der Haas."

"I've got nothing to say," Robinson said. "And I have the right to call my lawyer."

Kugler smiled. "I think you have lots to say. You can start by explaining why you were using a fake name to check in. As for your lawyer, well, we'll entertain your request, but I don't think the law will be on your side for too long."

***

Ayden, together with Isabelle and Guy, arrived in Geneva on a heli-taxi arranged by Cavallo. It landed at Geneva Airport, where they were greeted by Detective Kugler and escorted to a safe apartment at *Rue de Lausanne*. Two officers took turns guarding the lobby. An appointment had been arranged to meet Chief Inspector Guillaume the next day.

Ayden woke up the next morning around seven to the sound of tram bells. He rose slowly and pulled back the curtain to an ornate environment, with pedestrians moving out of the way as the public transport passed the line.

He went into the bathroom, washed up, and then entered the kitchen, where he found the other two.

"Kugler told me yesterday a car will pick us up by 9:30," Ayden said, yawning. He looked at Guy dipping an Oreo into his coffee. "You don't have to go if you don't want to. How's the leg?"

"The Italian doctor did a fine job. They gave me some painkillers. I'm a bit tired, so I think I'll stay back and rest," Guy said.

"Get as much rest as you can." Isabelle slotted another pod into the coffee machine. She turned it on after setting a cup in place. The machine began to gurgle as the aroma of espresso filled the kitchen.

"Isabelle, have you been memorizing what you're going to tell the Swiss police?" Ayden said.

"*Oui*, and I'm going to use my best perfume too. Even women cannot resist it."

"Brilliant."

The doorbell rang.

Ayden looked at his watch. "Thought Kugler said 9:30."

Isabelle took a final sip of the coffee, then crossed the hallway to the door. As she put her hand on the knob, Ayden dragged her to the side.

"The signal was three knocks. They were ordered not to ring the doorbell," Ayden whispered.

Isabelle nodded.

"Where's your gun?" Ayden asked.

"In the bedroom."

"Mine's on the bedside table. Go get mine while I let Guy know," Ayden said.

Ayden led Guy to the opposite side of the door. Isabelle appeared with their guns.

The doorbell rang again.

Ayden signaled Isabelle to respond.

"Who is it?" Isabelle said, both hands clasping her weapon.

"The car is here to take you to the police station," a man's voice said.

"It's a bit early, don't you think?"

"Change of plans—we're taking you to a different location for safety reasons. It's a little bit far from the city," the voice behind the door said.

"Okay, one moment please," Isabelle replied, and pointed to a moving shadow through the slit. She turned to Ayden. "What now?"

Ayden pointed to the kitchen. "Back door."

Retreating to the kitchen, they rushed through the back door into the stairwell. They stepped two floors down and stepped out into a corridor, then darted toward an elevator at the end of it. Guy struggled with his leg, trying to keep pace.

The lights indicated the elevator was three floors above them. Ayden cursed at the slowness.

They held their breath when the stairwell door opened. Just then, a door next to the elevator opened. An elderly couple stepped out of their apartment. Ayden sprang into the apartment before the door closed. He held the door to let everyone in, stunning the couple. He shut the door behind them and locked it.

They rushed to the balcony. Ayden pushed the curtain aside and slid the glass door open. He stepped out and peered down to a large pool. He turned and looked at Isabelle and Guy. "Go."

"What? Jump into the pool? It's winter, for God's sake! Don't forget my leg!" Guy cried.

Ayden stared at him. "That door isn't going to stop them."

"The worst part is nobody's recording this for YouTube." Guy climbed over the railing with Ayden's help. He took a deep breath and then plunged straight into the deep end. Ayden urged Isabelle to jump next. She climbed over and dived into the water headfirst with her arms straight above her head.

The door slammed open just as Ayden had one leg over the railing. He fired several rounds at the assailants, hitting one of them in his chest, shoulder, and pelvis. Unable to keep his balance, he slipped and landed on his back as he hit the water.

The other masked assailant stood on the balcony and fired at the pool indiscriminately. Underwater, his bullets left a trail of air pockets as they whizzed through. Ayden and the other two clung to the side of the wall for cover.

A minute later, Guy looked at his watch and indicated he needed to surface soon. Isabelle closed her eyes, trying to steady her breathing. Ayden signaled his intention to take out

INCOGNITO

the shooter. Springing out of the water, he fired at the assailant, hitting him in the chest. Crumpling on the balcony, his gun fell into the pool and sank to the bottom.

They broke the surface to see the attacker's arm jutting out of the balcony's railing.

Isabelle spit water from her mouth. "There might be more of them."

"I don't think so. They would have been here by now," Guy said, gasping.

Ayden looked up. "Who needs coffee with a morning like this? Let's go upstairs again and change into some fresh clothes."

The taxi arrived at the atrium of the police station at Boulevard Carl-Vogt and stopped in front of the glass doors. Past the entrance, murmurs and squeaky floors roiled the atmosphere. Ayden had contacted Detective Kugler to brief him on what had happened.

"My people are at the apartment now. We found the dead bodies and the gun in the pool," Kugler said as he led everyone upstairs to the squad room.

"They knew we were there," Ayden said.

"Do I look surprised?" Kugler said.

Kugler led them to the reception area. Below the traditional ceiling light panels, the interior within the white walls resounded with incessant telephone buzzing, and men and women scampering with folders, charge sheets, and transparent evidence bags. A few huddled in corners with coffee mugs. Discussions stretched from casual to serious. Tables away from them, a scruffy man in cuffs raised his voice at a detective as he tried to take a statement. A gym-built female cop entered, dragging a cuffed prostitute in a mean dress.

The detective pulled up a black plastic chair and sat in front of them. Moments later, everyone had a cup of cocoa in their hands. A uniformed female officer with a medic kit came and replaced Guy's wet bandage.

"By the way, we have Robinson in custody," Kugler said.

"Has he told you anything?" Ayden asked, clinging to the hot cup to keep his wrinkled fingers warm.

"He's a stubborn one," Kugler said. "It'll take time. He's been asking to call his lawyer.

"This arrest could hurt the pope if Robinson opens his mouth," Ayden reminded him of the stakes.

"We know that, but look around you — this is the office of the Swiss police, not the Swiss Guard," Kugler said.

"Ah, you don't care," Isabelle said.

"It's not that we don't care, but this matter has forced us to open several case files," Kugler said. "Don't forget, we're also cooperating with our neighbors."

"You know, they might try to kill Robinson if he opens his mouth," Isabelle said.

Kugler shook his head. "He's being guarded by some of my best. We need a few more hours, or days, with him." Kugler looked around, then said to Ayden in a soft voice, "You can't stay at the same apartment tonight."

"I'll check into a hotel," Ayden whispered in reply.

Guillaume approached. The introduction was quick. He pulled up a chair and sat down heavily beside Kugler. "Robinson's days as a newspaper editor are over. His lawyer is on the way. Hopefully, we can bargain with them. The usual — information for information. Speaking of which, I'd like to know who you people are."

Ayden glanced at Kugler, then back at Guillaume. "We're a group of specialists dispatched to find the pope."

Guillaume shook his head. "Who do you work for? How come there are no records of you? Are you even Greek?"

"We represent a Middle Eastern royal family. There are no records of us because they were erased to protect us," Ayden said.

"You expect me to believe this? Why should an Arab royal family care?"

"To prevent a modern crusade. As it is, there's a lot of tension in the Middle East and Europe between people. We were engaged because we operate quietly, and without bureaucracy and politicking. So, why should you not believe us?" Isabelle smiled.

"That's the truth." Ayden put the cup down.

"I don't know what to believe, but try not to encourage more trouble than you already brought to my country," Guillaume said.

"What about Van Der Haas?"

"It depends on what Robinson tells us. When his lawyer comes, we'll negotiate with him. I wonder what the Tribune de Geneva's board of directors will think after the newspaper's competitors run a story about their editor. I'll leave you in Kugler's good hands." He nodded once and walked away.

Ayden sniffed. "That was easy. Think my cold's coming back. Who's got aspirin?"

Chapter Nineteen

Benzinger stood outside the coffee shop that evening in a small lane in Amsterdam's Handboogstraat neighborhood. Bounced lights from the neon signs advertising coffee shops, bars, restaurants, and small hotels gave a psychedelic effect. He walked in through the coffee shop's glass door. None of the patrons gave him a second look. They didn't notice—they didn't care; eyes half shut, smiling weakly. Hands held rolled up weed joints and hashish while balancing their drinks. The interior's eclectic décor, which included quirky posters, kept the happy atmosphere afloat.

A voluptuous blonde waitress approached Benzinger. He told her he was there to meet Van Der Haas in the back room. She ushered him down a dim paneled corridor to the back of the coffee shop. A little further before the end of the hallway she stopped. She flicked a light switch on the wall, and the door slid open, revealing a flight of wooden stairs down. They descended, and the panel shut behind them. They proceeded into another hallway and walked toward a green door at the end of it. When they reached the door, the waitress opened it. The door opened to a smoky, subdued atmosphere room with rugs, cushy couches, and fancy bolsters, with soft music piped in to keep the mood. About a dozen people, men and women, sat around the room. A few propped against a stack of pillows, others reclined with their elbows resting on bolsters and poufs. The flaccid atmosphere clashed with the sense of urgency inside Benzinger.

Van Der Haas, with two buttons of his shirt open and shoes off, reclined sideways at a corner on a large pillow. He pinched rolled marijuana between his fingers and inhaled deeply. He blinked at Benzinger, then exhaled. His bodyguard, the giant, sat nearby against the wall with a pillow propped behind his back, reading a magazine. He looked up, nodded at Benzinger, and continued reading.

"Sit down, sit down," Van Der Haas said.

"I hate the smell. Can we talk somewhere else?" Benzinger asked, standing in front of the Dutchman.

"Sit down," Van Der Haas said. "You won't die from breathing secondhand smoke."

The waitress exited.

Benzinger sat with his back against the wall, crossing his legs.

Van Der Haas smiled. "I'm most sensible when I'm having one of these." He offered one of the rolled cigarettes on a silver tray in front of him to Benzinger, who waved his hand dismissively. "I like the disguise, by the way. You look good with a brown beard and that hairstyle."

"It's the same one I used to meet Zanebono in Rome," Benzinger said.

"It's about Theo Robinson, isn't it?" Van Der Haas said.

"Yes, we have to sort the problem," Benzinger said.

Van Der Haas inhaled another puff and slowly blew out the white smoke. "The police know about me, but how much do they know? They can't touch me."

"They can make things awkward, especially for me if Theo talks. My country won't like it. It could have repercussions."

"His loyalty to us is unquestionable," Van Der Haas said.

"Your friend is not trained to withstand long hours of interrogation. He will crack. I know you don't like what I'm saying."

Benzinger caught the giant's side glance at him before resuming his reading.

Van Der Haas sighed. "Let me think about it."

"There is no time," Benzinger said.

Van Der Haas remained silent for a moment, then said, "The decision is yours."

"It will be swift," Benzinger said.

***

Benzinger paced his breath every few seconds through the neoprene mask as he slinked along the ceiling's metal framework. He took his time, weighing each step, knowing if he put his gloved hands on a tile instead of the grid he would plummet to the ground. As he advanced forward, he could hear voices below, an interchangeable tone that went from high to low, and then climbed again. The voices belonged to several men, one he recognized as Robinson's. The other two were his interrogators. The voices grew louder as he settled above them. He listened to the conversation for a while. The relentless barrage of questions thrown at Robinson sounded like a runaway train before it crashed on impact.

In this instance, Robinson was the beginning of a dynamite fuse the cops had lit. To prevent an explosion, the fire must not travel to the end. Robinson had to go. Even though he didn't know where they hid the pope, he knew too much—enough to implicate a lot of people. The newspaper editor had always been faithful to their cause. He was liked by all. But he was also expendable. Even so, they would honor him.

Benzinger knew shortly the interrogators would leave the room. They always did, maybe to take a piss, get some more coffee, or hold a postmortem before initiating Plan B if the interrogation had failed.

He heard the door open and shut. He knew, however,

Robinson was not completely alone in the room. A guard would be posted to watch him, to make sure he didn't try to harm himself.

Benzinger removed the suppressed gun from the single strap fastened to his thigh. Quietly, he slid the ceiling sheet to the side, creating a slit, enough to slip the barrel through. He peeked down below. Robinson had his back to him, elbows on the table, his face in his hands. A video cam on a tripod stood an inch away from the table. The uniformed officer, arms folded, leaned in a corner, watching Robinson.

The policeman pitched forward and hit the ground. The bullet had taken him in the forehead. Robinson turned and looked up. Eyes ablaze, he transitioned from shock to anger, and then to fear.

The bullet smashed though Robinson's left eye. For a fraction of a second he jolted, wobbled in uncertainty between life and death, then cocked his head backward and slumped to the right side of the chair.

Benzinger tucked the weapon back into its strap. He eased the tile back into place, then turned and slipped away across the rails, ignoring the growing chaos below. Reaching another section of the ceiling, he slid a sheet aside and peeped below into a toilet. He lowered himself into the cubicle, its door locked from inside. His office attire hung against the door. Standing on the cistern's lid, he pushed the tile back to its place. He switched clothes before unlocking the door.

***

Housekeeping at the *Mandarin Oriental Geneva* had been instructed not to bother them. Even so, Ayden had overslept. He checked the time on his wristwatch. 10:30 a.m. He turned to find Isabelle tucked under a blanket in the next bed. Guy was not in his bed. He assumed he was in the bathroom.

The hotel phone on the side table buzzed. Ayden answered lazily.

"Demetrious?" Kugler's voice sounded bothered. "Robinson is dead."

"What?"

"He was shot while we were interrogating him."

"At the police station?"

"Yes. The killer came through the ceiling."

"Did the interrogators learn anything before he died?" Ayden inquired.

"Not much, Robinson was stubborn. The cops needed a few more hours with him," Kugler said.

Ayden noticed a note tucked underneath his Android phone. "Gordon Bennett!"

"What? Who's Gordon Bennet?" Kugler asked.

"Just an expression. I'll have to call you back," Ayden said, staring at the message.

Gone to see Anna.
Back soon.
Cheers, Guy.

***

It was Saturday, and Guy expected Anna to be at home. He had made a quick stop at a cake shop to get some pastry. He knew how much she loved cakes.

He opened the door and entered the small apartment. The curtains were still shut, and he assumed she was still asleep. He saw her shoes on the floor and her handbag on the sofa, along with a few shopping bags. He smiled to himself. He placed the cake box on the table and crept to the bedroom.

He opened the bedroom door and found her tucked under the blanket. He took a step forward, knelt down, and kissed her on the cheek.

Guy jerked up and staggered backward, slumping against the wall. He tried to scream, but the void held him in its grip.

Anna's head fell and hit the floor, rolling once. Her face stared at him with eyes and mouth opened.

Guy closed his eyes and opened them again seconds later, checking to see if he was imagining things. He struggled to get up, leveraging on a thigh. He fell again. He pressed his hands harder against the wall as he pulled his weight up. Gasping, he bent over and vomited on the carpet. He straightened up after and took a deep breath.

Voices.

He hid in the built-in wardrobe, jostling clothes as he did, then remained as still as he could. He tried to calm his breathing or they would hear him.

He watched one of them enter the room. Gun in his hand, the man looked around. He motioned to the edge of the bed and then knelt down to look under it. He got up and turned to the wardrobe.

Seeing the door start to open, Guy pushed against it and lunged forward, landing on the man and grabbing him by the neck. Hooking an arm around the man's neck, Guy grabbed his gun arm and repeatedly slammed it on the floor until the gun slipped from the man's hand. Guy picked up the weapon and pointed the muzzle at the man's head.

Three more assailants with suppressed guns entered the room.

"Back off now or he dies," Guy yelled.

The three assailants stepped back out into the living room.

As Guy stood, he dragged the man to his feet by his collar and then pushed him out of the bedroom. Using the captive as a shield, he turned toward the kitchen. As he neared the entrance, he released a stream of bullets at the other three standing in front of him. One of the gunmen fell against the curtain, pulling the cloth down. The remaining two dodged, slamming their bodies to the floor behind the sofa.

Guy shot the man he was holding in the side of his head, then rushed into the kitchen. He opened the window and climbed out. He lowered his body over the ledge, clinging by his hands for a moment. He dropped to the next ledge and then the next. He felt like he was drowning in a spin cycle, but he knew he shouldn't give in into his emotions.

He landed on the tiled pavement and bolted across the short cement path to the back gate. It led him to a quiet street. He ran up the pavement toward the tram stop about two hundred meters as a tram rattled on its track. He pushed his exhausted body to gain pace, slamming one foot in front of the other, kicking stone chips, twigs, and pieces of broken glass, enduring the pain as it rose up into his calf.

The tram passed him and stopped momentarily. A few people alighted and others climbed aboard. Guy arrived just as the carriage's sliding doors were closing. He leaped through and fell on the floor, almost hitting his head on a pole. He looked around. Eyes gave him looks of disdain.

***

"Guy?" Ayden stared at him outside his hotel room. "What's wrong?"

Looking disheveled, Guy fell to his knees and began to cry. His reaction shocked Ayden, who raised him up and brought him into the room.

Ayden sat him down on the bed. "What happened?"

"They —" He began to hyperventilate. "They —"

"What?"

"They killed Anna," Guy said, tears welling up in his eyes. "They cut her head off, man. Motherfuckers cut her head off!"

Ayden locked his fingers behind his back and breathed deeply. He walked around the room several times to gather his thoughts. The room was silent for several minutes. He then went to the side table and picked up his cell phone. He called Kugler and spoke to him for more than a minute.

"Don't cave in, man," Ayden told Guy after hanging up.

"This is my fault." Guy pressed his hands to his face. "I should've been more discreet about my relationship with her. They knew where to find her."

"Think with your head, not your heart. I know it's not easy, but you must. Understand?"

Guy tapped Ayden on the shoulder. "I can't put what I feel into words, but I hear you, man. By the way, when the time comes, don't stop me."

"I won't."

CHAPTER TWENTY

Guy sat opposite Kugler in his cubicle at the squad room giving a statement, while Ayden and Isabelle waited for him in the waiting area. Technically, Ferde Borsok didn't exist, so Kugler agreed not to make his statement formal.

"I feel sorry for Guy." Isabelle thumped her chest twice and crossed her heart.

Ayden stared at her. "Me too. He's going to find it hard to stay focused, so we've got to watch him."

"He'll live," Isabelle said.

"This is a different kind of pain," Ayden said, leaning back.

Isabelle took out her phone and clicked the Google app. "Ouf, the news about the pope is still going strong."

Ayden leaned closer to read the article. There was an old photo of the pope in his white robe wearing the Pectoral Cross.

Ayden continued to look at the photo. Suddenly his brain increased in alertness. He felt energetic, excited, and alive. "Why didn't I see it earlier?" he said cathartically.

"Pardon?"

"I think I might know where the pope is," Ayden said.

"*Excusez moi?*"

"Later, Guy's coming. Don't say anything in front of Kugler," Ayden whispered.

They stood as Guy approached with Kugler.

INCOGNITO

***

Guy replayed in his mind what Ayden had told him earlier. He should stay focused and not cave in. If anything, he should consider preparing a cold dish. People who spoke about revenge being ugly didn't know what they were talking about. It would be ugly if one prescribed it to a mortal. But revenge is never wrong when dealing with evil hiding in a mortal's shell. Those men who killed Anna were evil. For as sure as Anna rested in the morgue's cold storage, she was rooting for him to do unto them. The League's assignment, like any other, was always professional. In this instance, the rules had just changed.

Ayden looked at Guy sympathetically. "Everything okay?"

"Yeah." Guy stared at the floor after the monosyllable reply.

"You can leave now if you want," Kugler told Ayden. "I'll arrange a car to send you back to the hotel." He placed a hand on Guy's shoulder. "Take it easy. I know it's hard."

"Think we'll go get some fresh air, check out the sights and sounds of Geneva," Ayden said.

"You need to be careful. They've probably assigned more assassins," Kugler said.

"We've survived this far," Ayden replied.

They ended up at a small café near the police station. Outside the perspiring window, a golden glaze coated the rounded perimeters of the street junction as the mild sun descended. The streets teemed with pedestrians. Traffic ran in tandem with cars, motorcycles, scooters, trams, and buses.

Isabelle looked at Ayden as she hung her jacket behind the chair. "Tell us."

"Tell us what?" Guy glanced at her as he pulled a chair out.

"He said he knows where the pope is," Isabelle said, sitting down.

Guy shifted his attention to Ayden. "You do?"

"Maybe." Ayden folded his jacket and sat down. "All this

time…I mean, all this time the answer was there. But I didn't see it until now." He took out his phone and clicked on Google Images to a photo of the pope. He turned the screen to face Guy and Isabelle. "Cardinal Bartolomeo told me when the kidnappers gave him the Pectoral Cross the chain was damaged. He said some of the circular links looked dented. What if it was done on purpose?" Ayden took a sip of the latte.

"What should we be looking for?" Guy's eyebrows clashed with each other.

"We need x-ray glasses maybe?" Isabelle sounded irritated.

"Bartolomeo told me the pope was kidnapped a week before the Vatican decided to announce it publicly. So he had ample time to do it."

"Do what?" Isabelle scratched her hair. "I don't understand."

"The chain is Morse code," Ayden said. "That explains the dents on it. He created those dents to look like dots and dashes. The pope learned Morse code as a boy in the French resistance. He just gave us his location."

INCOGNITO

CHAPTER TWENTY-ONE

The view from Ayden's fifth-floor hotel room at the *Mandarin Oriental Geneva* reflected the surrounding lights on the River Rhone's edges as darkness smothered the city. Ayden sat crossed-legged on the bed, leaning against the headboard. Guy rested on the bed beside him, with Isabelle sitting at the edge facing Ayden.

Ayden autodialed Cavallo's number. He raised his brows when the phone rang. He didn't expect it after failing to reach him several times in the past.

"*Pronto,*" Cavallo answered.

"Hello, Cavallo, I need something from you," Ayden said. "It's a bit awkward."

"What is it?"

"Can you send over the pope's Pectoral Cross? I'd like to see it."

"Send over what?"

"The Pectoral Cross."

"Why? You can see it on the Internet."

"I have to see the real thing. I have my reasons. Trust me, Cavallo. I need to see it, like right now."

"But you're in Geneva." Cavallo breathed heavily in frustration. "I don't even know where it is."

"I know where it is. It's in Bartolomeo's desk drawer. He wanted to send it to the craftsman for repair."

"What's wrong with it?"

"The chain is dented. But send it to me as it is. It could be a clue," Ayden said.

"Okay, tomorrow evening. Best I can do. Expect a call from one of my agents. He'll let you know when he arrives. Where are you staying?"

"The *Mandarin Oriental Geneva*."

The next day at 5 p.m., two of Cavallo's agents met Ayden in the hotel's lobby. They had called in advance to let him know what they looked like and what they were wearing.

"Please don't lose it," one of the agents said, handing over a small velvet bag.

"This is too important for me to mess around with," Ayden said.

Back in his room, Ayden sat on the bed and removed the Pectoral Cross from the bag. It was designed with Jesus embedded on it and a dove on top. At the bottom was Mother Mary, and some other people kneeling and praying. He pulled the chain out through the bail, separating it from the crucifix, and then lay it out in front of him with the roller and toggle at both ends. Isabelle sat cross-legged at the edge of the bed with a pen and a blank piece of paper in her lap, supported by a leather-bound room service menu. Resting on the other bed, Guy watched him transcribe the dots and dashes to her.

When they were done, Isabelle handed the piece of paper to Ayden. He unplugged the iPad from the dock charger on the bedside table. He then searched for a Morse code translator on Google. After finding a reliable link, he keyed in the protocol.

"Voila!"

28. 555948 BT 33.976048

Ayden turned the iPad's screen to show the others the result.

"It's latitude and longitude coordinates," Isabelle said.

"You're absolutely right." Ayden smiled. "I see the French military taught you well."

"Among other things," she sneered.

"Now let's see what we get," Ayden said as he typed in the key words "map coordinates" on the Google page. It led him to several links, including a latitude and longitude finder. The particular link took him to an interactive map tool. He keyed in the set of numbers and letters again in the search features and hit the *convert* button.

The page unfolded to an interactive map. The cursor turned into an arrow and zoomed into a place mark: a mountainous desert terrain. A red dot popped up, highlighting a location. He dragged the cursor above the dot and clicked on it. "Well, well, so that's where they are," he muttered. "Egypt."

Saint Catherine Monastery
Mount Sinai, Egypt

Ayden stirred the next morning as the reddening sun rose behind the snow-capped mountains. He covered his face with the thick blanket as the rays seared his face. He pressed the light function on his digital watch. 7:00 a.m.

He felt someone pulling his blanket. Isabelle, sitting at the edge of his bed, stared at him. He dragged himself to a sitting position on the edge of the bed and yawned.

"*Bon matin.*" Isabelle wished him a good morning in French.

"Yeah, good morning." Ayden yawned again. "What is it?"

"We leave for Egypt today," Isabelle said.

"What?"

She put her hands on her hip. "Wake up, brush your teeth. We go, now."

"What about Guy?" Ayden said.

"Look at his leg. He's not qualified for the next adventure,"

Isabelle said.

"Yeah, I'll stay here," Guy said. "Besides, they've got Netflix."

"What about our weapons?" Ayden wondered.

"No weapons. We play it by ear. But we'll take Guy's bag of tricks," Isabelle said.

The Turkish Airlines flight rattled in turbulence with a raging sandstorm underneath as it descended into the blurred, sandy runway at Egypt's *Sharm el-Sheikh International Airport* in the Sinai region. Inside the cabin Ayden braced himself, ignoring the spilled beverages and jostling luggage. He was conscious of the fact accidents occurred more during takeoff and landing.

The cabin crew had been warned to return to their seats. From Ayden's vantage point in the middle aisle, a blonde Turkish flight attendant sat muttering a few words under her breath. No doubt she was praying for a safe landing.

The flight was generally empty except for a few European tourists. Unsettling news about the Middle East had forced governments to issue travel warnings, encouraging their citizens to avoid "all but essential travel" to the region. For regulars, the warnings had become white noise in the background as they eagerly waited to get to their destination: the beach resorts and scuba diving spots.

By the time the landing gear opened and locked, dust had blanketed the plane's windows.

"Look at the dust. Can we even land? How's the pilot going to see?" Isabelle, sitting across the aisle from Ayden, stared out the window.

"The plane has wipers like a car," Ayden replied. "You didn't know that?"

"Don't be silly. Of course I know," she said.

The plane bumped and thudded as the wheels hit the ground. Ayden's heart skipped a beat, and he hoped not to see the contents of his stomach. The aircraft continued to maneuver on the grainy tarmac before coming to a stop about a hundred and fifty meters from the terminal building.

The captain informed everyone through the intercom that the airport was temporarily closed. All flights had been cancelled until the weather conditions improved. Passengers were advised to check with the airline counter about rescheduling their return. They were also advised to cover their faces before exiting to prevent being assailed by the storm.

A senior flight attendant stood by the cabin door ready to disarm it. She picked up the intercom phone and waited for approval. The door opened a minute later.

The orange-copper sky had blotted out the sun, limiting visibility as they descended the stairwell. The gusting north winds seared through the hot air mercilessly.

"This place looks like Mars." Isabelle squinted through her fingers as she and the other arriving passengers plodded through the sand veil toward the terminal building.

Ayden didn't answer. He was busy protecting his eyes with his hands against the tempest carrying twigs and other debris. The passengers covered their faces and bodies against the stinging particles with handkerchiefs, T-shirts, sweaters, plastic bags, sunglasses, and hats.

A chorus of sighs went up once the new arrivals stepped inside the airport. The respite was short-lived. Some people voiced their dismay when they saw uniformed officers snapping their fingers as they directed passengers to the respective counters.

With carry-on bags only, they skipped the baggage carousel after passing the immigration hall. A middle-aged, mustached Egyptian man in a black leather jacket and denim jeans held a placard sign with Ayden's name. Isabelle had arranged with a tour company for a private transfer to the monastery, a three and a half hour drive.

The Egyptian driver, with a long, thin face, wore a brown

baseball cap and black Ray-Bans. He stood with a cluster of airport greeters. He smiled as Ayden approached. "Welcome." The Egyptian didn't remove his shades, and gave his name only as Mahmoud. He suggested waiting inside the airport before going on the road, as the storm had not subsided. The delay was inevitable. They could use the time they had to freshen up, he suggested.

They sat upstairs in a café with almost all the tables full. Voices grumbled when some passengers were told the Wi-Fi service was unavailable.

"Of all places, Egypt. People will really think the Muslims had a hand in the pope's kidnapping," Isabelle mumbled, slurping on a soda.

"I'm sure Cavallo and everybody else will come up with some excuse," Ayden said.

Mahmoud returned two hours later. "We can go now."

They were greeted outside by a smack of hot air moving down from the semi-shrouded red mountains nestling in the near distance. The wind dragged sheets of newspapers, plastic bags, and cans across the sand-coated pavement. Water bottles they'd purchased from the café earlier in hand, they walked to a dusty Cherokee parked nearby.

Mahmoud opened the side door and bid them to enter.

"Is it safe to be on the road? Will the storm come back?" Ayden asked as he stepped inside the vehicle.

"Don't worry, no *broblem*." Mahmoud waved his hand with the keys between his fingers. He pointed to the sky. "Trust Allah." Ayden noticed the man had a problem pronouncing the letter P, as in the case with most Arabs.

"Yes, have faith in Allah. I understand. No problem." Ayden smiled. He knew from his encounters with Middle Easterners that unless they had received a formal Western education, he should expect everyone to replace every English word that began with P with a B, because there is no P in the Arabic alphabet.

Sand began to lift in the air as the Cherokee sped out of the airport to the highway. About twenty minutes into the ride, the 4x4 slowed down in a tourist town defended by craggy mountains. Mahmoud pulled into a McDonald's, then turned and looked at Ayden.

"I go toilet. You go? You want drinks? Burger?"

"Thanks, Mahmoud, we're fine."

Mahmoud unintentionally slammed the door as he exited the vehicle, startling Ayden and Isabelle. About five minutes later, he exited the restaurant carrying a brown bag and walked back to the car.

He adjusted his Ray-Bans and cap and started the engine. Within ten minutes back into the journey, Isabelle fell asleep. Ayden, however, who felt rested, was eager to reach his destination as fast as the vehicle could take him.

A whistling wind accompanied them on the road even though all the windows were closed. A few vehicles passed them along the flat road edged with craggy mountains, boulders, and ligneous plains.

Ayden leaned forward behind the driver. "Were you born in *Sharm el Sheikh*, Mahmoud?"

"Yes, I was born here in a village," Mahmoud replied while munching a burger. Ayden could hardly hear him with his mouth full.

"Have you always worked in the tour business?"

"Yes. I like it very much. I like people. Good job."

"Have you ever travelled outside of Egypt?"

"No, just Cairo."

"Where would you like to go if you had the chance? Dubai? Paris? London? New York?"

"I like, err…see all country. I like most Paris. Eiffel Tower is very tall, very nice. Yes, everything nice."

"I like travelling too. I'd like to see the world. I've got a traveler's heart," Ayden said. "So I see we've got things in common."

"Very nice. The world is very nice. Praise to God."

Ayden sat back. Something was wrong. Mahmoud's reply made him uneasy. It was odd to hear the Egyptian say Paris instead of *Baris*. What happened to the Bs? It was hard to tell with his mouth full, but his tone sounded different. Not that Ayden had known Mahmoud for a long time, but he noticed the little things. One of the languages he had studied back on the secret island was Arabic, and he remembered the lessons well.

When the man had come out of McDonald's his walk was somewhat different. He walked with heavy footsteps, unlike Mahmoud, who had a light way of moving. One logical explanation: the man behind the wheel, despite the cap and sunglasses, was not Mahmoud. And Ayden doubted if he was taking them to their location.

Chapter Twenty-Two

Ayden nudged Isabelle beside him.

She woke up, rubbing her eyes. "Are we there yet?"

"No." Ayden looked straight ahead as he slipped her a scribbled note.

Trouble. The driver is not Mahmoud.

Isabelle straightened and gave Ayden a sideways glance, followed by a nod.

"How long more before we reached the monastery, Mahmoud? About an hour and a half or so, you think?" Ayden quizzed.

"Yes, about there."

"Could we stop the car for a moment? Toilet time."

"Okay. But please hide behind rock. Don't let any people see what you doing."

"Okay, sure," Ayden said.

Mahmoud, or whoever he was, stopped the car at the side of the road facing a small lagoon bordered by a large rock and a mountain wall. Ayden and Isabelle got out and scuttled toward a conclave of giant rocks with small waves slapping against them.

"Hey, you go man and woman together?" Mahmoud exclaimed.

"You never know. Maybe there's a snake or scorpion, so I have to protect her." Ayden faked his laughter.

"Ya, you're right, you're right." Mahmoud took out a cigarette and tried to light it up in the strong wind.

They proceeded behind the rocks.

"What happened to the real Mahmoud?" Isabelle asked Ayden once they were hidden from view.

"Something happened back at McDonald's," Ayden said. "That guy can pronounce the letter P, but Mahmoud couldn't."

"So what do you want to do?"

"Get rid of him."

They emerged from behind the rock and headed back to the vehicle. The wind started to pick up. The driver threw the cigarette on the ground and stubbed it into the sand. They came beside him. Just as he was about to get into the driver's seat, Ayden turned him around and swung a right. The punch knocked the sunglasses and cap off the man's face. He fell backward, knocked out.

"We don't have anything to tie him up with," Ayden said.

"Leave him," Isabelle said. She knelt beside the man and frisked him. There was nothing on him except a box of cigarettes and a cheap lighter.

Ayden noticed a slight shade of blond hair at the back of the man's neck. "Look." He pointed. "He dyed his hair." He studied the man's complexion and ran his finger across his cheek, leaving a fair line.

"Don't tell me," Isabelle said. "They followed us?"

"Not sure. Let's go before he wakes up."

Ayden sat in the driver's seat with Isabelle beside him. He inserted the key into the engine but didn't start the car yet. He slid his phone out of his pocket and activated the GPS mode.

Wending their way along the canyon, the mouth of the corridor led to a *cheval de frise* about three hundred meters ahead.

About twenty Egyptian soldiers stood behind the armed blockade, flanked by two armored personnel carriers. They waved at them to slow down.

"What do we do, Ayden?" Isabelle asked.

"Stop and play tourist," Ayden said. He lowered his window after bringing the vehicle to a stop. Walkie-talkies crackled back and forth in the background as several soldiers in dusty, desert camo moved toward them.

"*Bassport blease*," an officer demanded, standing outside his window. His insignia looked different from the other soldiers near him. Two stars decorated his shoulder plates, indicating he was either a lieutenant or a captain.

Ayden handed them over.

The officer studied the vehicle. He got another to record the license number. "*Thiz Cherokee iz rental*?" he inquired.

"Yes, it's a rental," Ayden answered.

"*Who you rent from, blease*?"

"Umm…Hertz," Ayden lied.

"Are you sure?" The officer looked through Ayden.

"Yes."

"No Hertz in Sharm." The officer raised his weapon and took several steps back. He uttered several words in Arabic to his men as they encircled the vehicle, weapons raised.

"Get out now!" A soldier pointed his rifle at Ayden's face. "Raise your hands and don't make nervous."

They obeyed.

The officer scrutinized their passports. "Greek?" He raised his eyes and stared at Ayden.

Ayden nodded. "Yes."

The officer pointed his finger at Isabelle. "This lady is from Belgium?"

"Yes, she is," Ayden said.

The soldier squinted. "You're husband and wife?"

"No, we're friends. We work together in Switzerland," Ayden said.

"So you're girlfriend and boyfriend?" The officer stuck his tongue out, and then became serious again. He exchanged some words with the other soldiers and then looked at Ayden. "This *blace*, Sinai, now have many *broblem*, lots of *broblem*. You know this from *newsbaber*, I think. Terrorism is number one *broblem* here. Now you say you take this vehicle from Hertz, but we've no Hertz in Sinai. *Blease* give me good answer. If no good answer, we make arrest now. You understand? So show me your vehicle rental receipt."

Eyes straight, Isabelle whispered into Ayden's ear. "I think he's asking us for a bribe. That's how it works in Egypt, so I hear."

Ayden flashed a smile at the officer. "We borrowed this Cherokee from a tour company. Their driver, Mahmoud, is not well, and so the tour company gave us the keys if we promised to take care of it," Ayden said, hoping his lie sounded believable.

The soldier's eyes widened. "So why you say from Hertz? You make lie."

"I didn't want to make it complicated for you," Ayden said.

The officer grinned. "We know this vehicle. Everyday come to this road with Mahmoud. Now, you're driving it. You said the company gave you the keys. Not possible. We received a radio call earlier that Mahmoud was found dead in the McDonald's toilet. He was strangled. You kill him."

"Okay, okay, the truth is, we stopped at McDonald's hours ago," Ayden said, raising his hands with open palms. "Mahmoud went to the toilet. Then another driver, disguised as Mahmoud, took his place. I became suspicious. So I punched the guy out and we left him a few kilometers behind. I think he was trying to kidnap us. That's the truth."

"*Merde*," Isabelle muttered, eyes rolling.

"Duck under the vehicle when I say go," Ayden said,

squinting at a cat high up in the rocks. "Something is about to happen."

"What?"

"Get ready."

The soldier interrupted them. "I think you take Mahmoud's Cherokee and you hurt him."

"That's not what happened," Ayden said.

The officer looked at the other soldiers. "Arrest them!"

Ayden and Isabelle were ordered to turn and face the vehicle with their hands behind their backs. Three soldiers approached with cuffs as others guarded them.

Small rocks and debris tumbled onto the surface in front of them. By reflex, everyone turned and looked up. A furry little face with large ears hid behind a mid-size rock on the rocky wall's ledge. A fennec fox.

One of the soldiers noticed Isabelle looking at it. "Nothing to see — turn around," he said. Those were his last words. His body went limp and he dropped to his knees, weapon dropping from his hand, helmet rolling as he hit the ground.

"Duck!" Ayden pointed at the fennec. A rifle's barrel protruded through the stuffed furry creature's gaped mouth.

The other soldiers scrambled for position, gesticulating and shouting orders as they fired. None of the shots hit the target, who was well hidden behind the rocks. The vibrations loosened some of the bigger ones, forcing them to tumble.

Nearby, another sniper had taken up position. His first shot reverberated off the rocks, echoing in the stillness. The officer yelled at everyone to rush to the APC behind the barricade. As they ran for cover, an earsplitting cracking sound echoed across the desert air. It was a speeding orb of fiery light.

Ayden and Isabelle slipped underneath the Cherokee, and under the hail of bullets raking the soldiers, hacking tiny chunks of flesh from their faces, necks, limbs and bodies. A bullet punched through a soldier's neck and exploded out of his back. Others fell in a thrashing heap, lacing blood in the air from burst veins.

The noises around them became muffled, accompanied by a buzzing inside their heads. A distance away, one of the armored vehicles was in flames. A cloud of black smoke rose sluggishly in the air.

A swirling trail of dust followed a thunder of Jeeps heading their way, loaded with a dozen armed men wearing head scarfs and goggles. The Egyptian officer ordered his men into the other APC. Leaving the wounded and dying behind, the armored vehicle roared, spewing smoke and lunging ahead on the road.

About forty meters to their left, a man stood in one of the Jeeps, holding its roll bar. Wearing a green scarf to cover his face and head, leaving a slit for the eyes, he pointed to the fleeing APC at the far end of the road. A militiaman with a grenade launcher stood, leveled the weapon at its target, and fired. The rocket struck the back of the armored transport, which trailed sparks and spurting fireballs as it slowed down to a stop. A soldier staggered out of the top deck and collapsed.

"Take a rifle!" Ayden yelled, seeing several AK-47s strewn on the ground near a group of dead soldiers.

They crawled out and took the weapons, along with the extra magazines and some grenades in the tactical pouches.

"These desert pirates don't look too friendly," Isabelle said, pointing to the newcomers on the Jeeps.

Ayden jumped into the vehicle and started the engine, gunning it as he sped off in the direction of the burning APC. He pressed the pedal down, pushing them back into their seats as the men in Jeeps sped up from the left side of the desert road. Tires squealed as he swerved past the APC, driving partially into the desert before resuming on the tar again. As their pursuers drew closer, Isabelle opened her window and leaned out, firing at will. Facing retaliatory gunfire, she ducked under the backseat.

From Ayden's rearview, he saw a man lean against the front Jeep's roll bar with an RPG on his shoulder, aiming at them. Ayden swerved the vehicle sharply into the desert without slowing down. The propelled rocket missed the vehicle, eventually exhausting its flight path and sloping to impact a clump of rocks. The tremendous explosion blew flames, rock fragments, and sand flying in all directions. As the Cherokee drove on the sandy expanse, the female GPS voice became confused, spinning the virtual map madly on his phone screen and repeatedly advising major route changes.

The second Jeep suddenly overtook the first. Gaining speed, the driver angled closer to the side of the Cherokee. As the Jeep came closer, the men on board opened fire. The bullets kept coming, crashing into the 4x4's metal and glass. A bullet zinged through the windshield, cracking the glass.

"Too close!" Ayden said. He felt another bullet penetrate into the front tire on the passenger's side, forcing the vehicle to swerve to the left. He steadied the vehicle as it rasped across the open terrain, bouncing over mounds of sand. He floored the accelerator, pushing the vehicle to its limit as it leaped forward.

Looking behind him, he saw the Jeeps had split up to perform a pincer movement.

"'Nade them when they sandwich us," Ayden said, holding the steering wheel steady.

Isabelle unpinned a grenade and held down the grip.

Ayden watched the vehicles draw closer, calculating in his mind the throwing distance Isabelle needed for the grenade to have success. He braced himself. As the Jeeps neared, he gave the signal.

Trusting Ayden's judgement, Isabelle tossed grenades out of the windows on both sides, one at a time. The first grenade hit the right back wheel of a Jeep. Flipping over onto its side, the Jeep exploded into a massive ball of fire. The velocity of the second grenade explosion split the Jeep into two parts, sending some men and their limbs tumbling through the air.

Ayden brought the vehicle to a dead stop, jumped out, and ducked behind the car, pointing the AK at the two Jeeps. Isabelle crawled out from one side and crouched behind the back tire, weapons ready. When the smoldering dust cloud had cleared, they approached the burning vehicles with their weapons raised. The sound of someone coughing alerted them. Ayden turned to see a man on the ground, body covered in blood. They approached and stood in front of him.

Isabelle knelt down and removed the scarf that covered his face. The injured man was a European with blond hair and blue eyes. She looked up at Ayden. "Another one. I was expecting to see an Arab face."

"Just like our imposter driver." Ayden knelt beside Isabelle and stared at the man. "What're you doing in Egypt?"

The injured man turned his head, shut his eyes, and faded.

They stood and stared in silence at the desert, feeling its cold stillness soak into their bones as the wind blew dust to cover the sporadic patches of fire. Ayden removed the revolver in the dead man's holster and took the extra magazines in his pouch. Isabelle had managed to salvage a few more as well.

Somewhere in the vast sands, a jackal howled and shrieked as the wind joined the sensation of biting the air.

"I don't like that sound," Isabelle said.

"Neither do I. Let's go," Ayden said, turning.

They quickly changed the tire, and then cleared the pieces of broken glass in the backseat. Isabelle then helped Ayden remove the shattered windshield. He grabbed one of the bags in the backspace and removed two black robes inside it, along with a disguise kit. After donning the robes over their casual attire, they helped each other adjust their fake moustaches, beards, and hats.

"Leave the rifles under the car seat, but take the handguns."

Ayden got into the car and pressed a button to raise the window on his side. The driver's window was the only one not broken. But it didn't spare him the chills as the sun sank behind a dune, launching dust higher into the atmosphere.

Driving back toward the tar road, sand hissed around them as wind whipped their faces, plastering blisters to their lips, filling their hair, trickling down inside their clothes, skulking along their noses and throats. Isabelle pressed her eyes shut and pulled up her robe against her mouth, cutting the assault by half.

The GPS functioned normally again, guiding them along a path bordering between sand and a stony vastness as the vehicle snaked through lines of boulders. They passed curvaceous tracks as they advanced, at times having to careen around desert rocks. The endless winding and unchanging scenery made Isabelle eventually fall asleep.

Ayden slowed down the vehicle as he entered a small, quiet dirt road. He came near the right side of a short running wall and parked. He removed his phone from the car mount and slipped it into his pocket. Then he turned to look at Isabelle. He tapped her twice. "We're here — wake up."

They sauntered casually toward the ancient hermitage. The wind rose high, stirring leaves as the tall cypress trees shuffled and swayed. They meandered along a path covered by sparse greenery along the short stone border walls, which led to the monastery's main entrance beside the old portal. The monastery's girded red granite walls stood citadel high, and ringed by jagged mountain peaks on three sides. A wooden bay window protruded from high above.

Centuries before, the monastery was built on this location to disguise itself among the mountains in order to stop marauding bandits from reaching it. Those days one had to climb the mountain to reach it. Emperor Justinian built it back in 527 A.D. The place had undergone changes since then, of course. It had

241

even come under the protection of the Prophet Muhammad, and Napoleon had a hand in its refurbishment later. The burning bush was supposed to have occurred there, but no one knew for sure.

"Sure this is the place?" Isabelle admired the surroundings. "It's hard to imagine."

"Don't think I'm mistaken, but I don't want to assume anything," Ayden said.

"I'm trying to make sense of this. This is a Greek monastery, but this is Egypt. Did the Egyptians and the Greeks conspire to kidnap the pope? You know what I'm trying to say?"

"What I do know is the Egyptian government closed the place to visitors after some bomb threats were made," Ayden said. "Then again, it could be an excuse to deter outsiders from coming here."

Six armed Egyptian soldiers stood in front of the gate. One among them stepped forward and raised his hand as Ayden and Isabelle approached.

"I don't think showing my legs would be appropriate at this time," Isabelle said.

Ayden looked at her. "I'm not showing mine either. Well, you never know these days. Then again, this is Egypt—you'd be safer wearing a kippah than trying to fly a rainbow flag."

Standing in front of the guard, Ayden explained in English that they were visiting monks from a Greek island. The excuse sounded convincing enough for the guard to let them pass.

Inside the compound, a monastic chant echoed off the walls, bouncing off a cluster of buildings: chapels, a refectory, and annexes—both square and rectangular in shapes—with rooftops and verandahs, a bell tower, a basilica with granite columns with foliage separating several aisles.

They arrived at the Chapel of the Burning Bush behind the altar of the basilica. Nearby, a sprawling bush hung over a stone fence covering its roots. Isabelle raised her hand to touch it.

"Think those costumes could fool me, did you?"

They turned to find an unarmed man in an outfit resembling an archeologist looking at them.

"Who're you?" Ayden asked.

A cold breeze kicked up a layer of dust and blew across the ground. Isabelle blew into her own eyes and rubbed the particles off her face. "Notice the Russian accent?" she asked Ayden.

"I did, yes," Ayden said.

Hurried footsteps were heard behind them. Ayden and Isabelle turned to find eight muscular men in the same type of clothing as Benzinger. The two specialists slipped their hands into their pockets under their robes.

"Don't take out your weapons. This is holy ground," Benzinger said. "Unless you want to attract the Egyptian guards outside, let's keep it quiet. You're going to have a tough time explaining to them why you're wearing disguises. On the other hand, we've got permission to be here."

"I'm sure you do. So, is the pope here?" Ayden asked, removing his fake moustache and beard.

"Getting warmer."

Isabelle removed her moustache and beard and kept them in one of the side pockets. "You're Russian?"

Benzinger nodded. "I've been working with your friends, Chief Inspector Guillaume and Detective Kugler. I'm the public relations consultant with the Geneva police."

"So you're the one," Ayden said.

"Kugler made the mistake of whispering too loudly. Stupid man," Benzinger said. "I found out by chance, snooping around here and there. The plan was to capture one of you on the train. Hopefully that would make you back off. We failed, thanks to you."

"What's this got to do with Russia?" Ayden asked.

"Well, since you've made it this far, I guess you deserve to know what's going on. Follow me," Benzinger said.

The men behind them approached and removed their weapons and phones. They led them to an off-white rectangular building with a semi-detached *minaret*, a tower with a balcony used to call Muslims to prayer. It was located in the northern corner with a small courtyard in front of it. The tower stood beside a clay-colored church bell tower.

"This mosque was built during the Fatimid Dynasty, completed around 1106," Benzinger said. "Mount Sinai is also identified by Muslims as *Jebel Musa,* or Mount Moses in English. For them, as for Christians and Jews, this is the place where God made a covenant with his people, handing down the tablets. In 628 a document signed by the Prophet Muhammad known as the *Ashtiname,* or Holy Testament, exempted the monks from military service and tax. It also called upon Muslims to give them help. As a reciprocal gesture, the monastery converted a chapel into a mosque."

"So you're good student of history, big deal," Ayden said, walking behind Benzinger.

"You have to be if you're going to pretend to be an archaeologist." Benzinger rapped the mosque's door entrance twice and waited. The door unlocked slowly with two wrinkled hands holding it. An old, hunched man wearing a brown robe and a white *haji* cap appeared. Benzinger greeted him in the few Arabic words he knew, then gestured for everyone to enter.

With daylight pouring through the few windows, they stepped upon plastic sheets covering the carpet as they moved toward the minbar, the Islamic pulpit.

The old man shut the door and locked it.

Benzinger stopped at the side of the pulpit. He placed a hand on the panel and pushed it sideways. A motion-sensing light brightened the space inside, revealing a steel ladder fastened

INCOGNITO

to a stony wall leading below. Benzinger glanced at Ayden and pointed at the ladder. He shuffled through the small space and held the sides of the ladder as he climbed down. Ayden and Isabelle followed.

Lights on one side of the wall lit the way along the precipice. Even so, it didn't give comfort looking down into the abyss. The warm temperature sent trickles of sweat down Ayden's sides and spine. They landed on a fenced-in metal pad fastened to a rock face beside the ladder. A silver shuttle elevator stood at the end of the pad's edge with its doors open.

Ayden jumped off the ladder onto the solid platform. He stepped aside to give Isabelle room. They stood beside each other and looked at the shuttle.

"Are we going to meet pharaoh or what?" Isabelle stared at the elevator.

"This will take us all the way down," Benzinger explained.

They stepped into the elevator and the temperature became cooler all of a sudden. A box with two buttons—red above the green—jutted at the side of the door. Benzinger pressed the green button. The shuttle's transparent doors slid closed automatically, then opened again seconds later.

Ayden looked around. "Did we even move?"

Without feeling the descent, they had descended to a station behind a brightly lit white tunnel bordered by a circular glass door. The glass door parted with a fizzy gas sound, leading them into a silver metal capsule with seats on both sides. They entered and took seats beside each other. The glass doors shut.

"Nothing's happening," Isabelle said.

"This is a hyper loop," Benzinger said.

Isabelle flinched. "A what?"

"A hyper loop, Miss Ignorant, takes you from one place to another in a matter of—"

The glass doors in front of them whisked open.

245

"Seconds," Benzinger completed his sentence as he stepped out.

"Very impressive," Isabelle said. "It's so fast I didn't even get a chance to tell you what a son of a bitch you are."

Benzinger frowned. "Don't try to work my emotions."

"Please excuse my friend," Ayden said. "According to her medical reports, she has an allergy to bastards."

"Say what you like, at the end of the day I'll have the last laugh. Or should I say, the last bullet." Benzinger smiled.

"We'll see," Ayden said. "We'll see."

They ascended on a platform with rubber tile covering the floor. In front of them was a large metallic door. It opened to reveal two armed guards standing in front of them.

Chapter Twenty-Three

Behind the door was an earthen catacomb with a metallic path and grid of glowing tubes running along the walls. The two armed guards stepped aside to let them pass.

They walked in utter silence as the square-shaped, concrete tunnels winded through innumerable turns, two guards stationed at every turn. The length widened when they reached a dug-out entrance with grated steel steps. They descended to a multi-level bridge, which connected to other warrens and a suspended platform across an excavation area. Fifteen feet below them, mini tractors and cranes moved around lifting piles of rocks and dirt into dump trucks under the watchful eyes of armed soldiers. Sparks flew and metal screeched against the granite marble walls as men in protective masks drilled into them. Others pounded blocks with hammers.

They turned right and ambled along the platform. It led to a carved-out room in the rocky wall with a seamless glass window. They stepped on a shorter confluence to reach the room. The door slid open.

They found themselves in a room with green rubber protective flooring. Perforated lamps encircled the ceiling, making the interior bright.

Benzinger gestured for them to sit.

Ayden sat down at a round white table. "What do you do

here exactly?"

"This is our Middle East base of operations," Benzinger said. "We're constructing tunnels to reach Libya, Saudi Arabia, Lebanon, and even Israel and Palestine. We're continuing to build more hyper loop tunnels to reach all these countries."

Isabelle folded her arms. "So the Egyptian authorities think you're doing archaeology work."

Benzinger smiled deviously. "Searching for the remnants of Moses's tablets. People are afraid nowadays to come to Egypt because of terrorism. We approached the Egyptians and offered them an opportunity to work with us. We convinced them that finding bits and pieces of Moses's tablets would improve their country's tourism. Our real intention, of course, is something else."

"What's your real intention?" Ayden asked.

Benzinger pointed outside the window. "These tunnels lead to several military bases being constructed, including submarine pens and underground air bases. They're all expected to be ready in five years. By then, we'll be able to come and go as we please without detection."

"You want to sandwich Europe," Ayden said.

Benzinger smiled. "That's correct. We're concerned about the missiles the Americans have installed in Europe aimed at Russia."

"You don't need Sword's help to do that," Isabelle said. "They've got a different agenda."

"We want to dismember NATO, starting with Turkey, being the weakest nation of the pact. It's not a European nation anymore, nor is it Christian. Its alliance with Europe is fragile, and it walks on a tightrope between Europe and the Arab world. Turkey is NATO's Achilles heel. Turkey is under strain after what happened recently. It's all messy. Don't be surprised if it gets sacked from NATO. For now, we'll start with Turkey."

"Ah, the win-win. Somehow I suspected there was more to the story. It just didn't make sense to me that Sword would open a front against Turkey," Ayden said. "Obviously Sword doesn't know about your country's big plan."

"These idiots think we're building tunnels and bases to secure our Middle East operations."

"Where's the pope?"

Benzinger blinked. "In his cell."

Ayden leaned back. "What do you intend to do with us?"

Benzinger pointed again outside the window. "We've got lots of holes down there. Who knows? They might find you thousands of years from now and revere you as saints. Meanwhile, I'll put you in a cell until further notice."

"Fuck you," Isabelle raised her voice.

"That would be a pleasure," Benzinger said. "Alas, I don't have time. Now if you'll please follow the guards, they'll escort you to your suite."

The guards led Ayden and Isabelle to a stone-walled corridor with a grated floor and four metal doors on each side and one at the end, which one of the guards opened to reveal a small cell devoid of furniture.

Ayden sat against the wall, an elbow on a knee. "Got any brilliant ideas? Mr. Somebody knows our location, but without our phones he's not going to know we're in trouble unless we contact him."

"*Merde.* So much for technology," Isabelle said, sitting beside him.

They studied the room.

"*Bonne*, I've got an idea," she said proudly.

"Let's hear it."

"When the guards come in to take us away, I'll do a corner wall run, then somersault over the door and drop on them," she said.

"This is real life, not *The Matrix*," Ayden said.

"Hey, I come from the country that created *parkour*. You know *parkour*?"

"I've seen it on YouTube. This better work."

"But the timing must be precise," Isabelle said, removing her robe. "You stand near the door to back me up."

"Just don't break your back."

***

Tiny grains of sand shifted to one side of the road as the afternoon light caught the mountain ridges. An Egyptian officer with an AK-47 knelt, looking at a lifeless soldier on the desert checkpoint. His unit had been ordered to investigate after receiving a distress call. He had arrived with three personnel carriers.

The clean-shaven military officer's eyes scanned the environment, strewn with dead comrades, weapons, and bullet casings. He picked up one of the casings and examined it. A few soldiers stood around him. The constant desert wind failed to sweep the smell of death away as the soldiers began picking up the dead.

A soldier with a large walkie-talkie approached. "Sir, the guards at Saint Catherine's Monastery said a group of monks arrived in the stolen Cherokee."

The officer stood and looked at the soldier. "Get reinforcement. Tell them to go straight to the monastery and await further orders."

***

The noise of boots clumping outside the metal door alerted Ayden and Isabelle.

"Okay, Isabelle, they're coming." Ayden stood.

"This is it—do or die," Isabelle said.

Isabelle jumped up and stood in position at the sound of keys being turned in the lock. With all her leg strength, she rushed to the corner and ploughed one foot against the left wall as her right leg climb the other side. She repeated the process once more, then spun over the door as it opened. She landed with her weight slamming the three bodies to the floor.

Ayden rushed forward and grabbed the weapons after the guards collapsed with Isabelle on top of them. As the guards struggled to get up, Ayden hit them with a rifle's butt. They fell back down, unconscious.

Isabelle rolled over and grabbed the extra weapon while Ayden dragged the guards into the cell. They removed the extra magazines. Ayden then took the ring of keys from one of the guards.

"I bet one of these keys opens the pope's cell," Ayden said.

"Let's find out," Isabelle said, then hesitated. "Wait a minute. You forgot something."

Ayden looked at her. "What?"

She pointed to the guards. "It's a good idea to look like them."

They stripped the guards and put on the khakis. Isabelle took a bandana from one of the guards and tied it around her hair to complete her new disguise.

Ayden then locked the cell door and led them along the hallway with their weapons extended. He began fumbling with the keys and slid each into the lock of the first cell door on his left. One fit. He turned it and pulled the door open. It was empty. He tried the next one and the next. He tugged the final door and found a withered body, looking gloomy and unshaven, in a dirty black cassock huddled in a corner.

Pope Gregoire looked up. "What now?"

Ayden rushed in and knelt in front of him as Isabelle guarded the entrance.

"My name is Demetrious Mallas," Ayden said. "I've come to rescue you."

"How did you find me?" Pope Gregoire asked.

Ayden smiled. "I deciphered your Morse code message."

The pope smiled faintly. "I used my teeth to flatten some of the links, hoping someone would notice it. Good thing I still have strong teeth." He looked at Ayden with compassionate eyes. "It's a miracle you managed to decipher it—you're truly a Godsend."

Ayden didn't respond to the remark. "Let's get out of here." Ayden lifted the pope. "Sorry to ask this, but where do you do your business?"

"Business?"

"Toilet."

"They take me outside whenever I need to go, past the excavation area. Why do you ask?"

"If anyone stops us, that's going to be our initial excuse."

Ayden took the lead as they crossed the metal bridge. They ignored the drilling and pounding as they neared the excavation area. Just then, two guards appeared at the carved entrance. They descended the short stairwell and crunched toward them. One of the guards, carrying a weapon with its muzzle down, stopped them. "Where you taking him?" the guard asked in Russian.

"Toilet," Ayden replied in the same language. "He smells."

The guard nodded and let them pass.

Ayden didn't say another word. He held the pope tightly as they climbed the flight of stairs. They began retracing their path back to the hyper loop station, every once in a while checking for unexpected surprises.

"The toilet excuse isn't going to work anymore," Isabelle said. "I'd like to remind you there are guards at every corner."

Nearing the tunnel intersection, they stopped as shadows were cast upon the wall in front of them. Ayden signaled for Isabelle to subdue them.

The two shadows on the wall became three. The onslaught was quick with immediate punches and kicks, followed by rifle butting to the heads. The shadows on the wall then became one.

INCOGNITO

"You can come out now," Isabelle said.

Ayden raised the pope and stepped forward into the center of the intersection. "Best His Holiness put on real clothes," he said.

Isabelle began stripping one of the guards.

Ayden turned to Pope Gregoire. "We need you to put on this attire, to let them think we're archaeologists."

"Okay," Pope Gregoire said. He put on the pants first under the robe, and then slipped into the shirt after disrobing.

They kept walking through the empty tunnels, every once in a while passing some guards. None gave them a second look.

They reached the large metallic door that led to the hyper loop. This time, however, there were more guards stationed there. The guards raised their weapons and pointed at them while one of them spoke into a walkie-talkie.

"Yes, we found them," the guard with the walkie-talkie reported in Russian, which Ayden understood.

The walkie-talkie crackled. Benzinger's voice came through. "Shoot them."

The guard looked at Pope Gregoire. "What about the pope?"

The metallic doors parted, with several dozen Egyptian soldiers rushing in, weapons leveled at Benzinger's men, who instantly surrendered looking at the sheer number.

The clean-shaven Egyptian officer stepped forward. "What's going on here?" He looked at Ayden and Isabelle, then finally at Pope Gregoire. He took a few steps forward, and then recoiled. "Your face. You look familiar...*El Baba Vatikaan*?"

Ayden smiled. "That's him—the pope of the Vatican."

Chapter Twenty-Four

Egypt Destroys Dozens of Terrorists Tunnels

The Egyptian army announced that it had destroyed twenty-five terror tunnels between the Sinai and several Arab countries. "Egyptian forces, with the help of our neighboring allies, discovered and successfully destroyed these tunnel networks that could have been used for smuggling and terror networks," army spokesman Brigadier General Alaa Gamal said in a press statement. The brigadier general added that the destroyed tunnels were equipped with railroad tracks to help ease smuggling efforts, while sections led to underground bases for communications and storage.

Wearing a fake moustache and beard, his hair dyed light brown, Benzinger sat in a small Dusseldorf café near the glass window reading the newspaper article. Though the street outside was tranquil, he glanced up at every person entering the café. Beside him, two young German women were cheerfully murmuring and giggling as they chatted about a range of subjects, including their boyfriends.

Benzinger's phone rang. The number on the screen was unfamiliar.

"Benzinger," a familiar voice said.

"Zanebono. Indeed, this is a surprise. Where've you been

INCOGNITO

hiding? We were wondering what happened to you after the bank heist. We read about it in the papers. According to reports, you disappeared from work the next day and never returned. The police have been looking for you. Speculation is that you might be involved, especially since they found your wallet in the vault. How careless of you. We thought, possibly, you got greedy. We had an agreement, Zanebono — get us our money, get back your life."

"You think it's easy to be on the run with fifty million dollars while the police are looking for you? I did more than just move house, I moved to another country. Now that I feel safe and secure, I decided to call you to let you know where the money is."

"Very nice of you. I hope it's not a trick," Benzinger said.

"No tricks. It's in a cabin in the German forest," Zanebono said.

Benzinger smiled to himself. "Give me directions."

***

A pack of howling wolves in the distance broke the stillness of the German forest as Ayden peered out the window of the log cabin. He checked the time on his watch: 2 a.m. They should be here soon. Behind Ayden, the crackling fireplace rejuvenated his tired limbs.

A light flickered against the impenetrable dark. A car stopped in front of the cabin. The lights went off. Benzinger and two others got out. Ayden recognized one of the men as the peppered-haired limo driver who had picked him up at the airport in Geneva. The other man's face was unfamiliar. He was about the same height as Benzinger, with Nordic features. Ayden crossed to a chair in front of the fireplace and sat down, hiding his face under an ivy cap.

The door slammed open. The limo driver pulled out a laser-guided, silenced pistol and aimed it at Ayden's cap. "Take off your hat."

Ayden complied, removing the hat slowly.

"You," the limo driver growled.

"Ah, Demetrious," Benzinger said. "The last person I expected to see. What kind of a deal did Zanebono make with you?"

"Not with me, but with the Vatican intelligence agency. Zanebono has a new identity—he's long gone. We knew you'd take the bait. I wondered what happened to you after Egypt." Ayden shifted his eyes to the limo driver. "I remember what you did to me."

"I didn't bury you deep enough. My mistake," the limo driver sneered.

Benzinger scanned the room. "Just you alone? Where are the Italians, the Swiss, and your friends?

Ayden gestured for them to sit down. "It's cozier like this—just a few of us."

They sat in front of him. The limo driver continued to point the gun at Ayden.

"What do you want?" Benzinger asked.

Guy entered the cabin. Benzinger and the two other men turned.

Benzinger looked at Ayden again. "You brought your ugly looking friend along, I see."

Guy raised his hand, which held a small device with a flickering red light. He pressed a button on the device. The chair the limo driver sat in exploded, sending chunks of metal into his legs and buttocks. The gun slipped from his hand and bounced on the floor. Blood poured as from a leaking wine barrel. The limo driver screamed as he fell, bucking spastically on the floor, his hands thrashing, his body contorting up and back. The screams turned to moans and, minutes later, short gasps. Then, he was still. No one was certain if he was dead or alive.

"You sick bastard," the Nordic-looking man said.

"Don't move, we rigged all the chairs," Ayden said. As he

headed toward the door, he stopped in front of Benzinger and picked up the car keys in the masses of flesh on the floor.

Benzinger gave him a fixed stare. "My people will never rest until they get you."

"Well, good luck to them." Ayden looked at Guy. "Ready?"

Guy smiled. "Ready."

They stepped out but left the door open. They walked to the vehicle, opened the doors, and stood there for a while...waiting.

The howling grew louder, and closer. Moments later, the sound of breaking twigs creaked through the matted darkness. As the rustling sounds of stealthy movements intensified, they got into the car and shut the doors. Ayden adjusted the rearview mirror to see behind. Bright amber-colored eyes blazed in the darkness, and then they vanished.

Ayden and Guy looked at the porch. There were six, staring through the open door, crouching to spring.

***

Ayden weaseled his way into an outside table near the entrance of a cafe-bar at Neil's Yard. It was one of the many outlets tucked off an alley near London's Covent Garden. Waiters cheerfully took orders as young men and women with fancy hairdos, body ornaments, and stylish frames chatted animatedly around him. A few read while munching on crackers and scooping desserts. Others chatted with one another over matters that either caused them to frown or chuckle.

He ordered a steak sandwich lunch with a glass of beer in this pleasant spring weather. He was in no hurry to order dessert. He had the whole afternoon to himself. He picked up his iPad and checked the news.

Pope Found Safe and Well After Search

Vatican City (AP): Pope Gregoire the XVII, who went missing

three months ago, was found in the fishing village of Portofino on Sunday evening. Last seen waving to the crowd from his window, the pope explained to the police the bizarre nature of his disappearance.

The police have blamed the fascist terrorist organization, Sword, for the kidnapping, although the reason remains a mystery. The pope was rescued by Italy's elite counterterrorism team in a joint task force with the Swiss police and Interpol.

A video link below the article gave an update on Pope Gregoire. Ayden clicked it to watch.

High above Saint Peter's Square, a carpet rolled out of the pope's window and hung on the ledge. A podium appeared and Pope Gregoire arrived behind it a few minutes later. The crowd cheered and chanted. The pope began to speak in Italian, and later repeated his message in English and French. When he finished, he waved and raised both hands upward, offering a few flying kisses in between.

Ayden then clicked on the *Times* app icon. The headline read: *Three terrorists found dead in German forest.* The article went on to say the remains of three Sword terrorists had been found in a remote forest cabin near the Swiss-German border. They apparently had been making some kind of bomb and ended blowing themselves up by accident. Carcasses of wolves were also found in the cabin.

On another news link, the Vatican had officially apologized to Turkey for the comment made by Altimari during a press conference. The smile on Ayden's ruddy face reflected on the iPad's screen. He leaned forward, picked up the glass of beer that had just arrived, and brought the glass to his lips as the forefinger of his other hand clicked on the next story. A famous Hollywood celebrity had just punched a movie director during an interview. Singer Adele was in Tokyo doing a concert.

Sleep the night before was perfect after soaking his tired

body into a hot tub, and then mending some of his bruises with medicated cream. The bullet graze on his shoulder had healed, but a slight scar remained. Physical scars needed more time to fade away, or they could be permanent reminders of one's life story. Maria continued to remain at the back of his mind. So did the question of God's existence. He also questioned his role in the League. Perhaps it was time to move on, if the council allowed him. It was an organization that operated on its own set of laws. He had still not grown accustomed to their brand of justice. He had been conditioned to believe there was only one kind of system based on arbitrary rules accompanied by certain norms that allowed a wider society to function. The league did not give him that sense of security and strength. He felt as if he were running down an endless corridor that made it difficult to enter the gates of nirvana. It had presented a life not easier, nor safer. He was nameless, always watching his back, living in a labyrinth of lies and pretenses. How did he lose his past?

He began to reminisce about his childhood, about a time when he went with his parents to Brighton. Fun days. How did he end up drifting away from them? He wondered about his other relatives, especially his cousins who were all around the same age as him. He remembered the weekends at his home with them, and sometimes at theirs. They played had police and thief, board games, and did every other thing kids did at that age. There were even sleepover sessions where they told ghost stories. Where did the time go? Where did he go? He wished he could meet them again. But it was forbidden. He was officially dead. They had moved on while he was stuck in a void. They were all probably married by now. He wondered if one of them had named a child after him. That would be nice.

He put the iPad on the table and removed his cell phone from his pocket. He typed in a message to Cavallo:

The pope looks fresh.
Hope all is well.

Cavallo replied within two minutes.

Good to hear from you, my friend. Yes, all good.
God works in mysterious ways. Sometimes he uses anonymous people.
Take care.
Peace.

***

Ayden opened the glass door into *Hotel Romantik's* foyer after arriving on the funicular to hear a familiar voice in an irritable tone. A man in a red winter hoodie stood in front of the long counter, arguing with the hotel receptionist.

"I need a room with a mountain view," the man complained.

"Sir, as I have said, all our rooms have mountain views," the male hotel receptionist explained in a calm demeanor.

"But you gave me the back mountain view. I want a room with a frontal view," the man said.

"I'm sorry, sir, we cannot do that. You should've specified earlier. All our rooms are presently fully booked," the receptionist said.

Ayden stepped forward. "Mate, it's all the same — front, back, sideways." He pointed at the snow covering the mountainous terrain through the glass panels. "Besides, you're not going to spend the whole time in your room, are you?"

The man turned and gave an amiable smile. "I know, I was just making conversation with the hotel receptionist. Nice seeing you again." Guy gave Ayden a tight hug.

Ayden smiled. "Not too tight. I'm still aching all over."

"You've come to the right place," Guy said.

"She checked in yet?" Ayden asked, referring to Isabelle.

INCOGNITO

"*Bonjour*," a familiar female voice interrupted them.

They turned to find Isabelle stepping in. She wore a knitted black hat, her hair tied up behind her, a purple winter jacket, and jeans with high boots. They both gave her a hug, one at a time.

"This is going to be a fun week," Isabelle said.

"Did you ever visit Milan?" Ayden smiled.

"Ah, you remembered," Isabelle said. "Where did you think I got this outfit from?" She spun around once to show off her apparel.

"Nice."

"Why did you choose this resort?"

"When I saw this place before Cavallo rescued us on the helicopter, I told myself to come back. Something about this place—it just feels like a good place for a holiday," Ayden said.

Guy tapped his forehead. "While we were being shot at, you found time to day dream?"

"It was just a second or two—I was focused the rest of the time," Ayden said. "Hey, we're alive, aren't we?"

"We're going skiing tomorrow, yes?" Isabelle said.

"You bet your French ass." Guy smiled. "Oops, sorry! I didn't mean—"

Isabelle smiled. "It's okay."

Ayden put a hand on his hip. "Let's sit outside for a while and enjoy the view. Just in case, I brought some aspirin if anybody needs it."

***

The mysterious man in ski gear, a hand lingering over coffee, sat outside the small, secluded hotel, which faced directly in front of the railway at the foot of the Morteratsch glacier. Around him, people enjoyed leisurely lunches while chatting. He watched other guests come and go as passing waiters served, took new orders, and cleared tables. From behind ski sunglasses, he looked at his watch, expecting his appointment to arrive any minute now.

The train arrived on time. His eyes roved over the alighting passengers. In the crowd, he recognized a face: a man around fifty in a thick brown overcoat. He also kept his eyes hidden behind a pair of sunglasses.

The man approached his table and sat down opposite him. He ordered a glass of beer.

"It's been a long time," the mysterious man said in Russian.

"It was five years since we last met, yes? I don't remember it being a pleasant occasion. I also don't expect today to be different," the man replied in Russian. "So come to the point, what does NATO want from Russia?"

"We'll forget this incident ever took place if you stop bothering Turkey," the mysterious man said. "The tunnels have been destroyed, and we have your men in custody—courtesy of the Egyptian army. We'll release them on condition."

The Russian sneered. "We won't forget this day NATO threatened us."

A waiter came with his beer. He took a sip and sat the thick glass down.

"NATO didn't threaten you...the United States did," the mysterious man said.

The Russian took another sip of his drink. "Is that all?"

"That's it."

The Russian nodded. "What time is the next train?"

The mysterious man smiled. "Soon."

"Whatever happened to those three people?" the Russian asked.

"What three people?"

"Never mind. It's not important."

"Have a nice trip to wherever you're going next."

INCOGNITO

EPILOGUE

Mr. Somebody sat in the living room of his cottage reading the papers when a beeping sound came from his watch. He stood and crossed to the dining room cabinet on the right wall, opened the glass door, and turned a vase anti-clockwise. The cabinet parted. He walked through it and descended a series of steps as the wall behind him shut via an auto-sensor. He entered a bunker jammed with high-tech equipment. Mr. Somebody flicked a light switch, illuminating metal walls. He then took a seat in a black swivel chair in front of a computer. He typed in a code and the bright white letters on the monitor responded: access granted. He leaned back and waited.

A Guy Fawkes mask appeared on screen.

"Greetings, Mr. Somebody," the scrambled voice behind the mask said.

"Greetings," Mr. Somebody replied. "The mission is accomplished."

"Far from it, Mr. Somebody. There is still one more thing Ayden Tanner must do," the voice said.

Mr. Somebody nodded. "I understand."

***

London. 10 a.m. Ayden stood along Brompton Road in front of Barclays Bank, near the red letterbox. It had started to drizzle, but he didn't mind. Farther down, the street was lined with

Arab-owned sports cars outside Harrods as shoppers clogged the pavement. Passersby stopped to take photos of the super cars with Middle East license plates. The car owners had been warned against blaring their horns and revving their engines, so it was a quiet showoff until the drizzling turned to a downpour. Everyone wildly clambered into their cars and drove away.

Just then, a windowless van pulled up and stopped in front of Ayden. Its back doors opened to a reveal a black curtain. Ayden pushed the curtain aside and stepped into the high-tech interior that looked more like a compact version of a space shuttle control room. The doors shut automatically behind him.

Mr. Somebody, wearing a maroon bowler hat and a black tie suit, greeted him as he sat at a small bolted desk facing a laptop.

"Good to see you again," Mr. Somebody said. "How's the cold?"

"It comes and goes." Ayden sat beside him, an elbow leaning on the desk's edge. He felt the van move.

"Anonymous found the millions Rabolini stole. He laundered it to Singapore," Mr. Somebody said.

Ayden squinted. "You could've told me that on the phone. Why are we meeting?"

"The assignment is not over yet," Mr. Somebody said.

Ayden gave a tight smile. "You want me to take on the Russians? I was just thinking about having a nice salt bath, maybe even doing some painting."

"Leave the Russians to NATO," Mr. Somebody said.

"So what is it?"

"Van Der Haas," Mr. Somebody said. "I've booked you a flight to The Netherlands. Here's your new passport." He picked up a small maroon booklet on the desk and handed it to Ayden. "Mr. Hans Hoedemaekers."

Ayden smirked. "Hmmm…"

***

The sparkle of spring's sun glistened on the purple Lexus's body as it drew up in the forecourt at the *Binnenhof*, the grand lakefront complex at The Hague. The doors of the two SUVs flanking the vehicle opened. Several stone-faced bodyguards in dark shades and black suits burst out, wielding an array of automatic weapons.

The men encircled the Lexus with their backs to it, their eyes roving in all directions. Luuk the giant stepped out, followed by several others. Van Der Haas, looking distinguished in a dark suit, then emerged from the vehicle. He coughed as he regarded the bodyguards, who then marched him into the building.

A hush fell upon the opulent lobby. People gave way and gawked at the entourage hovering near the Dutch senator as he and his bodyguards moved across the lobby, intent on the elevator.

The doors of the elevator opened. The senator stepped in, accompanied by the giant and a few aides, while others guarded the doors.

The elevator seemed suspended in space, though the numbers reflected the ascent. Inside, nobody spoke — there was no need.

The doors parted and the guards escorted their charge along the corridor. When they came to the end of the corridor, the giant took out a keycard and inserted it into the thin horizontal slot in the door. It wouldn't budge. The giant looked at Van Der Haas, then tried again.

The door opened with a slight click.

According to witnesses in a newspaper report, the flames and smoke coming out of the building after the explosion could be seen from twenty blocks away.

In other news, hundreds of charity organizations around the world reported receiving mysterious donations from an anonymous donor totaling tens of millions of dollars.

The End

Born and raised in Singapore, Khaled is a former magazine journalist with local and international exposure. His articles have also been published and syndicated to newspapers worldwide. Khaled's debut thriller novel, Smokescreen, was listed "Thriller of the Month" on e-thriller.com's September 2014 issue. The author is a member of the International Thriller Writers, and the UK Crime Writers Association. Khaled is an avid traveler and believes in being kind to all animals, great and small.

Author's Website: www.khaledtalibthriller.com

Printed in Great Britain
by Amazon